Soul Catcher

By

Diane Rzepka

The characters and events in this book are fictitious. Any similarity to real persons, living or dead, is coincidental and not intended by the author.

ISBNs: 979-8-9991596-1-8 (Paperback), 979-8-9991596-0-1 (ebook)

To those who encouraged and supported me through this process, I appreciate you.

To my sisters, you are my greatest support. Thank you for being there.

Chapter One

I pulled away from the profiling as a tear fell down my face. The tear didn't belong to me. It represented the last warm drop of life before Sherry Sweeny took her final breath.

I turned my eyes toward the lifeless body lying beside me in the cold, damp grass. "I'm sorry for what he did to you," I choked out. Twelve times, that monster stabbed her. Twelve times, the knife sank into her chest.

As I immersed myself in her thoughts, absorbing her last memories, I went through everything she experienced, taking in every emotion and impact she endured from her attacker. The pain was excruciating, and the fear—an all-consuming dread—as she fought desperately for her life. Yet, his dominance was undeniable, and as she recognized that death was just a breath away, her final tear dropped.

I lifted my gaze to the starlit sky, striving to count the stars. I had to recenter my mind. Time moved too fast, and I had a job to do. But as I reached five, my thoughts turned to each stab that struck her body. I squeezed my eyes shut, straining to break free from the emotional connection. It wasn't for lack of empathy. I felt for this poor girl.

Called in to assist another horrifying case, my body responded as expected. Depending on the profiling I had to perform, the physical experience of dying would ease before I came out of it. Unfortunately for me, I discovered long ago that I had a gift. Or at least that is how some people would refer to it. In cases like these, I begged to differ.

I could enter the victim's mind and discover how a person died. But it was no picnic learning what it was like to get stabbed, shot, or even strangled. I temporarily became the victim. Regardless of how they died, I experienced all of it. I saw everything they saw and knew all that they knew. Then I would pull out as the person took their final breath. I would deliver the facts and help provide justice the victim deserved. I only have to recover from the shock of witnessing the death, and convince my body and brain that it didn't actually happen to me, and that was difficult.

My current predicament with this profiling, however, floated on an emotional level. The trauma lingered. Single, lonely women trying to foresee a future with a man who would end up murdering them usually leave an impression on me, but I had to press on. Solve this case, and I won't be able to do that if I don't concentrate on getting back to normal.

A cool breeze brushed my cheeks as the trees swayed ominously above. Their gentle rustling produced a welcome tune to ease her screams that still deafened my thoughts. I commanded my mind and body to calm and focus. I focused on the trees above, swaying as their leaves brushed against each other, sounding like soft waves on a sandy beach. Cicadas bellowed a lovely tune, and the sound of a couple of frogs nearby helped me relax to the music of nature's orchestra.

I reached out on either side until my fingers grazed the soft grass and floated my palms over the delicate blades as they tickled my skin. I tried another breath, which formed more easily now —a good sign that my body was returning at a gradual pace back to the land of the living. Mud, with a nauseating hint of iron, scented the air. For years, I endured the stench of blood from many profiles, and still, that odor made me sick to my stomach.

I turned back and studied Sherry's face. "I swear we will do everything in our power to find him," I whispered. I offered a reassuring smile to the once-promising young girl. I hoped wherever her soul went, she would know peace.

"Hey, kid, are you back?" Captain Julian Marcus approached from a few feet away. He moved with caution, aware that my return to reality was a delicate process. I pulled my focus away from Sherry and shifted it toward my boss. I spotted movement behind him and saw the forensic team waiting off to the side for Julian's cue.

"Yeah, I'm back, mostly," I assured him. I reached out my hand, gesturing for him to help me up. He lifted me from the ground and eased me against a nearby tree. My legs were like dead weight as the shock and tension from the profiling lingered. I told him what happened to Sherry, recounting each moment as she experienced them, and the monster that killed her— his name, description, and how she knew him.

"He took her on a second date, introduced himself as Evan Hanes. He claimed to work in IT and moved to the city." My heart sank a little more with every thought I pulled from her. She met him on a dating app, and assumed everything went great, that is, until he decided to murder her." I glanced over at her body. "She just wanted to find love."

"Anything about the attack you can tell us?" Mike, the Medical Examiner, chimed in. His role served more to verify the evidence as I presented it to him. Unfortunately for him, I took away most of the discovery work because I simply told them what happened once I tapped into the victim's memories.

"Uh, yeah, she scratched him with her ring. Over there." I pointed toward a thick patch of grass a few feet from the body. "She slipped it off her hand, determined not to let him get away with it, and tossed it into the grass after she scratched him up." Smart girl.

Mike and his team took detailed notes while I recounted everything I remembered, securing the details to build a solid case. One of his investigators approached the spot where the ring fell and shone his flashlight through the tall grass, searching.

"I found it," he said.

He photographed the ring lying in the grass, then pulled out a plastic evidence bag and secured the ring inside. After I provided them all with a detailed account of what happened, along with a complete description of Sherry's killer, the team gathered any vital evidence and prepared Sherry's body for transport to the morgue.

It was nearing midnight, but the moon shone so brightly that it cast a gentle light, conveniently illuminating their work. A homeless man found Sherry's body behind a strip mall and called it in, and with my help, it didn't take long to finish up. As they carefully lifted her into the post-mortem bag and onto the gurney, I couldn't help but gasp. The moon's soft, iridescent glow highlighted Sherry's features, as Mike zipped the bag over her head. With a heartbreaking reminder of the beautiful young woman, full of dreams yet to be lived, I made her a solid promise that we would find the monster responsible for this. I always kept my promises.

Chapter Two

Two days have passed since the tragic murder of Sherry Sweeney. The forensic team collected evidence at the crime scene after an intense search for Evan Hanes, also known as Dylan Lawson. We apprehended the guy—another victory for the department, and I kept my promise to Sherry.

So why can't I sleep? I swallowed hard against the crippling anxiety pulsing through my body. I pulled my pillow over my eyes, praying the extra weight would push out the chaos searing through my mind. The other night, the cicadas bellowed a welcome sound, helping me ease back into my routine. Tonight, their incessant high-pitched buzz reverberated outside my bedroom window, making me go mad. My house sat in a wooded area, making it the perfect location for the Cicada Performing Arts.

I fancied opening my window and, as if I stood as a maestro conducting my choir, unloading my Glock into the bushes with Beethoven's Fifth guiding me along. I let out a half-amused, half-hysterical chuckle. The cicada choir faded out, then in, at a loud, high pitch. I was half expecting the clang of a cymbal or the deafening boom of a snare drum to finalize the performance, but the buzzing kept on.

"Wine sounds good right about now. That might help."

I slipped into my oversized slippers, pulled on my robe, and sped for the kitchen. I snatched a glass out of the cabinet and my favorite bottle of Merlot. I removed the stopper and let the sweet liquid fill three-quarters of the glass. I inhaled and chugged. The wine flowed down my throat, coating me like a warm blanket from the inside. With little tolerance for alcohol, my body reacted to the sensation after a couple of minutes when a subtle warmth spread down into my stomach, releasing the tension. Sleep would return in no time.

As I took another gulp, my cell phone rang unexpectedly, causing me to spit out part of the last sip. I reached for the phone and pressed the talk key, intending to yell at the caller.

"Ms. Natalie Rhine?" a male voice asked from the other end.

"Yes," I answered.

"I'm Agent Chris Rodgers."

Federal? "What can I do for you, Agent Rodgers?" My words echoed into the glass as I drank down what was left.

"I need your assistance on a case of vast importance."

"Oh?" I muttered, pouring more wine into the glass. "Must be important if the feds are calling me."

"I need people who can support our investigation. It's my understanding that your team has a high solve rate and ensures a quick turnaround time."

A part of me wanted to beam with pride, but his implication told me he didn't know how my "team" operated.

"I already spoke with your supervisor." Agent Rodgers drew in a breath. "Are you willing to help or not?"

I ground my teeth. "And what did my supervisor approve?"

The sound of a chair scraping against the floor echoed in the background. “He guaranteed me that your expertise would be invaluable, as you have a remarkable ability to pick up on what others might miss. I will fill you in when you arrive. I arranged a flight for you from Baltimore-Washington Airport to Newark. Two of my men will escort you from the airport upon your arrival. I need you here ASAP."

I couldn't help but grin from ear to ear. Oh Julian. A great way to give the agent what he wants.

I focused on his voice—subdued but intense, almost intimidating—the kind often used during a ransom call. "It will take me an hour to drive to BWI airport. How long do you expect to keep me around?"

"We’ll have you back in your office before lunch. Do what you must to get on the plane and be quick about it." The urgency in his voice piqued my curiosity, but his arrogance annoyed me. "I assume punctuality is another of your many qualities."

I ground my teeth again, this time adding a faint grumble. "I’m on my way.”

"Don't keep me waiting." The cell phone screen lit up, indicating that the call ended.

I rechecked the clock before dialing my boss's cell number. Julian answered on the first ring.

"I take it the FBI called you?” he breathed into the phone.

“Yeah, a charismatic Agent Rodgers. He said he spoke to you, needing me to work on a case of significant importance.”

“He wanted the whole team, but I can’t spare everyone, so I told him I would send you in my place.”

I hesitated. “Wait! You mean you’re not coming with me?”

“No, I have my work to attend to. But I just talked with Mike. He's sending one of his crew with you to assist.”

“And you think that’s a good idea?” I ran my hand through my hair as anxious tension built in the pit of my stomach. “Julian, he'll find out how I solve these cases. What happened to keeping me a secret?”

Julian groaned into the phone, “Apparently, he already knows. Don’t ask me how,” he breathed out, his annoyance evident. “You know the rules, Nat. Do what you gotta do, provide the details, and get back as soon as possible.”

“The Feds are going to owe me for this."

Julian yawned into the phone. "He woke me from the best sleep ever; they will owe us both,” then disconnected the call.

I peered into my empty wine glass, oblivious to having drunk it all. Disappointed that my warm bed would not be on my agenda, I put the bottle back and headed for the shower. I endured five minutes of icy water to help ease the effects of alcohol. My stomach turned; whether it was from the alcohol or my anxiety about being called into a case outside my comfort zone, I couldn’t decide. Probably both. I regretted not following my first instinct to use my gun and unleash hell on my bushes. If only I didn’t have neighbors.

The cool spray helped me contemplate the case before me. You would think working with the FBI would be exciting, but dealing with my department rocked a few nerves. Now I get to work with agents who believed they earned a spot higher up the food chain—that's a different level of arrogance. Lucky me.

Jumping out of the shower, I rummaged through my closet, donned a suitable outfit, swiped my wallet and keys, and ran out the door.

The drive to the airport went as expected, with little traffic on the roads at this early hour. I sped and left my car in the short-term parking area. When I walked up to the service counter, I discovered a private jet awaited me. For once, a perk to my job.

"There's another person who is supposed to join me," I told the rep.

"Ah, yes, I believe he is just over there," the woman indicated over my shoulder.

I turned and saw a familiar face approaching me.

"Hello, Ms. Rhine," David said, offering a friendly smile and carrying a small case.

I smiled. "Hi, David. And you know you can call me Natalie," I assured him.

"Oh yeah, I know. Just being courteous," he said, looking awkward and a bit uncomfortable.

If I had to take a guess, I'd say this case is outside both of our comfort zones. "OK. We're ready." I turned back toward the rep who directed us to where we needed to go.

My mouth dropped open when we reached the terminal and boarded the jet. The cabin comprised an impressive amount of space. I chose a seat and contemplated a catnap. David took a seat across from me and reclined, without hesitation. A childish grin crossed his face as he, too, enjoyed the comforts of the job. Once the steward secured the door, the jet taxied to the tarmac, and we were up in the air in no time. Thirty minutes later, the captain's voice announced our arrival.

I stretched my arms and gazed out the window at New Jersey. The sun seeped through a layer of thin overcast clouds, creating a solid glare against the windows. I pulled myself up from the seat, thanked the captain and steward, and waited as the door opened with David behind me.

Two men slouched against a black Ford Expedition as we descended the stairs, exchanging glares as they walked toward the plane to meet us.

"Ms. Rhine?" A tall, stocky man approached with purpose, displaying his FBI badge for identification. He wore a standard FBI ensemble: a fitted black suit jacket that accentuated his broad shoulders. Beneath that was a crisp white shirt that contrasted sharply with the dark fabric, and sleek aviator sunglasses that concealed his eyes, adding to his imposing demeanor.

His expression was serious, conveying authority and resolve, convincing me that I was all bark and no bite in comparison. The man had thick, dark hair that was neatly combed back, and a strong jawline that hinted at both determination and strength—he seemed ideally suited to play the role of a superhero in some action-packed film.

"Yes, I am," I said, showing my credentials.

"I'm Agent Nicks, and this is Agent Sorrentino. After you."

"David," he said behind me, introducing himself.

Much leaner and more conventional than the other, the second man nodded, escorted me to the car's passenger side, and ushered me to sit in the back while Nicks got into the driver's seat. David hopped into the back seat beside me. We wasted no time and zipped out of the airport into the light Saturday morning traffic.

My head ached from sleep deprivation and the sudden change in my day's activities. I rested against the back seat window. A mixture of cold and warmth touched my skin as I gazed out the glass, watching homes and businesses pass by, block after block. New Jersey differed from rural Maryland, which lacked ample land and efficient means of travel from one place to another. Jersey's houses are built on top of one another, dozens of parked cars fill the roadways, and nearly as many potholes.

"Where are we going? " I asked, observing the number of streetlights and road signs we passed.

Dozens of residences whirred by, stirring a hint of dizziness behind my eyes. I never enjoyed riding in the backseat; motion sickness always kicked in, and I didn't want to worsen my current predicament. My attention shifted toward Agent Nicks's face in the rearview mirror as he fixated on the road. The other drummed his fingers on the car door, humming a tune. David sat quietly, gazing out the window and tapping his fingers on his knee. I couldn't shake the feeling that I was out of my element.

"You'll know when we arrive," Nicks replied with arrogance.

I stifled a chuckle. "Feds," I murmured. Why did I have to answer the phone? I lay my head back against the seat, craving more wine. I cursed those damn cicadas that kept me awake and prayed that this new case would go well; not wanting to appear useless to a group of uptight Federal Agents and make my boss look bad.

"I don't suppose you'll fill us in on this case. It must be important if you guys called us in?" I provoked.

Neither answered. Nicks just focused on driving while Sorrentino kept humming.

The stuffiness of the vehicle and the overpowering scent of men's cologne heightened my agitation. I tried to open the window, but nothing happened. I wanted fresh air. I knocked on the glass for Nicks to unlock it. Nicks peered at me in the rearview mirror, his eyes shifting from the road to me while maintaining his intimidating stare. After a long pause, he pressed the button on his door and lowered my window halfway.

"Thanks," disregarding his superiority.

I inhaled the crisp autumn air and redirected my senses to the views whizzing by. Initially, the houses clustered together in pairs, resembling duplexes with minimal space for driveways or yards on either side. However, as we drove further, the space began to improve. The neighborhoods we passed through flourished remarkably with tall maple trees, adorned with vibrant red, orange, and yellow leaves. The foliage brightened the diverse driveways and complemented the more luxurious homes.

We ventured into a charming neighborhood, embodying a typical Saturday morning suburban lifestyle. Elderly couples sipped coffee in their robes on their front porches, while joggers with dogs and baby strollers strode along the sidewalks, creating a picturesque scene of contented living.

Agent Sorrentino stirred in his seat. "The house is at the end of this road on a cul-de-sac," he said. It belongs to Congressman Edward Floyd, who is now deceased, and the reason for your presence. Last night, he hosted a formal gathering in his home to honor an upcoming election."

My eyes darted to the back of the man's head sitting in front of me. "A Congressman? Interesting." Finally, some answers.

"He's not just a congressman; he took down a major money laundering operation a couple of years ago, resulting in the arrests of several prominent political figures, including a few mayors, state legislators, and others of political interest." Pride flowed from Sorrentino's voice as he addressed the Congressman.

"Before long, he proposed an act that would crack down hard on those participating in public corruption. We believe his actions may be related to his death. Many people affected by the bust would want him dead, including those overseas whose operations came to an abrupt halt."

I recalled the news broadcasting a significant arrest a while back—about an undercover operation revealing millions of dollars in international money laundering and political bribes. This developed into one of the most important political scandals in New Jersey's history, garnering international headlines.

Floyd, yes. Dubbed Flaming Floyd because he would always come on strong-- no calm media talk, no smiles, or jokes. He would approach a podium and get to business with his passionate language and animated gestures. I let out a low snort. That's putting it nicely.

"When the police and medics arrived, they found his wife hysterical. She said that once the party ended, the Congressman told her to go to bed while he finalized some paperwork in his office. Four hours later, she awoke to a loud noise, went downstairs, and found him face down in a pool of his blood on the office floor. She called 9-1-1, but when the paramedics arrived, Floyd had already died.

"Did forensics determine the cause of death?"

"From what they found, a significant wound to his neck caused him to bleed out. There's no murder weapon, no signs of struggle, and most items seem to be in their places, except for the couch, which moved from his fall."

"And now, Madame Cleo, everyone is waiting for you to solve the mystery of his death," Nicks added. The two men exchanged a look I recognized- skeptics, not keen on having someone like me do their work. I've learned that most law officials did not want a profiler like me hanging around.

My popularity as a profiler soared over the past few years. Given the risks associated with using my services, Julian wanted to keep my work confidential. I didn't carry a badge, so I acted more as a consultant. Psychics didn't often get invites to solve cases. However, my particular talents enabled me to provide details that most ordinary human beings couldn't, and that led us to sufficient evidence to close cases according to the law.

Murder cases in Julian's department closed at an exponential rate. Curious onlookers tried to sneak a peek, and when rumors began to circulate about my role on the team, all eyes turned to me.

"Here we are, the wonderful land of Oz," Sorrentino said, waving to the guard monitoring the entrance.

I scanned and spotted all the security around the house, monitoring the personnel on the premises who kept the swarming reporters out.

The house resembled a beautiful mansion before half a dozen uniforms cluttered it with yellow tape. Enormous white pillars outlined the entire front, and a sumptuous garden added color and charm. French doors added a glamorous touch to the home, offering a pleasant view of the chandelier hanging inside. The house retained its beauty, except for the forensic team and law enforcement stamping out its gracefulness.

The SUV came to a sudden halt. I gripped the door handle to steady myself. Sorrentino got out and opened the door for me, but walked away before I muttered a thank you. I aimed a provoked glance at Nicks. He scrutinized me from the mirror, unmoved by my stare, and exited the vehicle.

The noise struck me like a wave as I stepped out of the SUV. At first, shouts from the invasive reporters and conversations among authorized personnel erupted, but as their eyes turned toward me, the talking faded to a whisper. Even though I should be used to this, it made me uncomfortable. Once again, I became the center of attention as I walked up the front porch stairs past the mass speculation.

"Do they know you?" David muttered in my ear.

I turned toward him and shrugged. "I guess so."

David and I followed our escorts up the pathway toward the front door. A half-dozen cold stares followed me up the walkway and into the house. I searched a few of those faces and discerned between the skeptics and those who believed. The latter seemed more shocked as I sauntered past them, making me question my popularity even more.

When I entered through the French doors, the home's inner luxury took my breath away. The chandelier dangled above my head with much greater mass than it showed through the bay window. The rooms were tastefully decorated with intricately arranged art pieces. Soft red and gold colors adorned the furniture and flooring, while subtle animal prints complemented the interior, creating a style I liked. I couldn't imagine Flaming Floyd residing in a place like this; he must have hired a decorator or married one.

I moved through several rooms down a hallway toward the rear of the house. I passed a brightly lit dining room, a billiard room, and a sitting room where an attractive woman sat in a chaise lounge. She hugged an accent pillow in one hand and cupped her mouth with the other. Her long, pale pink robe bore crimson red patches, and as my eyes roamed over her frame, she captured my curiosity with her gaze fixed out the window.

Over the years, my attempts at detective work taught me how to read a person's emotions. Her face reflected a fit of silent anger. She resembled a beautiful photorealistic painting crafted by an artist with tales of woes.

Three men stayed in the room with her. Two officers stood off to the side, whispering to each other. The woman in the chair adjusted herself and locked eyes with me. She brushed away the damp lines along her cheek and nudged the third man sitting on an ottoman, his hand resting on her knee. He stood up when he spotted me in the doorway. He said nothing but nodded toward the door, and I followed him out of the room and down the hallway.

"I assume you're Ms. Rhine?" he asked in a familiar voice.

"I am. And you must be Agent Rodgers." I surveyed the man whose voice interrupted my morning drinking binge. He stood tall in my presence, an authoritative quality in my book and one I wished I possessed myself.

Rodgers glanced over my shoulder. "And you are?"

"David. Forensics." David reached out to shake his hand, but Rodgers ignored him.

"Your boss gave me the impression that I would get a top investigative team on this, but from what I learned, you're the one behind all those solved cases." Rodgers shook his head at me. "I don't believe in psychics."

"Duly noted. Anything else?" I asked, meeting his eyes while raising my head and subtly rising on my toes to appear taller. I tried to remain calm and prevent my face from showing any irritation.

"Yes." He peered at me. "Don't mess up my crime scene."

I let out a long, irritated breath. "I'm well accustomed to the procedure. As you already know, this isn't my first case," I smirked. "For the record, I don't want to be here any more than you do, but you called me."

Agent Rodgers' unamused glare bore down on me, but I brushed it off. "Besides, I assumed your crew would have already gathered any evidence and finished up. There's no reason to waste any more time. We'll do what we need to do and be off," I gestured toward David.

"Make protocol your number one priority," Agent Rodgers said, holding eye contact.

"Solving the case is my number one priority. The protocol comes second, but I will add that to my list of attributes." I stood firmly against his presence and motioned for him to lead.

He muttered something through his teeth and brushed past me. I turned on my heels and followed. He led us to another set of French doors that opened into a spacious office. My eyes adjusted to the light streaming in through the wall of windows, and I couldn't help but admire how it added a particular brilliance to the room.

The office retained an elegant, masculine touch. My eyes grazed the floor-to-ceiling bookshelves, which housed multiple awards. Behind the desk sat a shadow box filled with medals and photographs of a man posing in military attire. As expected, an American flag hung proudly in the corner. A plush, dark mahogany leather couch rested before a cherry oak desk, and between the sofa and the desk lay Congressman Floyd.

Along with Nicks and Sorrentino, a few more agents strode into the office. "This is ridiculous," Agent Nicks said to another in a mumbled voice.

"Is the room going to spin because I just filled up on steak and eggs?" boasted another as he patted his belly. A couple of them tried to cover up their grins and muffled laughs.

I rolled my eyes and glared at Rodgērs. "You know I don't have to be here. We can leave, and maybe you'll figure this out on your own. Maybe not."

Rodgers glared right back at me. "Knock it off, all of you," he said.

The laughter stopped. The agents exchanged looks, shrugged their shoulders, and smirked at me with their ignorant faces.

I smiled. "Good. Now that that is settled, you all need to leave, but bring me something to lie across the floor before you do," I demanded.

The agent with a heavy frame spoke up. "Well, now listen here, darling. Don't think you can come in here and give the orders."

“Oh, here we go,” I hissed as a slight headache emerged. I rubbed my eyes, irritated by the need to explain again, and addressed Agent Rodgers, ignoring the other agents.

"You summoned us here, and to do what I must, I cannot allow any disturbances," I said, gazing down at the Congressman's body. "I've never made the room spin, but things happen." I crossed my arms and gave Rodgers a cautious stare.

Rodgers met me with his perpetual stare for the second time since my arrival. "Fine. Let's get this over with, shall we? You heard Ms. Rhine's order: everybody out!" he demanded.

"Chris, are you kidding?" the heavy-set agent asked.

"I want this room cleared in 30 seconds."

The others stood around, looking dumbfounded.

"20 seconds!"

The agents picked up the pace and left, with Nicks and Sorrentino shuffling out last. "Call us if you need anything," Sorrentino assured him.

"Yeah, just leave, will you? I have no desire to endure this humiliation," Rodgers said, pushing him out. "Don't let me catch anyone trying to sneak a peek. We wouldn't want to interrupt her ability to talk to the dead," he said, sounding disgusted.

I disregarded the agent's last remark and circled the body, treading carefully around the pool of dried blood on the floor.

"I wouldn't advise you to stay either," I cautioned.

"Don't push your luck," he slammed the door.

I smirked. "Fine. Your health."

“And what about him?” Rodgers gestured toward David. He knew the ropes and kept some distance between us, fading into a wallflower to avoid interacting with our friendly host.

“He knows what he needs to do. Pay him no mind,” I said.

Rodgers rested his hands at his hips and scoffed. "Let me introduce you to Congressman Edward Floyd. He earned a lot of respect around these parts," he said, standing a few feet from the victim and looking down at him with sorrowful eyes. "I've known him and his wife for many years. He dedicated himself to dismantling the corrupt elements that plague us, and this is the price he pays for his courage."

I turned my attention from the lifeless body to Rodgers. The depth of his respect and genuine sorrow for his friend was poignant. Regardless of any tension between us, I wanted to help him. Losing a friend is a tragedy, and I knew that if I faced a similar loss, I too would lash out at everyone around me in my grief.

The sudden knock on the door startled him. Sorrentino waited on the other side with a folded plastic sheet. Rodgers snatched the sheet and slammed the door in the agent's face. He tossed the sheet at me, and I grabbed it before it hit me.

"Is there anything you'd like to ask me?" I sensed his agitation and met his stare. He flinched as if expecting the jack-in-the-box to spring out at any moment.

He straightened. "Your technique sounds ludicrous, talking to the dead or something like that. I'm not buying it."

I waved him back to give myself more space. "Wait. Give it time. You will." David tried to stifle a laugh, and we both turned toward him. He shook it off and pretended to focus on his equipment.

I refocused on the middle-aged man's body, lying belly-down with his face cocked to the side. His hand rested just short of his neck. He appeared to have died trying to keep pressure on the wound that opened his throat. The blood pouring from his fatal injury covered a portion of the floor.

I peered over at the agent and asked, "Why can't your team solve this case? I'm brought in when all else fails."

Agent Rodgers lowered his shoulders. "This isn't just anybody. We want answers now. I don't want to waste any time nailing the son of a bitch that did this. Do what I brought you here for."

I scoffed, shook my head, and mumbled, "Feds" yet again as I shoved the leather couch farther away, spread out the plastic sheet, and laid it on the floor next to the body. I positioned myself, adjusting my line of sight to match the lifeless eyes of the Congressman.

The agent's voice interjected. "All right, Ms. Rhine, make a believer out of me," he said, standing over me with both hands resting on his waist.

"Shh," I hissed. I propped myself up on my elbows, observing Agent Rodgers. His flaring nostrils betrayed his attempts to regulate his breathing, while a subtle twitch in his right eye gave him away.

"You are not to speak or move, and if you can tone down your loud breathing, that would be great. No matter what happens, you do not interfere! Do you understand?"

"Sure thing," he said, fidgeting with his suit jacket. "By all means…begin. This should be interesting, assuming you are what they say you are."

I shook my head and then lay flat on the floor. Profiling varies on a case-by-case basis; it is sensitive, but overall, straightforward. The hardest part is controlling my breathing and concentrating on the objective. It's almost like I fall asleep and wake up inside the victim's mind. Meditating on the physical process of death is an impossible practice for most, but my abilities made me a pro at making my body theoretically die.

I took as long as I required to creep inside. I'm used to this by now—hundreds of cases. People of all ages, genders, and races. From every form of assault - stabbings, shootings, suffocations, burning, drowning.

I didn't approach the victims with fear. I used to experience an intense pull when standing a few feet from the dead, as if someone tugged on me with a rope, but that faded over time. I still tolerated a strong urge to dig a hole in their minds and explore, but I taught myself to deny it when I wanted to.

Most of the deaths pulled at my heartstrings when I discovered their innocence, while I secretly applauded the deaths of those who enjoyed their evil ways. Ultimately, I handled the investigation with an unbiased purpose and professionalism. My job is to find out who killed them, help bring their killers to justice, and solve the case. So far, I have maintained a perfect record.

However, I now find myself in the home of what I assume is a murdered politician. The Congressman's death presents another case to solve, another sorry corpse needing to tell me his story. My mind adjusts to the slow and steady disconnection from the world around me. I let my arms relax at my sides, palms open. My head, shoulders, and back contort to the hardwood floor beneath me.

It took me years of practice to achieve the perfect meditative state by reading books and attending yoga classes. I released from my surroundings and allowed the air to fill my lungs. Taking deeper, more effective breaths, I cleared my mind and let myself drift away from my consciousness and into the mind of the man next to me. The cold tingling in my fingers brought me back, but I slipped inside once more as I refocused.

Hello Congressman.

Chapter Three

David studied the woman before him. His keen eyesight captured the periodic twitches of her fingers—nothing too noteworthy. Still, he found himself immersed in the increasing speed of her eyes moving beneath her eyelids; he witnessed rapid eye movement before, but nothing like this. He shifted to survey her face, releasing a breath he didn't realize he was holding in while keeping a close eye on a puzzled Agent Rodgers.

The whole precinct gossiped about Natalie Rhine and her methods as if they were still in high school. Julian was naïve to think he could keep her a secret. Someone like Natalie couldn't be hidden away. She amazed and captivated him, drawing awareness wherever she went.

Natalie's body quivered like an animal caught in a dream. Her skin paled, and her lips and cheeks changed from soft olive to a clammy white-blue hue. She resembled someone who went for a dip in frigid water. He shuddered from the coldness sinking into his bones, as the air in the room plunged twenty degrees.

Her entire body moved in unison with the twitching of her eyes. David found it strange how she moved, as if she opened a hole and was drilling down into it. His eyes moved from side to side, trying to keep pace with her motions. With increased speed, they caused a sharp throbbing at the corners.

Agent Rodgers hobbled back in surprise as Natalie's eyes burst open, revealing only the whites. David couldn't help but let a smile creep across his face, as he was familiar with this process. Rodgers would witness a glorious scene that would burn into his memory for the remainder of his days.

The hair on the back of his neck stood in fevered anticipation. Natalie's body convulsed like an earthquake erupting beneath her. Rodgers gasped for air, stunned by the unexpected movement.

Taking a few steps back and kneeling on the floor, he went through the motions of gasping for breath as if the room filled up with smoke. He never knew how she did it, but the environment changed when she went to the other side. The temperature in the room dropped. The air would thin out, and it almost seemed like his lungs would collapse if he didn't take proper precautions.

He weighed the option of warning Agent Rodgers to follow suit, but Rodgers, being a pompous prick, deserved to suffer through it. David relished the opportunity to gain an extra edge.

Natalie's head turned toward the body next to her. Her face mirrored the dead face of the Congressman. The movement went slow yet fast all at once. The Congressman's lifeless eyes snapped open, aligning with Natalie's perpetual stare. Floyd's body began to convulse in tandem with hers, responding to her movements with equal force, like a puppet on its strings.

Rodger pressed against his chest, and David knew all too well the burning sensation he experienced. He even noted Rodger's eyes reddened, but he didn't blink, or perhaps he couldn't blink. When David first witnessed one of her profiling sessions, Mike ordered him to wait in another room, but he snuck in and hid behind some furniture. He never forgot the discomfort he experienced, as if sharp pins were driving his eyelids open or cutting him off from blinking.

When his body couldn't perform the natural act of drawing air into his lungs, he thought he would suffocate. It was then he understood why Julian didn't want anyone else around when she did her thing. It hurt like hell how she sucked the life out of the room. He just couldn't understand how she did it.

Both bodies moved: one person declared dead. The other, he couldn't tell. Natalie's ability to extract the victim's memories turned into a dramatic spectacle as her eyes latched onto the Congressman's unending stare. His body shook and twitched as if reacting to a command.

Rodgers tried to yell out, clearly fighting for air, and fell to the floor. She did warn him.

What seemed like minutes lasted seconds when both bodies stopped convulsing. The Congressman returned to a corpse, and his body slumped back onto the hardwood. Natalie turned her face away from him. Her body relaxed as the room shifted from an intense, adrenaline-sucking atmosphere to an eerie calmness. The stunned agent pulled his focus from the two bodies and scanned the room, catching David's amused grin.

"Impossible!" the agent choked out as air filtered back through the room. Rodgers turned and vomited to the side, still holding his chest and steadying his breathing.

The other team declared the Congressman's death hours ago, yet his body moved in a rhythm on its own- impossible by any natural law.

The sounds of the other agents running toward the room echoed off the walls. David didn't want them to see him like this, but the stiffness in his legs and arms prevented him from getting up quickly. However, with all his might, he managed to pull himself into a kneeling position and then stand up using a small table beside him. He still had to figure out how to manage the physical response to these proficiencies. It took some of the joy away from watching her.

Natalie lounged on the floor, her skin returning to its normal color, no longer resembling the walking dead. When she opened her eyes and glared at Rodgers, David realized for the first time the color of her eyes—deep blue, especially since just moments ago, those same eyes unveiled the purest of white.

The door crashed open, and several figures swarmed into the room. "Chris, are you all right? What happened?" they all demanded. Rodgers couldn't pull his attention away from Natalie, who seemed as comfortable as a cat sprawled on the floor.

"Chris!"

"Nicks, help me up," Rodgers gasped. David sensed the room grow warmer, and the tension in his muscles melted away. The agents glanced between David and Natalie, ready to make an arrest. Rodgers reached for Nicks, shook his head, and urged them to assist him outside. A few agents lingered, no doubt expecting answers. David helped Natalie to her feet and offered her a bottle of water from his case. The others seemed unsure of what to do.

"What happened?" David asked.

"Well," Natalie said, taking a sip. "I wouldn't recommend letting the lady of the house rush out the door anytime soon."

Chapter Four

I bellowed with laughter, "Agent Rodgers clutched his hand to his chest. His men rushed to his side, helping him to his feet. I made myself comfortable, watching the stream of suits pouring into the room."

I told my story to Detective Jeffrey Sands, who hung on every word I spoke. I arrived back in town around noon and headed to the office. Jeff waited at his desk to hear all about the gory details of my latest case. I always enjoyed giving him more information than necessary. He respected my work and never regarded me as a freak of nature.

"Please tell me he wet himself. I beg you." His auburn beard revealed the smile of an amused little boy stuck inside the body of a mid-forty-year-old man begging for more.

"Sorry, bud, but I do believe he puked. That's a first for me."

"Still, awesome."

"I told them it was Miss Scarlet, in the library with the knife," I said. "Those other agents stood around, dumbfounded."

"Then what?" Jeffrey asked.

"I suggested Rodgers and his boys ask the wife about her dirty little secret that the Congressman discovered right before he bled to death; she can also tell him where she hid the knife."

"Oh, come on, the wife? I figured a mob-supported Democrat took him out," Jeff jolted away from his desk, throwing his pen down like a twelve-year-old.

"You are such a Republican," I laughed. "But no, I think they believed that as well, hence the rush to get the case solved, but it turns out...the usual suspect."

"So, they doubted you, huh? Feds!" Jeff smirked.

I grinned. "I swear you and I might be related."

"I bet Detective Rodgers called and chewed out the captain for you making a fool of him."

"No doubt," I stretched my arms, working on my fourth wind for the day with little nap time between heading to Jersey, solving the case, and returning home. My body still recovered from the long night and the never-ending morning. "I warned Rodgers from the beginning to leave the room, but the guy insisted. If he ends up having to visit a cardiologist or develops a fear of dead people, that's on him."

"It's never that simple. You're damned if you do and damned if you don't," Jeff warned.

"Well, Rodgers is FBI, after all. I can't tell him how to run his crime scene."

Jeff threw me an unconvincing nod. "That may be all well and good, but there are rules to your profiling. No witnesses!" He dangled his finger at me. "I can attest to the almost heart attack I experienced when I stood guard over you for the first time. I can handle the moving dead bodies; I don't like the wrecking ball to my chest."

"I think I've said sorry a million times over," I said, more argumentative than sincere. "I didn't know how much energy it takes to do what I do. I'm on the inside when it happens, not standing around watching."

"I'm over it. I'm just saying, be prepared for Julian to bring the rain," Jeff said, aiming a paper ball at a garbage can and nailing his throw for the dozenth time.

I glanced at the open door of my boss's empty office. Luckily, Julian was nowhere to be seen. I took a sigh of relief; this should keep me safe from the downpour for now. Jeff is right, though; I'll get reamed about the Congressman case sooner or later. No witnesses. Julian's rule.

I wasn't certain why. Perhaps it was the unnatural effects my profiling caused to the surrounding atmosphere. Or maybe Julian just wanted to keep me to himself. Psychics were a sin in the law enforcement world. No self-respecting cop wanted to get caught using one. I, however, was a different breed.

"And speaking of rain…is a heavy storm cloud hovering inside your mind?" Jeff's voice reduced to that of a depressed spokesperson for an antidepressant commercial.

I rolled my eyes. "Don't remind me," I said, glancing at the clock. Dr. Lance opened a time slot and scheduled me for when I got back from Jersey — a usual practice to attend a psychiatrist appointment with my least favorite individual after every profile. The goal is to help keep me level-headed and human after experiencing being shot or stabbed or whatever happened to the latest victim.

Jeff didn't hide his sarcasm. "When do you have to visit the good doctor?"

"I'm supposed to meet him in an hour." I prayed that time would stop.

"Well, just think, not only will you enjoy that bundle of sunshine, but you'll relive it all over again during your debrief."

I arched an eyebrow at Jeff. "Thanks for the encouragement. I'll remember that," I said with a wry smile as I stuffed my things into my satchel. "I should grab a bite to eat before sitting in that depressing office. Who knows how long I'll be stuck there this time?" I sighed.

"Good luck," Jeff sang out. "Let me know when visiting hours are at the psych ward."

Jeff is not only my coworker, but also my best friend—actually, he is my only friend—so I didn't hesitate to give him the middle finger as I walked away.

Chapter Five

I checked my watch and compared it to the clock on the wall as I waited at the empty psychiatrist's office. The receptionist informed me the doctor would be out in a minute, fifteen minutes ago.

The secretary hunched over in her chair. Her posture appeared pained, no doubt from years of service, enduring a rusty, squeaky piece of furniture that offered her no support. An old book propped up one of the desk's corner legs to help keep it balanced. Even her name tag, which used to say Mrs. Clara Rice, lost a few vowels during her career as a psychiatrist's assistant. She focused on the typewriter before her, paying me no mind. Unstable people are a dime a dozen to her; my reputation didn't faze her.

I paced around the waiting room, examining the remaining artifacts that populated it. Against the wall, wood-framed chairs sat with cushions so old that the floral patterns resembled a poor imitation of a Van Gogh painting. The carpet displayed worn circles from the restless feet that settled while waiting to be seen.

With the money this man charges, at least he can remove the hideous wallpaper and paint the walls. This place is more depressing than depression itself.

"Ms. Rhine. You can go in now." The delicate voice from behind the desk spoke.

Clara tried to use the desk to help lift herself out of her chair.

"It's okay, sweetie. I can get the door myself," I said, moving quickly. She smiled a lovely, homely smile, settled back into her chair, and refocused on her work. I wondered why she still worked at her age, rather than retiring at home; she must be in her eighties. I scanned the dilapidated waiting room and reflected on what a cheapskate her boss is. If he wouldn't pay to update this, he's not going to pay into her retirement.

The doctor's office on the other side of the door displayed a more refined, yet archaic space, except for the oversized leather plush chair sitting right in the middle. Dr. Lance sat at his desk, scribbling in his notebook as I walked in.

"Natalie, good to see you," he perked up from behind his desk.

"No offense, but I wish I could say the same."

He ignored my remark. "Well, I'm glad you made it back all right. Flight okay?"

"Coming back, the lovely little jet hit every turbulence possible—quite nauseating. It doesn't help to fly with a headache and lack of sleep," I said, plopping into my regular seat and making myself as comfortable as possible. Those pills you prescribed aren't working anymore."

I slunk back into the plush leather chair across from the doctor's usual spot. I used my feet to pull the matching ottoman toward me and rested them on top, making myself as comfortable as possible.

The psychiatrist moved to his small, square, metal-framed chair with metal armrests and a black, worn leather cushion. Why the hell would he spend his workday in that uncomfortable-looking chair?

"I'm afraid I can't raise the dosage on your pills." He examined me through furrowed brows and then reviewed the notes before him. "Did you try the breathing exercises I suggested?"

"Yep. Doesn't help," I replied.

He shuffled through his notes, "We'll just have to figure out something else then, won't we? Although I hate to be the bearer of bad news, we are running out of options. The faster I write a script, the quicker you write it off in your system."

"Well, you're the professional. You know best," I said. I considered the man sitting across from me. I never accepted the idea of meeting with a psychiatrist. He can declare me unfit, claim I'm suicidal, or suggest I'm on the verge of a complete mental breakdown, and my job as a consultant would be over.

The persistent clicking of the typewriter echoed through the door, each sharp tap resonating in the silence. The sound crept under my skin, compelling me to twitch with every keystroke. I burrowed into the couch, fighting the desire to give the office an extensive makeover.

“Question,” I asked.

“Hmm.”

“I've been curious to know; do you not believe in modern-day computers? I mean, what's with the typewriter? I love antiques, but you would think that a computer would help keep you better organized in your work.”

Lance peered at me over the rim of his glasses. “How often do computers break down, and all information disappears? It's better to stick with what we're used to. No need to change what's not broken."

I perked up. "Oh, so then there's no need for me to be here. Great!"

He smirked. "Nice try."

Dr. Lance showcased his typical pristine appearance, complete with pressed khaki pants, a white button-down shirt, and a dark blue tie, all topped with a cardigan sweater. I estimated him to be in his mid-to-upper fifties. He neatly combed his hair to cover the slight balding, and his meticulously shaved skin revealed a flawless tone and texture. He wore glasses perched high on his nose, which made him resemble a less handsome Stanley Tucci.

"So, tell me how this recent case went. I heard through the grapevine that you scared the daylights out of an FBI agent," he asked, pen poised, ready to write. I knew Julian would have spoken to him already. I can barely finish profiling without Julian shoving Lance in my face.

I thought back to this morning and let out a laugh. "Yeah, I did. I'm guessing the agent will need some time off for a while. Rodgers still appeared a bit ill when I left." A thought struck me, and I perked up. "Hey, I have an idea, maybe he should come and talk with you?" I offered with a sarcastic wink.

He humored me with a courtesy grin. "Why did you let him stay?"

I shrugged and eased back again. "Agent Rodgers insisted, saying he didn't want me messing up his crime scene."

He maintained a firm voice. "But if I have to guess, I will say he voiced his opinion, you didn't like it, and you wanted to make a fool out of him. Am I close?" he asked, giving me his typical, I-know-you-better-than-you-think stare.

"I can't make the man leave if he doesn't want to. Rodgers knew from the beginning what I was capable of, but he tried to play stupid," I defended. I folded my hands together and sank further into the chair.

Lance smiled half-amusedly. "I'm sure you made quite the spectacle, but we're not here to talk about the agent, so let's move on."

"Fine with me. What else do you want to discuss?" I asked.

"Let's continue with the profiling you performed. How are you after this one?"

I tried to keep my answers as simple as possible. I hated talking about the profiling. I wanted to move on from those experiences, not dredge them up, but Julian ordered these sessions to help clear my mind and allow me to come to terms with each case. Julian barked out his command: "You talk, he listens, get the emotions and stress off your chest. Help him, help you. It's for your own sake." I didn't have the heart to tell him it didn't work that way.

"Fine. Floyd didn't see it coming. His wife hated him for getting her lover sent to prison. She made her move, and he suffered for it."

Dr. Lance scribbled some notes before looking back up at me. "Did you experience any residual fear? Anxiety?"

My foot shook back and forth while my fingers drummed against each other. I stopped moving, cursing my lack of poker skills. "When I emerged from his profiling, it took me a minute or two to recover. That's about it."

He tipped his head in slight agitation. "Natalie, you make his death sound so mundane."

His tone put me on edge. I recalled the profiling moment when Floyd grasped his throat. I swallowed hard to prevent my body from reliving the experience again.

Flamin' Floyd was a respectable man. He promoted himself as unstoppable and fierce, but still just a man. He loved his country, job, and wife, and would sacrifice everything for her. The moment he met his wife's cold eyes, a wave of devastation crashed over him as she gripped the blade in her hand. He couldn't comprehend how it came down to this—he didn't deserve such a fate.

"I'm sorry; I didn't mean to make it seem that way," I said.

Dr. Lance gave me a stern look. "Yes, you did."

My mouth fell open. "Well, if I did, it's because you have a habit of implying that I am a heartless, death-loving psycho, so I might as well spare you the trouble?"

He shuffled in his chair. He laid the pen down on the notebook, making direct eye contact. "First, I have never concluded that you are a 'heartless, death-loving psycho.' Second, most people can't handle death as it is. It terrifies them even more when death comes violently through murder. Natalie, you bear witness to these deaths. You experience what they experience in every manner. That is not something an ordinary person can face and then walk away claiming they felt nothing from it."

He intertwined his fingers to match mine. "These appointments are supposed to help you, but you turn to stone every time you walk in. You make yourself sound unbothered by your cases, or you try to convince me that everything is fine with you, and I know that isn't reality. I've been in this business for a long time. I'm skilled at reading people," he said, not trying to hide his smugness.

Because I don't want to lose my job! "Okay, fine. The case broke my heart like most others. I wanted to lash out at his wife, but I can't. At least I can live knowing I didn't let her get away with it." I sat up, resting my head in my hands. "I would give anything to be normal, but I'm stuck with this curse. I didn't ask for this," I said. "Call it an act of God."

The room fell silent for a minute. The lines on Lance's face tightened in a dramatic focus and eventually softened. "Natalie, I have worked with you for over three years, and you have changed, as if you are losing years of your life with every profiling, which worries me. When we first met, you were curious and eager to lend a hand. I think the issue is that you came off a bit too eager. You accepted everything Julian threw at you, and I believe that became overwhelming." He surveyed me with apologetic eyes. "I understand you have to confront death all the time, but each case takes a piece of your sanity with it, and whether you believe me or not, I'm trying to prevent that from happening."

Dr. Lance relaxed his arms and legs, showing signs of remorse. The atmosphere in the room became so quiet that each tap, tap, tap of Mrs. Rice's keyboard permeated through the door and echoed in my ears. I cringed and wanted to cover my ears from the relentless taping, begging in my head for her to stop.

Keep that from happening? He couldn't keep Sherry Sweeney from being murdered by a person she wanted to get to know. He couldn't keep Monica Pearson from killing her parents and then herself. He couldn't keep Matthew

Avery from following through on a bully's demand that he hang himself.

Please don't remind me that I'm unlike anyone else; I'm already aware of that.

The words echoed through my cupped hands. I compelled myself to endure yet another session of lies. I tell him I'm not crazy—a lie. I tell him I can cope—a lie. I say to him that death doesn't affect me—a lie. The truth is, I can sense those people here with me now. They are all living inside my head, drowning in my consciousness.

I thought the goal was to let them go, but their presence lingered. I never told anyone that. Lance would declare me as compromised in some mental capacity. Then, it would all be over for me. I needed this job to make sense of everything. Without it, these deaths would consume every part of me.

Restlessness worked its way under my skin. "I struggle with being different. It would be easier to embrace being me if I read tarot cards or openly discussed experiences with lost loved ones. Still, unfortunately, that's not my reality."

My focus trailed to the notebook sitting in his lap. I glimpsed his messy handwriting but couldn't make out any words. What would I give to read that notebook? To read his mind? I didn't hate this man, regardless of the help he claimed he wanted to give; he terrified me.

"I admit I still consider my ability a curse, but at least I can use it to do good in this world." I lifted my feet off the ottoman and sat poised with my hands tucked between my legs, all to shield my discomfort.

"I can help bring people to justice and assist their families in finding peace. Yes, it's scary to experience death, but I make it clear that it's not me dying. I come back. I always come back. My awareness kicks in, and I can disconnect myself, knowing it's time to return. Set the matter right."

Dr. Lance appeared more at ease. I prayed he listened, comprehended every word, and did not let textbook theories take precedence over his understanding.

"It's not easy, but knowing I can make a difference helps me put those pieces back together." I tossed in my best pleading, doe-eyed performance. Placating him became more difficult with each session. Every death was personal to me; I couldn't help it; I'm human. "It gives me purpose in life."

He studied me, remaining silent. He tilted his head to the left. His eyes seemed to grasp some understanding of my argument, which I hope is believable and compassionate, despite the topic of conversation.

He twirled his pen between his fingers. "All right. I'm having trouble figuring out how you manage all this. Most people would be in a psych ward by now, but perhaps that's a bonus to your gifts. Maybe you can cope with death in a way the rest of us can only dream of," he said, attempting to reassure me, "but you need to take it easy."

Lance clicked his pen, tucked it inside his sweater, and scanned his notes. He seemed to concede. I won the battle. Another thought struck me—maybe I can slip inside the minds of the living and the dead. Can I control him to see it my way? I doubted it. I didn't need to pass the psych ward and head directly toward a maximum-security prison.

"Don't take what I said too personally. Natalie, you may have an extraordinary gift that makes me skeptical, but you are still a human, young lady." He sounded like Julian.

"You keep pushing yourself too far, and I'm afraid that one day you'll reach the point of no return. Let's not allow that to happen, okay?"

"Got it. I'm human," I wanted to roll my eyes at Lance. There's nothing quite like sitting in a shrink's office, listening to his diagnosis that I already gave myself. I shuffled in my seat, unsure if that meant the appointment was over. He sighed and tossed his pen and notepad onto the table beside him. He tipped his head back and rubbed his eyes.

"Did you have a chance to talk to Julian since you've been back?" he asked, adjusting his glasses and standing up. I mirrored his movements, pushing myself out of the chair to stand beside him. "I'm heading back to the office after this," I said.

He picked up the pen and notepad, walked over to his desk, and set them down on the smooth, polished surface. "Well, do me a favor if you would. I know you're close to Julian. Make sure you're confiding in someone you trust. It's true what people say: talking always helps."

"I'll try."

"I want you to take a few days off and go out this weekend. Have fun, drink responsibly, and relax with your friends. Remove work from your mind. I'll tell Julian to give you the time off. You need it."

Friends? I let out a laugh, but quickly stopped myself.

Lance's attention darted to me. "Is that an agreement?"

I bit my lower lip. "Not sure. I'm usually on call, so good luck getting Julian to allow it."

"Don't worry about Julian. I'll talk to him. You need to rest; if he wants to keep you around, I will insist he gives you some time away from work."

"Oh," I said, unconvinced that Julian would. Not wanting to waste another minute, I agreed to the doctor's request and turned to leave.

"Natalie?"

I stopped right when I got to the door. "Yes?"

"How is your family? You haven't spoken much of them?" he asked.

"They're fine. I'll take my accrued time off to visit with them and my friends." I tried to hide the sarcasm in my voice.

"Good. Well, I hope you enjoy the rest of your weekend."

I turned away from him, giving a final once-over at the decrepit room, and walked out. It's a good thing he didn't pursue a career in interior decorating.

Chapter Six

"Hey, Rhine, great job on the Congressman case," a voice shouted from a few desks away. Tony Mosley reclined back in his desk chair while a rookie chatted with him.

Tony is the department's most experienced detective. He is a no-holds-barred kind of guy, preferring to tackle challenging cases directly, with a specialty in gang murders. There is something about him that made me keep my distance. He is neither disrespectful nor opposed to my work; Tony enjoyed the chase and wanted all the accolades for himself. His attention deficit disorder fueled this ambition, and he excelled in it.

The other detectives performed well, but Julian allowed them the first twelve hours rather than the first forty-eight. Julian would pull me in to wrap things up if they didn't solve the case after a day. Tony accepted this, even placing bets on whether he would crack the case. His way of tracking down the culprit is as unorthodox as mine. When they say there is always one in the group - not including me - he would be that one. As long as Tony adhered to the law, no one challenged him.

As I smiled and gave him a thumbs-up, I saw the mess of paperwork that seemed to overflow across his cluttered desk. The papers were haphazardly stacked, some partially covered by open folders and others adorned with scribbles. My focus shifted to the documents in front of him, drawing my curiosity about what he might be working on. Tony, ever the master of subtlety, shrugged and flashed a half-grin that seemed to say it all, hinting that the contents were off-limits. It was his clever way of establishing boundaries, reminding me to keep my curiosity in check.

"Thanks," I said. "Let me know when you need anything," I smirked and checked my watch, calling him out on his game.

I scanned the office, curious about who else acquired a new workload, and spotted several desks covered similarly.

Was there a crime spree while I was in Jersey? I dropped my satchel and let it hit my desk with a loud thump. I scanned the room again with a sense of urgency and was ready to take action. If there are more cases, I can help. Of course, the only problem is that, aside from Julian, no one asked for my help.

Over the years, a rift developed between my coworkers and me. They all wanted to pursue their police detective work the old-fashioned way, and who am I to tell them otherwise? The problem is that the old-fashioned method took time, and cases often went cold. Once Julian recognized how useful I could be, he would have me step in and solve their cases minutes after they spent hours and even days working on them.

I looked down at my clean, empty desk and then over at the others. I held nothing more than a one-subject notebook filled with scribbles of questionable artwork, my favorite pen, and a Post-it note hanging from my computer monitor with "C ME ASAP" written on it. My stomach turned; Julian's notes are not the accessory you wanted on your desk.

I peeked at his office door and recognized his shadow behind the glass. I couldn't imagine Julian would be mad at me, but you never know his mood from one moment to the next.

My eyes darted around the room, zoning in on the chronic eavesdroppers who will insist on having a front row seat to my time with the boss. A few times, I stumbled upon conversations not meant for my ears.

"Natalie needs to leave the police work to us, real detectives. She only got in because Julian is interested in her," one voice remarked.

"Yeah, and we all know what that means," another would add. They would laugh and fall silent the moment I came within earshot.

I never understood why they couldn't accept that we are all on the same team. It makes no difference who solves the case as long as it gets solved. Instead, they whine to the boss. I told them to handle the crimes of the living and leave the dead to me. Most of the office didn't take that well.

I flopped down in my chair, acting a bit childish and worried as if I'd be stuck grounded forever.

"I see dead people," an eerie voice sounded from behind my shoulder.

When I turned, a cutout of Haley Joel Osment attached to a popsicle stick loomed over me. "I see dead people," he recited.

I fought back a smile. Leave it to Jeff to lift me out of my almost defeated mood. "It's not like that ever gets old," I said, snatching up Haley Joel and tossing him aside.

"Hey! He's my best prop yet," Jeff said.

"I disagree. I'm still a fan of the hand buzzer." I sat back in my chair and let the moment sink in before we both started laughing.

"Oh yeah." Jeff scanned the faces of those present in the office. His eyes glazed over, reminiscing about the time he asked me to wear a hand buzzer as a gag. It would zap people the instant I touched them with my hand. Then, he would jump in and scold me for trying to eat their souls before lunch. "I think we broke a record for causing the most anxiety attacks in such a short time," he said, whispering through stifled laughter as he glanced at a few unsuspecting coworkers sitting at their desks.

"Ah, memories." I was about to remind him of another great joke we played on our uptight coworkers when a slight gust of wind rushed across my arms. Jeff's focus reallocated toward his monitor with such speed that I immediately believed something interesting had flashed across his screen.

"What does ASAP mean to you, Ms. Rhine?" Julian's voice called from behind.

I glared at Jeff for the lack of warning and turned to face my Captain.

"Well, sir, I figured you wanted to consult me about the Congressman's profiling, so I thought it best to finalize my notes about the case before reporting to you." I tapped my notebook, hoping he wouldn't call my bluff. The only note he would find is my horrible caricature of Rodgers vomiting.

“I want to discuss your recent profiling with you, but I assure you that I have all the necessary notes.” Julian stood almost military-style. His superiority loomed over me, catching the attention of the others milling about.

"Well, in that case, lead the way," I said, maintaining my composure. He gestured for me to pass. I kept my cool as I walked toward his office. As I walked the green mile, dozens of eyes criticized my every step.

Written in large, scripted lettering, Captain Julian Marcus's name was displayed across his office door. I hovered close enough to make out the dot above the' I' in his name before he came up from behind and pushed the door open.

"So, how's your day going, chief?" I said, trying to act as if I had no reason to worry. I loathed getting pulled into his office like this. It was like being back in middle school, getting summoned into the principal's office for making Abby Cook pee herself in biology class.

Revenge was sweet when I made the frog she dissected do a little dance on the tray before her. Her face turned pale white, and Abby fainted. She deserved it for throwing a handful of dead bugs in my hair. I ended up grounded for a month.

Julian shut the door behind him with practiced gentleness. He grew tired of replacing the glass of his office door after slamming it during his mood swings. He opted for frosted glass, and although it reduced visibility, I detected a few extra bodies gravitating closer to the windowpane.

He moved behind his desk, pulled out his oversized black leather chair, and took a seat. The office had three other chairs, and I chose the one farthest away.

"Oh no, this one," he directed me toward the small seat in front of his desk. Most of the department labeled it the electric chair, and for a good reason.

My stomach turned, and a tingling sensation seared through my fingers. Julian received the nickname "The Judge" due to his manner of dealing with people. If anyone opposed him in the wrong way or questioned his authority, he would come down on them so hard you could hear the metaphorical gavel slicing through the air.

I walked over and sat down. Julian's eyes remained fixed on a letter resting in front of him. He scanned it again as if searching for something he missed. The second hand of a clock behind him raced around a few times before he laid the papers down, intertwined his fingers, and tilted back in his chair.

"How about you tell me what happened this morning?" he demanded rather than asked.

"Well, I went to Jersey as directed and solved the case."

"Just like that, huh? You went, you saw, you kicked ass?"

I couldn't help but smile. "Exactly."

"And how did things go with the agents? Good, I hope?"

I shrugged. "As expected, you know how it is. No one wanted me around. They expected this highly efficient team and ended up with little old, psychic me. Tensions flared. I did my job and left the case solved."

"Uh-huh, go on…," he urged.

Don't play dumb. I know why I'm sitting in Julian's office. I received plenty of warnings. Why bother avoiding the issue?

"And…Agent Rodgers wanted to stick around and monitor while I did the profiling." I kept my voice calm yet justified. My performance was no different from that of any other case. Julian is aware of how others viewed me. Most law officials didn't find my way of solving cases efficient; it simply isn't natural. The CSI unit despised me even more, convinced they would all be out of a job if I carried on with the profiling.

"You let him stay?" His demeanor stayed disconcertingly professional.

This is Julian; I let out a small sigh and reminded myself. He knows me and how I react in certain situations. Lying would be futile. "Let me guess. Agent Rodgers is still pretty sore at me, and that's what you've been reading."

"Pay no mind to what I've been reading. I want you to tell me what happened."

"Like I said, nothing out of the norm. I received a call, flew to Jersey, got walked on by just about everyone there-"

"And you let them get to you by acting out of line and doing the one thing I insist should not be done…you allowed an audience!"

"What would you have me do? His crime scene. His rules." I began to yell back but caught myself and lowered my voice, shooting a speculative glance toward the door.

"The guy almost had a heart attack!" He sat poised in his chair, ready to jump out and do his ritual walk around the office as he maintained the law of his land.

I straightened, defying the rules of the chair. "And that is my problem, how? Again, not a cop, and not FBI."

"You know how dangerous it is for others to be present. The last thing I need is the government coming down on me because one of my own sent a federal agent to the hospital, thus turning all heads to this department and getting my ass handed to me by some jackass wanting my job."

I struggled to hold his stare. Under any other circumstances, I enjoyed looking at him. He had about twelve years on me, but he was stunningly handsome. His steel-gray eyes would secretly make me swoon. He had a tanned complexion and a tall, lean frame that would make any woman, including me, feel protected. His thick chestnut brown hair made me want to run my fingers through it.

Looking like a young George Clooney, I could picture him on the front cover of a woman's romance novel, looking sexy with his head tipped to the side, wearing a suit jacket pulled back to reveal his badge, and a dress shirt tight around his muscled chest. I blinked. Stop it, Natalie!

"Agent Rodgers is a grown man. And last I checked, I can't tell an FBI agent where to go."

Julian pushed away from his desk. "How many times have I told you? When you're called in. You're in charge."

I turned away from him and peered out the window. Julian's office had the best view overlooking the bay. Whenever I am stuck late working on cases, I would sneak into his office to watch the beautiful sailboats and the sunset flickering off the calm water. While it may sound strange, Julian's office is my sanctuary—until moments like these. I responded out of principle, making my position clear. "Easier said than done. I'm not you. I don't possess a fancy title or a shiny badge. I solved the case, but I'm still dealing with the FBI's ignorance. I have enough issues of my own to worry about aside from Agent Rodgers."

It was like being back in Lance's office. Julian sat there and waited, just like a psychiatrist. I stood up, rebelling against the chair and its hidden meaning. There is no reason I should be in the hot seat.

"I did nothing wrong. The agents acted against me; I have every right to stand up to them. Rodgers knew the rules. He didn't follow them, yet I'm receiving the reprimand?"

I walked over to the window for a better view. The sights outside calmed me. The sun streamed in and warmed my skin through the glass. A moment later, a pair of hands brought another warming sensation across my shoulders.

"I'm sorry. I don't mean to yell. But truth be told, watching you is dangerous for those without any idea of what you can do."

"Well then, maybe you should have been there. Or better yet, don't pawn me off on other jurisdictions. The FBI called me. They gave me a ton of shit over it, and even after I solved the case, they still complained. Why do I even bother?"

His breathing halted. He wanted to say something, but then dismissed the subject, steering the conversation toward a more compassionate tone.

"Because it's who you are. It's what you do. And yes, you're right. I thought you would like the idea of showing those federal jackasses what you're capable of."

I found it hard to disagree with that. There was a fleeting sense of exhilaration at the idea of contributing to a federal investigation, and I wanted to make a difference, even if that included working alongside the FBI.

“These issues you're having. Tell me about them."

I didn't want to go through this again for the second time today, but Julian is a different kind of audience. He didn't study me the way Lance did. He transitioned from Captain Marcus, my boss, to Julian, my confidant, and maybe a bit more than that.

"Those dreams I told you about a while back started up again." Ruminating on the tormented screams and painful memories of past victims turned my stomach; my dreams leave me powerless to help them.

"When?" he asked.

"A few weeks ago." I turned to look up into those beautiful gray eyes. I grew to love and respect Julian. He is a diligent man and excellent at his job, but he is one of the few who truly knew me, appreciated my work, and treated me like a human being with feelings.

Julian brought me into the department. We worked closely together, but the others who strived to earn a badge acted against him for having me around, so we put on a professional demeanor. Yet our connection deepened over the years. I was too afraid to admit it, fearing rejection down the road.

"Have you talked to Dr. Lance about them?" he asked.

"No. I can't," I whispered.

"Why not? That's what he's there for." He moved his hands to my hair and ran his fingers through it. I allowed myself a moment of his closeness and savored the affection for as long as I could. I eased away from him, fearful that someone might burst through his door and catch us at any moment.

Julian quizzically tilted his head before propriety struck. He straightened himself and walked back behind his desk.

"For the record, you are not the only one getting reprimanded. Agent Rodgers attended a meeting in an office much larger than mine. He left a mess all over the crime scene."

I immediately smiled, picturing the agent's almost fetal-like position on the floor. "He sure did. I may have gotten a little excited about that, especially after his speech on strict protocol."

Julian gave me a playful nod as he picked up the sheet of paper and ran it through the shredder.

My smile faded. "Speaking of excitement, my wonderful psychiatrist told me I could have the rest of the weekend off until Tuesday. He said he would insist that you allow it."

"Is that so? He's the boss now?" Julian gave me a one-over and sighed as he pulled his chair out and took a seat. "But for once, I may give him the benefit of the doubt and comply," he smiled.

"Thanks. It will be nice to relax. If I report that I'm enjoying life, he might get off my back."

"Do you want me to speak with him?"

"No. It would just provoke him to find a way to torture me. He claims he's not, but I have my doubts. He's a shrink, after all. I swear, they always want to throw labels and diagnoses on people. I still think he's trying to paint me as this emotionally blocked psycho who messes with the dead."

"Are you?" His half-crooked smile and curious look caught me off guard.

"Julian! You know full well I have to eat souls to survive." I joked, trying to shake off the sudden tension in the pit of my stomach.

Damn, those eyes!

"He may be able to form an opinion and even a diagnosis, but when it comes to your job, that's my decision. If he even thinks about trying to take you away from me..." Julian said, giving me a sultry stare.

Again, he took me off guard. "Well then, the next time you talk to him, be sure to tell him I'm still normal and in control of my sanity," I instructed him. "Can I go now? I'm sure they're salivating at the thought of me getting canned."

We both eyed the door. It did seem quiet.

"Yes, you can go. I'll try to leave you alone during your time off."

"I appreciate that," I smiled, snagging one last glance at those eyes and composing myself before I headed out the door.

"Oh, and Natalie... when you go back out there, pretend I laid into you. I have a reputation to protect," he added, transforming his recent smile into a playful growl.

"Yes, sir. I'm sorry, sir; I will do better next time," I replied in an alarmed voice.

"You better. One more thing... dinner later?" he asked.

I responded with a sly smile and nod before opening the door and smirking at a few eavesdroppers, pretending to shuffle through their paperwork.

Sorry, everyone, not only did I not get fired, but I have a date with the boss. You're still stuck with the freak of nature. I kept my smile hidden from view as I left Julian's office and sauntered back to my desk. Jeff sat at his desk, waiting to learn what had transpired, expecting me to spill everything. I made it out for Julian's sake, like I got off with a nasty warning. I thought it best to omit a few minor details. I planned on filling my diary later with the truth and nothing but the truth.

My daydreams all but dissolved the moment I spotted Jeff sneak a hand inside his desk. He must have convinced himself that I needed cheering up after my time with Julian because Haley Joel Osment made another appearance.

"I see dead people," he said again.

"Is that the only thing you can come up with?" I asked.

Maintaining the creepy voice, he said, "Yes. That's all I remember from the movie."

I shook my head. "I swear I think you're crazier than I am."

Chapter Seven

David sat back as Mrs. Rice typed away behind her desk. The seventies-style typewriter occupied three-quarters of her workspace, and the little old lady's hair bounced with every keystroke. He smiled to himself as it reminded him to follow the bouncing ball.

"David," Dr. Lance peered out of his door, "you can come in now."

He diverted his thoughts to the man standing in the doorway. "Afternoon," he said, offering a simple nod as Lance stepped aside to let him into the office.

David eyed the chair but walked right past it, positioning himself against a window ledge. He relaxed, half-sitting, and crossed his arms while Lance took his usual place with his notepad in hand.

"So, how have you been?" Dr. Lance asked, ready to begin the meeting.

"About the same as last we met," David said.

Lance smiled, "I suppose that can be good, since you and your wife were here only two days ago. Anything change in the last couple of days?" He laid the notepad across his knee, and all David could make out was him noting the date at the top of the page.

David shook his head in response. "Not really." He couldn't even remember what they said during their marriage counseling session. His mind was still stuck on the earlier events. "I'm not here to discuss all that."

"So, what brings you in?"

David rubbed his chin. "Julian asked me to sit in on a case. With Natalie, you know." His eyes darted to Lance.

Lance nodded. "Yes. I heard the FBI contacted her to assist in solving a case. A big one, apparently. I'm assuming that's what you're referring to?"

"Yeah, well, it was frustrating, to say the least. The FBI didn't take our presence there too kindly. More so, her being there."

"They never do. To them, anyone who is not a federal agent is a meter maid."

David let out a snort. "Tell me about it. And they were awful to her."

"I hate to say that's no surprise. No one wants to take the poor girl seriously. People don't want to believe what they can't see." Dr. Lance said.

"It's funny you mention that because I think that's why I'm here. I know this isn't your usual topic, but do you believe in what she can do?"

Lance squinted. "Well, at first, being a man of science and all, it was hard to believe. But then, the more I heard about what people witnessed her do, the more I slowly accepted that she is everything people say she is. Why do you ask?"

David ran his hand through his hair. "Because I can't stop thinking about her ability."

"Ah. I get it." Lance eyed him, "I hope you aren't doing anything that would cause problems anywhere."

David sneered, "I know all the rules, and I'm always careful," he breathed out.

Lance resumed his incessant scribbling on his notepad. "That's probably for the best. I understand it can be dangerous for anyone around Natalie when she does her thing." He adjusted his glasses higher up his nose. "So, when you say you can't stop thinking about her, what do you mean?"

David lowered his hands to his side. "Oh, don't worry. I'm not fixating on her like that. She's plain, actually. It's more of an obsession with her ability to interact with dead people, if that's what you call what she does. What do you even call what she does?"

Lance's troubled brow gave David the impression that this doctor had no clue. "From what I understand, she interacts with the dead, as you said. So, when you watch her… are you afraid or uncomfortable around her? I assume you've seen her in action?"

"Yeah, and like, holy shit! No better words describe it—the adrenaline rush when she makes the body move. It's so addicting; I can't take my eyes off her. And then the way the corpse responds to her, it's like, I don't know, a marionette, and she's holding the strings." David rubbed his forearm. "Seriously, just talking about her makes me giddy."

Lance sat still, his pen resting motionless in his fingers as he focused intently on David. "David, I must admit it's encouraging to see that Natalie has supporters who truly back her rather than undermine her. However, I can't help but feel that your interest in her is more than just professional. I'm hoping it's not veering toward obsession?"

David blinked a few times. "Hey, you told me to study her."

Lance was taken aback. "No, I did not. I never said the word study. I suggest you try to make friends. You and Natalie are in a line of work where you both handle heavy workloads that are mentally and physically exhausting, and could use some time away from the office. Natalie is an interesting woman—she is witty and enjoyable to converse with, someone who can help take your mind off all the negative aspects of your job. Plus, your wife mentioned that you still haven't made many friends since you are new to the area." He let out a long breath. "I'm starting to believe I caused a misunderstanding."

David extended his hands in defense. "There's no misunderstanding. Yeah, I guess you suggested an office friendship with her, but have you seen what she can do? She's intriguing."

Dr. Lance studied David above the rim of his glasses. "She's not a circus act or a piece of art hanging in a museum. If you try socializing with her as opposed to observing her from the sidelines, you can discover who she is, not just the anomaly most of the department labels her as."

"But she is an anomaly! It's like she can bring the dead back to life or something! Christ, doc, I joined that team to take a few pictures, gather evidence, and do my job, but I discovered a woman with superhuman powers. Wouldn't you consider that an anomaly? I don't know what it is… she's driving me crazy."

David moved to the chair and fell into it with a loud thump. Lance reallocated his a few inches.

"You know, for once, I have no idea what to say to you regarding Natalie. I had to take a moment to believe it all myself, and I never could figure out exactly what she could do. I don't have answers about her abilities or how she accomplishes what she does. I'm still trying to figure that all out. But I know for certain that she is most definitely human, a bright young woman with feelings, and someone who would love to have friendships with people who accept her. Given that you both work together, I hoped you would be one of those people. Was I wrong?"

David stood up from his chair, creating distance between them. "No."

"Good. I'm glad to hear that." Lance readjusted his chair, ensuring the chair's feet perfectly aligned with the indents on the carpet. "Now, the question is, where does this leave you with Michelle? Your wife revealed that she never gets to spend time with you because you always work. If not in the office, then in your workroom at home. You've only been with the team for over a year. It must have been difficult to accept that Natalie has an unusual talent, but I encouraged you to get to know her to promote a healthy work-life balance so you can get your marriage back on track."

David scoffed. "Healthy isn't the word I would choose regarding my work environment."

"Right, and I understand what you are saying, David. Working in forensics can be challenging." Dr. Lance rose from his chair, walked over to his desk, pushed aside a few books, and sat.

"Michelle and I have our good days and bad days. We could talk about that until we are blue in the face, and it still doesn't change the fact that it's marriage."

David paced the office, drumming his fingertips against his mouth as if deep in thought. He looked over at the psychiatrist and couldn't help noticing the tension on the doctor's face. "It's a shame you've never seen her in action. It's incredible!"

Lance adjusted his glasses. "Well, that answers my question. I fear I steered you in the wrong direction, and I apologize. I was trying to help you find a way to be more present in your marriage. Instead, I caused you to focus on another woman in an unhealthy way."

David grinned. "Don't worry, Doc. I'm not convinced you caused me to do anything. That was all her." He rubbed hard at his face. Having endured the same kind of day as Natalie, his bloodshot eyes told Lance he also had trouble sleeping.

Dr. Lance moved to the other side and opened a desk drawer, pretending to search for something.

David took a few steps, stopping short of Lance's desk." There's no need to prescribe anything to me, doc. She's my new drug."

"That's not very encouraging, David. We need to refocus your life. You walked in that door to help patch some issues in your marriage, but that no longer seems to be your end goal."

David let out a guttural laugh. "If it makes you feel better, doc, know I love my wife. I have simply developed a newfound love for my job. Perhaps you've helped more than you realize."

Lance drew back. "I don't understand how. I wish you could enlighten me on that one."

"Perhaps another time. I need to head back to work." David turned his back on him and moved toward the door.

"David!"

David turned for a moment as his hand reached for the doorknob.

"Natalie's special. Just remember that."

David smiled. "I couldn't agree more," he winked, and left the office.

Chapter Eight

I welcomed the breeze as it blew in from the inner harbor. The October weather in Maryland is warmer than usual. The Farmer's Almanac predicted a warmer-than-average fall but a chilly winter. I'm not too fond of the cold and snow, especially growing up in New York, with its bone-chilling winters and endless snow that lasts well into spring. I couldn't wait to move out of New York and into more comfortable conditions.

"Cold?" Julian asked, noticing me shaking as a chill crept through me.

"No, but it will be cold in a few months. Not looking forward to that."

"Are you kidding? That's my favorite time of year. I hate the heat," he said, looking over the menu.

I inhaled a long breath of air, along with the glorious mixture of smells, and sat back in my chair. Julian and I dined at a waterfront restaurant, sitting on the patio and enjoying the weather and the view.

Only a few boats stayed out at this time of year. It had been a cold and rainy September, and most boat owners had already docked and winterized their boats for the season. I spotted a few onlookers gazing at those who stuck it out a few more weeks. Jealousy flickered behind their eyes as the waves crashed against the docks. I couldn't blame them—perfect time for a boat ride, with temperatures in the low eighties.

As I scanned the lake, a crane caught my interest, gliding above the water with smoothness and grace. My inner photographer couldn't help but marvel at how the reflection perfectly mirrored the bird's graceful movements. Watching it, I contemplated whether I would prefer being the driver in the speedboat breaking through the water or the crane flying above. Both displayed freedom and a lifestyle I yearned for.

I snuck peeks at Julian, pretending to read the menu. We took a little time away from the office, and he suggested we meet for beers and all-you-can-eat crab cakes. We made it a point to pick a table tucked away in the corner in case other colleagues craved seafood.

I hid behind dark-framed sunglasses, enjoying the view of the man sitting before me. My eyes traced over his features. It was weird seeing him without his professional attire. His baby blue polo and khaki cargo shorts complemented his complexion, making him appear ten years younger.

"You okay?" he asked.

My cheeks flushed as Julian found me staring. "Uh-huh," I breathed, trying to cover it up by arranging the silverware and napkins on the table.

"Here are your drinks. Are you ready to order?" I eyed the waiter unintentionally, but he snagged my interest with his dark hair, friendly smile, and smoldering eyes. He must be somewhere in his early-to-mid-twenties, but he had a charisma that I bet made many girls blush. He was no Julian, but he was still attractive.

"I'll have your house burger and fries," I said, handing the menu back to the waiter without looking at it. He smiled at me and took the menu.

Julian viewed the options on the menu. When making choices, he excelled at making them for others rather than himself. "I'll take an order of snow crab legs and slaw and those crab cakes," he told Mr. Adorable, handing him his menu and easing back in his chair. The waiter nodded and strode away.

"If I knew you were not in the mood for seafood, I would have never asked you to meet me here."

I detected a hint of disappointment in his voice. "They have other things to eat besides seafood. Plus, I love being near the water," I replied.

I stared back at the lake, admiring its open beauty. It took me a long time to approach a body of water. My first death experience occurred when I was five years old. I wouldn't have called it an experience at that time. I had no idea what was happening. My older brother, Nathan, drowned in our family pool, and seeing his death through his eyes was something no child psychologist could explain. It may have been accidental, but it didn't matter; that traumatic incident messed me up in ways no child should ever endure.

"You need to step out of your comfort zone more. Try something new instead of sticking to the same old things," Julian said, forcing me away from my past.

His criticism indicated he didn't leave his imperial self at the office. He still wanted to tell me what to do without the suit and tie.

"It's just a burger. It's not a big deal," I saw where this conversation was headed, yet I stood my ground. I had a love for burgers, and that's not up for debate.

"It's not just about the burger, Natalie; it's everything else you do and don't do. You never go out and meet people or try to have a life. I'm shocked I got you to agree to come out with me."

My body strained as if it wanted to reduce down to nothing. "I'm sorry you feel that way," I mocked. "I'm just a homebody. I enjoy my solitude. Why is that wrong?" I glanced around to see if anyone sat nearby. The nearest couple sat at a table below us, devouring oysters as if they were their last meal. They stacked empty oyster shells on the table and stained their napkins with juice and hot sauce. I couldn't help wrinkling my nose at the sight.

I refocused on Julian. He would be an excellent catch for a woman of his age. Still, there's no denying our connection is stronger than a working relationship. We spent a lot of time together. In the beginning, I confided everything to him, but things changed when he insisted I work with a psychiatrist; it almost broke my heart. I never had any faith in psychiatrists. Dr. Lance had a way of making me feel like I wasn't in control of my life, which led me to want to socialize less.

“I'm just saying it would do you good for a little change.”

“Fine. I’ll get a cat,” I snapped. Julian scoffed as he took a sip of his beer.

I turned my focus back toward the water. A boat caught the attention of many diners with the roar of its engine. Two women stepped out and waited on the dock as the rest of their party parked and tied the boat to the pier. Their sunburned faces and excitable laughter made me envious.

"You have no idea what I would give to live a normal life."

"Natalie, you put up this tough-as-nails persona at work, but I watch you seek acceptance from others both in and outside the department. You say you've learned to accept who you are, but I'm unconvinced. You are your own worst enemy.

"Try being me. Everything changed once people realized what I could do. Jeff is the only one who sees me." I saw the hurt in his eyes as I dismissed his role in my life. "I mean, you understand me, too. However, that might also explain why I have issues at work. You are quite soft with me. Not that I'm complaining." I winked.

Julian tipped back in his chair, his head lowered as he examined me through his lashes.

"Would you call what I said earlier being soft on you? Because if you want, I can always turn it up a notch." He narrowed his eyes at me.

"Absolutely not. But still, it's not just the people I work with; I get it from everywhere. My own family treated me like a freak—my parents, my grandparents, and eventually, my sister. My parents blamed me for their divorce."

Julian narrowed his eyes. "How could that have been your fault? They couldn't handle the loss of your brother; they both placed the blame on each other for his death. No parent should have to bury a child."

"But they still had two daughters to look after. One wasn't old enough to walk, and another witnessed her dead brother being pulled from the swimming pool. My dad couldn't run away fast enough, and all my mother cared about was vodka and sleeping pills."

"But the blame lies with them, not you." Julian wanted to assure me, but a lifetime of confusion and guilt trumped any card he threw at me.

"To be honest, after my brother died, they treated me as if I weren't there. I was still a child. I had no idea what I had done and was as confused as anyone. The day my father left, he glared at me in a way I will never forget, and then he walked away. I never saw him again. The next thing I remember is my grandparents walking in the door and packing my things. I was five years old and could tell you when he left, where everyone stood, and what show played on the TV. No child should have memories like this."

Julian reached for my hand. "I'm sorry that this is hard for you, and I promise I didn't intend to take this conversation down this road. I wanted to let you know that people care about your well-being, regardless of what life throws at you. I'm one of them. And not all your coworkers are nervous around you. I learned some associates want to work with you more." He offered me a warm smile, and his gray eyes lit up.

Damn, those eyes.

Jeff must have been the one to put in a good word for me. I'm going to owe him.

Julian's demeanor changed. I knew he didn't want to have this discussion over dinner—we seldom have personal time together for obvious reasons. I'm sure the last thing he wanted was for our night to sour.

"If I recall, you weren't exactly calm when we first met," I smirked.

He snorted. "Yeah, I will never forget that moment either. I hear all this racket coming from the morgue and walk in to find a dead body flapping around and you doing who knows what right next to it. I think I pissed myself twice over," he said, letting out a slight rumble of laughter.

I smiled at him. "I remember you standing over me with the most horrified, confused, and downright hilarious expression on your face. I love how you substituted your gun for a metal tray. Till this day, I'm still relieved you'd rather strike me with a tray than shoot me."

"Well, what would you expect? I don't often see a corpse flailing its arms. A damned sight if I ever saw one, and yes, I may have had a lapse in judgment for a second and reached for the closest item. I remember not knowing which person to hit with it- the moving corpse or the crazy girl chilling out next to him. I could have sent you to the mental ward for getting freaky with a dead body," he snickered, pausing for a gulp of his beer.

He set the glass down, and pride crossed his face. "I still couldn't get over how easy it was to find our suspect after you told me about his murder. I was ready to put you under arrest for possessing knowledge you couldn't have had, but I had Mike follow through, and the evidence added up. But I knew what I witnessed, and it was incredible, so I encouraged you to work homicide," he said, raising his beer as if offering a toast.

I couldn't hide my playful smile. Julian is the reason I have a job, after all. "I was experimenting. I wanted to learn what I could do with this so-called gift. It was my first real experience with a human body where I took over." I said, drinking down my beer.

"It is a gift, Natalie, and a crazy one, but a gift regardless. Think of all the people who senselessly died, and you helped seek justice for them and their families. Think of all the cases that would go unsolved if you couldn't do what you do. If those people could speak to you one last time, I'm sure they would all say thank you."

I cringed and considered the restless souls floating around in my head, trapped inside me, and I had never once heard a thank you.

Julian's voice softened. "I am thankful for you," he said, sincerity in his eyes. And for maintaining our office's highest rank in solved crimes. You even make me look good to the FBI. I bet it frustrates them," he smiled and winked at me through his raised glass, swallowing the last of his beer.

"So, you're using me. What can I say? I'm here for you!" Easing back in my chair, I spotted Mr. Adorable approaching with a tray full of food, and my stomach answered with a growl.

"Here you go," the waiter said, placing dishes on the table.

"Now check out this burger; you can't tell me it doesn't make your mouth water. This place even gives you a pickle on the side," I said, picking up the pickle and taking a bite, puckering from the sour taste.

"That pickle's more than you can handle, their kid?" Julian said. He sat back for a moment, looking at me; his face softened as he held his eyes with mine. Julian's adoring gaze sent a schoolgirlish shiver down my spine.

He gave me one last smile and averted his attention to the food before him. He pulled his chair in and cracked open the legs of his dinner. I couldn't shake the unsettling fear that we were destined to remain nothing more than fleeting flirts and hidden moments. I hoped I was mistaken.

Chapter Nine

"Get away from me!" I shouted. I bolted upright in my bed, half-conscious and confused about my surroundings. My eyes opened halfway, arms flailing, beating away the bodiless images that stood before me moments ago. My pulse pounded through my skin as I scanned my room.

"Dammit," I breathed, placing my hand on my chest to steady my racing heart. Fucking dreams. The same one for weeks, but with each repetition, the dream became more real. Countless souls hovered above me, yet I clung to the knowledge that they are trapped and resolved to escape by any excruciating means.

I scanned the room, anticipating shadows to shift or something to tumble from a dresser or table.

"All right, enough of that. Relax," I told myself.

I wiped my eyes and ran my fingers through my semi-messy hair. The fan above me worked to cool my heated skin as beads of sweat rolled down my forehead. I worked to calm my nerves. Sleep would be challenging now. They would be waiting for me. I rubbed my eyes and reflected on my rendition of Nightmare on Elm Street. "And they say I have a gift…right..." I said aloud.

I surrendered to the struggle and kicked off the remaining covers. As I stood, I caught sight of myself in the dresser mirror. I almost didn't recognize the person staring back at me. The lack of sleep and stress caused dark circles to form under my eyes. I appeared sickly and pale, and… did I lose weight? I shook my head, fearing that I was starting to resemble their appearance. It was too much for any average person, and it was too much for me.

I started with the thermostat. Although the windows were open and it was in the low to mid-60s, my house felt stuffy and uncomfortable, lacking any breeze.

"Must…have…air," I bellowed as I fell against the wall and tapped on the control panel. The vent hummed to life, and the cool air caressed my skin. I lifted my arms as if showering in the chilly relief until my body cooled down. With my first stop completed, my dry throat reminded me it too needed attention.

Nightlights illuminated my path as I stepped into the kitchen, craving cold water to quench my thirst. I drank a full glass, letting the ice water sting my throat. Refilling the glass, I figured some late-night air would help calm whatever stirred in my soul.

I stepped out onto the front porch, inhaling the fresh air. I took a seat on my porch swing and admired the open space. The moonlight illuminated the yard, creating a glistening effect over the grass. If there's one thing I can say about living in the countryside, it's that it's beautiful.

Inhaling the damp air, my mind stayed blank for a short time before my dream resurfaced. I was standing in a dark room, surrounded by a circle of people. I could distinguish their familiar faces—young and old, short and tall; some dressed casually, while others wore suits and dresses. They all stared at me, waiting. I spun around and beheld them.

"What do you want?" I asked them. They stood silent and familiar. The circle tightened, but no one moved. My breathing changed as my body weakened, and I collapsed to the floor.

"Wait. What's going on?" I asked again, trying to force the words out through gasped breaths. Their expressions grew increasingly pained. Blood dripped off some, while others appeared to be suffocating, and the remainder stood in agony.

"I found your killer. It's going to be all right. You can be at peace now," I pleaded.

The people peered down at me, their expressions shifting from fear and torment to anger. Why are they angry at me? Their stares drove into me as if 200 pounds of solid weight pressed down on me. Tears formed at the corners of my eyes and flowed down the sides of my face. I stared back up at the crowd looking at me. What is happening to me?

Their profiles flooded my brain like a killer tidal wave. My body twitched in rhythm. My lungs burned, and the weight intensified as I entered connection mode.

"Dear God, stop this. I don't want to do this," I choked through the thick mucus filling my throat. Realization struck as I regarded each victim. They are going to make me profile all of them at once! They're pulling, beckoning me with an intensity I've never experienced before.

A scream tore from my lips as they drew nearer. Their eyes, white and glazed, bore into mine, chilling me to the core. A heavy pressure built in my head, as if my brain were about to turn to porridge: my body clenched with every new presence invading my thoughts.

"Please! Stop! Stop!" I cried out with my last breath.

I flinched as a tree limb cracked. The driveway spotlight illuminated, and the shadow of a raccoon darted across the pavement. As soon as it trotted into sight, it froze, noticing my presence.

I rubbed my arms and shook myself free from the horrific clutches that were dragging me into my nightmare. The mountain air is nice, but it's enough. I walked back into the house, securing the deadbolt, wishing I could do the same with my mind.

I turned the bathroom light on and faced myself in the mirror. Tired, bloodshot eyes glared back at me with every splash of cold water on my face, and then I dried off. Inside my medicine cabinet, two prescription bottles sat on the middle shelf- one for migraines and the other for sleeping pills. I snatched the bottle of sleeping pills and dumped two into my palm. Dr. Lance's voice mimicked in my head. The faster I write a script, the quicker you write it off in your system.

I dumped one more pill in my hand and swallowed all three tablets and a handful of water from the faucet. Placing the pills in the cabinet, I shut the cabinet. For a moment, a nervous tension came over me as I realized I had taken more than my allowed dosage, with my required dosage of only one pill as recommended.

Like mother, like daughter, said the small, anxious voice inside my head. Oh well. I craved peace, no dreams, no dead people, just pure, undisturbed slumber.

"Thank you, doctor," I said with a relieved tone as I turned off the bathroom light and went back to bed. The room temperature dropped to a more comfortable level. The cool sheets swathed against my skin as I slid underneath them, tugging them over my body and curling up into a fetal position against my pillow.

The deaths I profiled lingered in my head. "Leave me alone," I exhaled. I attempted to think of Julian — those gray eyes and handsome features — but yet another dead face came with every thought of him. Rolling over, I punched my pillows into the perfect shape and then uncovered my foot to let the air chill my toes. Maybe I should get a dog or a cat? Or some freaking fish? Something to talk to when I go into psycho mode.

"Fine. You win. I'm terrible at counting sheep. Instead, I will count you all." I kicked my legs in a childish tantrum, then straightened out and rested my arms across my chest. I stared up at the ceiling fan, watching it make its rotations.

The lady with the bloody hair. "One."

The man stabbed in his driveway. "Two."

The 15-year-old girl, all cut and bruised. "Three."

The boy with the…

Chapter Ten

"Leave me alone," I groaned at the furious vibrations at the other end of the bed. I waited a few seconds, hoping my cell phone would stop ringing, but it went off again as soon as the first several rings ended. Whoever is calling isn't going to give in.

"All right, already!" The phone vibrated toward me, just enough for me to make out the name on my caller ID. "Julian," I said as I nudged and squirmed my way over. "This better be important."

I swiped the answer button and laid the phone against my ear. I didn't say "hello" before Julian's voice yelled from the other side.

"I have been calling you for over an hour. Why the hell didn't you pick up?"

"Well, let's see," I said, rubbing my eyes. " It's, uh, oh yeah, in the middle of the night, when most people are sleeping," I yawned loudly into the phone.

"Well, get up," he demanded. A disturbance was going on in the background. "There's a new case, and I need you to be here."

"What's going on?" I stifled another yawn.

"There's been a triple homicide. It looks like a drive-by." Julian pulled away from the phone and hollered. "Put him inside a squad car if he can't control himself."

"Natalie, I need you here now."

"Julian, I think I need to sit this one out. I took a few of Dr. Lance's miracle sleeping pills."

"Are you kidding me?"

"I can barely move."

"Christ, Natalie. I need you. It's three kids. I'm sending Hopkins to pick you up. Drink a dozen pots of coffee if you have to. I need you here." The other line went silent, leaving him with the final say.

"I can't," I pleaded into dead air. I let the phone fall to the side of my head, my weakened fingers unable to hold on. My eyes closed during the exchange, and it wasn't until a loud banging rapped on my door that I pried them open again.

"What?" I cried out.

"Natalie, it's Mark. Julian sent me to get you," Officer Mark Hopkins persisted in knocking.

"Natalie's not here. Go away," I mouthed, aware that my bedroom is too far from the front door for him to hear me.

The knocking persisted, loud and unrelenting. Aware it would annoy the neighbors, I forced myself to get up, despite my body protesting as I moved my arms and swung my legs over the bed.

"All right, I'm coming. Give me a minute, would you?" I said more to myself.

"Sorry, Nat. Captain's orders," Mark shouted, still knocking. I guessed Julian must have told him about the pills, which would explain his determination to get me to answer the door.

My eyelids fought against me, resisting my will to open them. I pulled myself out of bed and went down the hall, pausing to lean against the wall as my head spun from sleep deprivation.

"You gonna make it?" he asked, spotting me through the glass window of the door.

"I'm almost there." I pushed myself to move again, lifting one foot in front of the other.

"I could break down the door if you want," he joked.

"Break my door, and I'll break you," I tried to quicken my pace. I had to cross about eight feet of floor space to reach the door, but in my current state, my mind told my legs it's more like fifty.

"Come on, Rhine. He's expecting you pronto."

I raised my arms, ready to catch myself just in case I lost my footing. I trudged across the wooden floor, touched the solid surface of my front door, and concentrated on unlocking the deadbolt. I slid to the side just enough to open the door and let Mark take care of the rest.

"Are you okay?" he asked, stepping inside and shutting the door behind him. He reached for my arm, thinking I might fall, and helped me to my couch.

"You caught me at a bad time," I responded, falling onto the cushions, grateful for the reprieve.

"Julian said to hurry. He also told me that I would need to load you up on caffeine. I figured you would be tired, being late, but I had no idea you would be this exhausted."

"I have to take pills to help me sleep. They keep all the dead people out of my head," I said, not realizing I spoke out loud.

Mark flinched and took a step back. "Oh, okay. Well, where do you keep your coffee? I can make it while you change."

Most other people I work with claimed to be comfortable around me until they were alone with me. Then it's a different story. Julian advised me to filter what I said around them, especially regarding dead people and my ability to handle them. Mark's quick shift in topic made me snort a tiny laugh.

He left me alone, made his way into my kitchen, switched on the light, and started opening cupboard doors and drawers. I figured he would find his way around and didn't need my help. I willed myself up into a standing position and headed back to my bedroom, moving as slowly as I did when I walked out.

I left the clothes I wore earlier on the floor instead of throwing them in the hamper. It took more than enough energy to remove my nightclothes and pull on my blouse and jeans. My shoes were on the floor across the room, and lacking all willpower, I figured my slippers would do just fine. I stepped into those and made my way back toward the kitchen.

The aroma of a fresh pot of brewing coffee evaded my nostrils. Mark stood at the counter, drumming his fingers against the granite countertop as the slow stream of brown liquid sanity filled the glass pot.

"How bad is it?" I asked for the sake of conversation.

He jerked at my voice, too engrossed in the coffee to notice I walked in and turned toward me. "It appears three are dead from gunshot wounds; it's a drive-by based on witnesses claiming they heard a car screeching, gunshots, and a car driving away."

I went to the cupboard and pulled out two travel mugs for the coffee. I sensed Mark tense a bit as I came up next to him. He shied away a couple of inches as if I were about to pickpocket him. "Relax, bud. I don't bite," I said, handing him the mugs.

"Sorry, Natalie. I don't have any issues with you. You're a great person, all. It's just this whole dead business. You know what I mean?"

"No. What do you mean?" I asked him with a subtle tease, although he didn't pick up on it.

"Well, last I checked, not everyone can speak to the dead except you, and the dead should stay dead."

"The dead do stay dead, and I don't speak to the dead. I jump into their minds, observe their last moments, and find out how they died. It's simple," I said matter-of-factly. He missed my sarcasm and pushed away from the counter, heading toward the front door.

"I have to be honest—it gives me the willies. I don't intend to be rude, but that's how I feel." He turned to face me, an apologetic look on his face.

"Okay, fine. I'll be careful around you. I promise I won't summon anyone, all right?" I said, maintaining my sarcasm.

"Good. I'll meet you in the car, but can you hurry it up? Julian keeps buzzing me, asking if we've left yet."

"Fine. I'll fill these up and be right out," I said, uncertain how I felt about his reaction toward me.

I loaded two travel mugs with coffee, secured the lids, and placed them in an insulated lunch bag. Then, I grabbed my wallet and keys.

The lights at the neighbor's house turned on, and shadows shuffled behind the window. Mrs. Kenzie is probably relaying every detail to her husband behind her.

"What else is new?" I asked under my breath and snorted a laugh before getting into the squad car. Mark didn't let me get situated before he shifted the car into drive and pressed on the gas, almost knocking over the lunch bag.

"Seriously," I said, looking at him. "You couldn't wait ten seconds for me to settle in?"

"Sorry. Captain's impatient and wants you there now."

We exchanged small talk during the ride to avoid uncomfortable silence. We arrived in Baltimore's inner city in a decent amount of time, and a considerable crowd was gathered around the scene. Julian stood among them, talking to Mike. He didn't appear happy to see me, or perhaps he didn't like my sluggish demeanor. Out of spite, I lingered in the car, finishing my first round of coffee and reaching for a second. The passenger door opened, and Julian stood beside me, looking as irritated as ever.

"Are we going to do this or what?" he asked.

"I won't be able to do a damn thing if I'm not fully awake. At this rate, I'll probably end up falling asleep during the profiling and leave you all convinced I'm dead," I said, wondering if that is possible.

"That's not funny." Julian eyed me from head to toe, stopping at my slippers. "How many did you take?"

I glared at him as I sipped more coffee and prayed I wouldn't need a bathroom. "I don't want to tell you. You're just going to yell at me."

"How many?" Julian's face tightened in annoyance at my unfortunate news.

"Uh. Maybe three."

He looked away from me, shaking his head in annoyance. "You are kidding me." Julian pulled the car door fully open and moved out of my way.

"Aren't we touchy?" I asked, sounding more drunk than tired as I handed him my coffee and pulled myself out. "Don't get mad at me. When you said I could have time off, I thought you meant I could take the time off. I anticipated getting a much-needed night's sleep and swallowed a little help. If I knew I was on call, I would have only taken one pill."

“I said I would try to give you time off. I didn't expect a triple homicide to show up at my feet.”

Julian ushered me out of the car and then slammed the door shut behind me, making me jerk. "Let's go," he demanded, wrapping his hand around my arm and leading me over to Mike.

Clumps of people stood on the other side of the street. Officers kept them at bay, controlling the crowd and preventing anyone from interfering. One man sat on the curb, swaying, consumed in a quiet struggle. Perhaps the pills kept me in a deprived state, but when the streetlamp illuminated his eyes in striking contrast, shifting from dark to bright, I could see the weight of his struggles.

"You coming?" Julian asked. I snapped out of it and steered my focus away from the man on the curb to Julian. When I caught up with him, Mike shared what his team pulled from the scene.

"We have three males here. Terrance Clemmons, age eighteen, two gunshot wounds to the chest and a third time in the abdomen." Mike gestured to the body closest to us. "This one here," he said, moving to the next body four feet away from the first, who is missing most of his face, "is Aaron Brown, age eighteen, shot once in the face."

My stomach turned a bit when I viewed the faceless body of young Aaron Brown. Underneath the bloodstains,

I spotted the swoosh symbol on his Nike T-shirt and matching basketball shorts. His branded sneakers and clothing indicated that the boy was passionate about sports and took pride in himself.

I carefully maneuvered around the second body and followed Mike's voice to the last one.

Mike continued, "This is Darrel Brown, sixteen, Aaron Brown's younger brother. He took one bullet to the back."

Darrel Brown dressed like his older brother, but his body was propped in an unusual pose for someone who was shot in the back.

"Was he moved?" I asked.

"Yes," Mike replied. "There's one more brother," he pointed toward the man sitting on the curb.

I peered back at the man wearing the blood-soaked t-shirt.

"Is that who you were shouting about on the phone?" I asked Julian.

"Yeah. When I arrived, the brother was trying to pick up the bodies, disrupting the scene. It took several officers to pull him away."

"Have you spoken to him?"

Mike spoke up, "We tried. He said he was sleeping when this happened. He stated that he has been working hard to help look after his brothers. His parents are gone, and he's been handling all the responsibilities of getting the older one into college on a scholarship. The younger one still had another year of high school but would have graduated early with honors. Good kids."

"Who's the third victim?"

Julian chimed in, "He lives a couple of blocks away. Neighbors insist he's to blame for all this. They said whenever he was around, trouble followed." His voice is less heartwarming than Mike's.

I examined the three boys as I would assess any victim before profiling. I only had to profile one, but whenever there was a case involving multiple murders, it was a matter of deciding which one would yield more answers. I chose the younger brother. He stood a few feet behind the other two and, with any luck, had a clear view of what occurred.

I nodded at Julian. From experience, he understood this was the sign I was about to begin. He nodded and instructed the officers to set up barriers around the perimeter. The onlookers speculated, curious about what we were doing. It took about five minutes, and several attendees assisted in sealing off the section. Julian also ensured that a few officers hovered close to the oldest brother if he grew curious.

Julian and Mike stayed inside the barrier with me. The intensity of the profiling wouldn't affect them being outdoors, but they still kept a few feet away. My eyes twitched from the usual migraines and lack of sleep, but the ache in my chest troubled me.

I knelt and studied Darrel Brown. My sympathy deepened with each passing moment. I could sense his energy radiating from his body, accompanied by an aura that reinforced Mike's belief: he was a good kid, hardworking, and driven. Sitting on the ground next to him, I paused and peered up at Julian.

"I'm sorry to do this to you again, but please come back to me, kid. That's all I ask," he said.

I gave him a reassuring smile and turned to lie on my stomach. I adjusted my head to meet Darrel Brown's eyes. I wanted to believe that Darrel could feel my presence, wherever he was, guiding him and assuring him everything would be all right.

I closed my eyes and focused on blocking the commotion behind the covers. The noise outside grew as people voiced their questions and concerns about the tarps. The officers guarding the crowd informed the curious onlookers that it was standard procedure. Most officers knew who I was and strained to catch a glimpse of me. I recognized them from previous cases, and I knew they were aware of me but had never witnessed my work to confirm the rumors.

I began my breathing technique, slow and steady. My body relaxed into the desired state, and I considered that the sleeping pills I had taken earlier were still working through my system. They would facilitate my entry, but I was apprehensive about the possibility of not being able to come out of the profiling.

For a moment, my dream flashed in my mind. I opened my eyes and gazed at the boy. "I'm sorry," I said to him, praying those were mere dreams and I wasn't trapping souls inside me.

My eyes stared at him, and then I started over. Within minutes, my body found a steady rhythm, and as expected, the pull surfaced. I told myself the boy was calling me inside, wanting me to understand why this happened to him. I reassured myself I was doing this for him and his brothers, hoping they would all find peace someday.

The pull intensified. The familiar tingling sensation that began in my fingers coursed through my arms and down my spine. The cold that followed seeped into my skin. It's okay, Darrel. Let me in.

Chapter Eleven

"What are you doing to my brother, you crazy bitch?" A man's shouts pulled me out of the profiling state. My body lurched from an agonizing shock, not my own. I was at the moment when the bullet pierced Darrel Brown. I gasped for breath as my body went through the motions of being shot.

Sensing something unusual, the oldest brother must have fought through several guards and forced his way into the tent. "Get him out of here!" Julian shouted at a few officers.

My blurred vision, accompanied by muffled yelling, was as if I were underwater. Amid the chaos, Julian attempted to push the brother away from me. The distress paralyzed me as my mind sent urgent signals to the rest of my body, indicating that I was in trauma mode.

With successful profiling, I would distance myself from the victim's last moments. The final phase, the disconnection, allowed my body to adjust before returning to consciousness- a respite that, inexplicably, was denied to me.

"Relax now. Adjust your bearings and let air fill those lungs," Julian demanded as if speaking to a child.

I struggled to comply. My body reacted as if it were undergoing rigor mortis. My lungs burned as if they were about to explode. Tears streamed down my cheeks as the shock engulfed me.

Mike's face sharpened as he knelt over me and fitted an oxygen mask over my nose and mouth. At first, I resisted him. The bullet wound felt genuine; the boy's pain became my own, and it didn't want to let go of me.

"He tried to protect his brother, and those bastards killed him," I cried through muffled coughs, wishing he could understand me despite the mask.

"We'll discuss all that in a moment. For now, Natalie, I need you to take a few deep breaths." Mike motioned for Julian to take the mask while he monitored my pulse.

"All right, slow and steady, you're almost there. Keep breathing," he instructed.

The shock and tension in my body turned into a dull ache and chill. "He was trying to protect his brother," I spoke again, attempting to shift my head toward Darrel. "They were good kids hanging out with the wrong person."

My eyes moved toward Terrance, and my anger toward him rose. He was selfish, wanting to act like a big man who took what he wanted. He pulled those brothers in. While he may not have been the one to kill them, he played a massive role in their deaths.

Mike tried to offer me a smile, but it came out forced and awkward. "This one was rough, but she's coming around," he told Julian, then turned to me. "Take your time, Natalie. I'll be ready when you are."

He stood and moved to the side, pretending to study the boy again. I reached for Julian, and he pulled me into his arms. His warmth flowed into my body. I didn't attempt to move, except to glare up at him. His hand brushed the side of my face, pushing the hair away from my eyes.

"You scared me. What the hell happened? I've never seen you come out of one like that before.

"I wasn't finished," I breathed out, still reeling from the air being ripped from my lungs.

"Shit." Julian tensed beneath me. "I'm sorry. The brother," Julian said, looking away. "He was supposed to be guarded. He's been interfering since I got here."

I mustered a smile in hopes of easing his worry. "Aside from the ghost trauma, I think I'll be okay." But that smile felt hollow; the hurt was genuine. I could tell Julian sensed the ache in my voice. I hurt—really hurt, and I know Julian could hear it in my voice.

Julian stayed with me to help ease the discomfort. I stayed in his lap, thankful he was between me and the cold pavement, and his body heat helped return my body to normal.

"Eh-hem." Both of us turned toward Mike. "Not that I want to disturb you, but in case you didn't notice, there's a mob going on out there, and the last thing we need is anyone accusing us of tampering with an investigation," he added, peeking out at the crowd.

"He's right. We need to wrap this up and get you home," Julian said, lifting me.

I pouted, reluctant to move, but the boy still needed my help. I slowly raised myself, using my palms to hold myself steady, with Julian supporting me, and turned toward the body. Darrel's form stayed distorted by the effects of the profiling. My heart raced when I saw the aftermath on his lifeless face.

"Oh, no, Julian, I left him like that!" I cried. The realization hit me. "That's why they're still with me. I trapped them."

"What are you talking about?" Julian asked, puzzled. He turned to Mike, who shrugged in confusion.

"All those victims," I muttered, raising my hand to my mouth, overwhelmed by my realization. "I trapped them. Don't you get it? They're stuck, and I did that to them. "

I couldn't take my eyes off the boy and the horrible expression on his face. What have I done? I didn't finish the profiling, and now he will remain this way in death. Confusion tore through me. Questions plagued my mind from every angle.

"I didn't allow him to die," I said, shaking my voice. "What if his soul is stuck this way? Julian, I have to do it again. I have to let him die," I said, moving toward Darrel Brown.

"Look at me!" Julian demanded. I pulled my gaze away from the boy's face. "You don't know any of that. I don't know how all that afterlife business works, but I don't believe you are causing him to endure an eternal death or whatever it is you claim to have caused. You are not going back in again; that last attempt nearly killed you."

I kept my eyes on him. He raised his hand to my face and wiped away tears from the corners of my eyes. Without even thinking, I reached out and hugged him. I sobbed, wrapping my arms around him and burying my face in his chest.

"Why do I feel like I stole from them?" I asked through muffled cries.

Julian accepted the hug, petted my head, and listened as I continued. "Maybe I am stealing their souls. Maybe I keep dreaming about them because they are trapped inside me, unable to move on because of what I did!" I pulled my head back and looked up at him. "People die, Julian, for whatever rhyme or reason. It's life, and they move on. I'm the one pulling them back, forcing them to stay." I pleaded with him to understand, but didn't receive the response I had hoped for.

"For God's sake, Natalie, we've been doing these profile assessments for a while now. What has caused this sudden change?" He searched my eyes, confusion etched on his face. "You have never acted this way."

I had never been pulled out before completing a profiling, so I didn't know what I was doing. "I told you, this one is different. And the dreams—all those people. They were still tormented." I felt myself sinking toward the pavement, but Julian caught me and pulled me back up.

“Natalie, stop. You’re overreacting and working yourself up. I think those pills did mess with you.”

I heard it in his voice, and it was written all over his face; he didn’t understand. He didn't bother trying. Were all those other people trying to tell me something? Or perhaps I'm finally losing my sanity, as Dr. Lance suggested I might.

I studied the corpse as if it were trying to crawl away, but he wasn't attempting to escape. He was trying to stay and protect his brother. Darrel. The boy was a good kid—they both were. Aaron was young and vibrant. He had goals and dreams of making his brother proud.

He planned to find his father, who had abandoned them years ago. Let him know about all he accomplished and how he missed out. He wanted to become a far better man than his father. But no more. His father will learn how his sons died due to foolish arrogance. He will never realize how hard they tried and how much they cared for each other.

My eyes drifted between the two brothers as I recalled their roles in the profiling. I knew it was a case of being in the wrong place at the wrong time for them.

I glanced at the first victim, the friend. My anger brewed, building inside me as a voice in my head shouted that it was his fault. He was young and wild, wanting to be free of rules and proper guidance. He even used intimidation to his advantage, but began boasting about his tenacity to the wrong people. They discovered him and enforced their own rules.

The brothers were innocent bystanders. Terrance was a bully and determined to keep them out. He called them 'kiddies with a curfew' and teased them about their older brother spanking them if they didn't go to bed. Darrel didn't give a damn about Terrance, but Aaron was bothered by it. He didn't want Terrance to think he was weak or controlled by his older brother, so he stayed out, sealing the fate of him and his little brother.

My body stiffened as I grabbed onto Julian's arms, and another terrifying thought occurred to me.

"What is it?" he asked.

"I pulled them apart. I took Darrel away from his brother. Stuck here, forever," I sobbed harder.

"Natalie, please snap out of it." His voice was soft yet condescending. "You don't know that. Your mind is playing tricks on you now, and you must tell it to quit. Tell us what happened, and we can wrap up, find whoever did this, and move on."

My confusion gave way to anger, and then to hurt. Julian made it clear he didn't believe me. He just wanted to wrap up, go, and collect another notch for his solved cases belt.

I pulled away from him, no longer enjoying the comfort I had moments ago. Neither Julian nor Mike cared about what those boys went through, who they were, or what they wanted in life. Not the way I did; neither of them knew the terror the younger brother felt when he witnessed his older brother getting shot, nor how he tried to protect him. Nothing else in the world mattered to him except saving his brother, and he ended up dying with a bullet in his back.

I lowered my head and wiped my eyes. I didn't want them to see me like this. I shook my head, signaling that I was okay. Mike stepped out, leaving Julian and me alone. Angry yells boomed, and more voices joined in when he reentered with additional forensic assistants ready to outline what happened. Mike held his clipboard in his hand, prepared to take notes. Julian moved to the side, relieved they were nearly finished.

"The shooting lasted less than two minutes from the arrival of the two males who instigated an argument with Terrance Clemmons until they sped away, leaving all three boys for dead."

I shut my eyes. My mind drifted back to Darrel's. I recounted everything about the two shooters, their names, and the make and model of the vehicle. What they argued about with Terrance, and what the boys were doing right before the guys in the car unloaded their weapons and sped off?

Whenever I started discussing the brothers and their fear, Mike would reel me in and remind me to stick to the facts. I struggled to "stick to the facts." I never anticipated this reaction, and I never expected to want to speak with a psychiatrist more than anyone else. I could share everything I wanted to express about this case, and he wouldn't interrupt me or tell me to stick to the facts. He would help me understand it better.

I watched Julian compare notes with Mike. Anger welled up inside me. To him, it was all just business.

"Christ, Natalie, relax… he's just doing his job," I said aloud, burying my face in my hands. I wish I hadn't answered Julian's call and had instead slept through the night without meeting Darrel Brown or his brother. Perhaps I wouldn't have made this horrible discovery, and could have believed I was doing the right thing for these people. The other detectives could have figured out who murdered them. Tony would have solved it, but Julian didn't give anyone else a chance.

"What's going on inside your head, kid? Are you all right?" Julian asked.

I raised my eyes to him as he stood over me, concern etched on his face, but I dismissed any belief that he cared.

"I'm fine," I said, running my fingers through my hair and applying extra pressure to my scalp to alleviate the pounding inside my head.

"In light of your return to all this, I disagree." He lifted my chin to meet his gaze.

I recoiled. "Are you my psychiatrist now?"

He let out a long breath. "It doesn't take a psychiatrist to see that you were having a breakdown of sorts. You weren't acting like yourself."

"How kind of you. Why don't you slap a straitjacket on me while you're at it?"

He rubbed his chin and gestured for Mike to leave. "I don't mean to be difficult, but nothing gets resolved if you're all emotional."

"Whatever you say," I whispered, crossing my arms to fend off the chill. I couldn't face Julian anymore; I wanted to run away. I dropped my face back into my hands, defeated. On second thought, I didn't want a shrink appointment. All I wanted now was to go home and cry this out. This was far from over. It felt more like the end of the beginning.

Chapter Twelve

It was after seven in the morning. My ride had left, and I assumed I had to wait for Julian to drive me home. I rocked back and forth on the curb, mimicking the movements of the traumatized brother. The crowd dispersed, and the bodies were taken to the morgue. I wanted to keep my distance from everyone, both the living and the dead. The thought never once occurred to me that I could harm the dead, but I found myself reviewing the profiling in my head. Did I take away that boy's peace?

"Natalie," Julian called my name. I ignored him. I wanted to be left alone to figure it out.

"Natalie, look at me," he said, raising his voice. He knelt in front of me and cupped his hands over mine. "I want you to meet with Lance. Things got out of hand earlier."

"I want to go home, jump in a hot shower, and sleep. I'll go to his office later."

Julian dropped his head. He was about to tell me something I didn't want to hear.

"I called him and told him what happened. When I asked him to clear his schedule, he got right on it." Julian nodded to my right.

Dr. Lance hovered off to the side, watching me.

"Are you serious? Now! I want to go home."

Julian assumed the boss's stance and stood his ground. "I'm not sure being isolated is the best idea for you." He studied me for a moment, took a breath, and apologized.

"I'm sorry. It was a triple homicide, and the victims were kids."

"Yeah, I understand, but the team could have solved this. You didn't need me. Tony would have jumped on it." Julian had no idea how much better off I would be alone and had no right to decide what was best for me.

He rubbed his tired eyes, forcing a resistance that showed he wasn't in the mood to argue. "Tony has a ridiculous caseload, and yes, I suppose the team could've handled this. But you would have resolved it much faster."

I viewed the blood-stained street where three young boys were murdered, and the empathy I felt for the brothers consumed me. I gave in. "I will go and talk to him. But this needs to stop. I want your word—time off. No profiling. No doctors. No angry phone calls in the middle of the night. None of it."

He raised his hand as if swearing on the bible. "You have my word. You need the rest, and I regret pushing you too far. I've become dependent on you and haven't considered your feelings." Regret rolled across Julian's face. He had become reliant on me. I played a significant role in his work. I was unsure whether that role was that of an angel or a demon. He had his way of using me, and I was too preoccupied with seeing him in a perfect light to pay any mind.

Dr. Lance strolled up to us, looking as if his patience had run out. "Morning," he muttered.

I turned to Lance, unable to hide my irritation at his presence. "You have some unusual work hours. How considerate of you to schedule me in at this time of day."

"I'm an early bird. I usually wake up at 4 a.m. to begin my day. That's the best time to gather my ideas," he said.

Besides, I was on my way to the office and was told that you both were still here, so I decided to swing by. If I were to fit you into my schedule, it would have to be as soon as possible. Julian's eyes stayed on mine. "Are you okay with going with him? I can pick you up later and take you home." He placed his hand on my shoulder. I sensed that he was worried about me. "But…" Julian added. "You take her to Trudy's," he said to Lance.

Trudy's was my favorite family-owned diner, a couple of blocks from the office. The owner made the best pumpkin and chocolate cream pies.

Lance didn't hesitate. "Why not? I could use a cup of coffee myself."

I scowled at them both, hoping either would reconsider. "Fine." I caved, too exhausted to argue.

"Coffee it is," Lance smiled, seeming eager to leave.

“Actually, I think I’ve had enough coffee to last me a long time. But some breakfast might help,” I chimed in.

Julian smiled and squeezed my arm as a sign of approval. “I’ll talk with you later.”

Dr. Lance offered to drive and directed me toward his car. I felt compelled to glance back at Julian with a final plea to keep me from going through this. He nodded and quickly walked away to finalize any last-minute tasks without further discussion.

Chapter Thirteen

David tucked his work camera in the equipment bag and checked around to see if anyone had witnessed him slipping another camera into a side slot. These photos were the best ones yet, so he protected them as if they were a prized possession.

You were in so much agony—you poor thing.

He zipped up the case, gathered the rest of his equipment, and walked toward his vehicle. Anticipation tingled down his arms and fingertips as his feet clopped against the pavement in a brisk walk. He would have to report to the lab and document the images. Those were acceptable, but his private photos taken with his camera were better. Developing the film would be a real treat.

David set all the equipment on the passenger seat, buckled himself in, and started the engine, keeping a watchful eye on the case at every moment. The roads were quiet, being a Monday morning. Pushing his foot harder on the gas pedal, he whipped down side roads, accelerating through lights before they turned red. He was only twelve minutes from the lab, but developing and documenting would take a few hours. Then, he would head home and spend a little quality time in his red room, savoring every moment.

He turned on the radio and searched the stations, stopping at 92.9. A smile crossed his face as he checked his rearview mirror when the song "Photograph" by Def Leppard blared through his speakers.

"Fitting," he said, eyeing the camera bag again and drumming the beat against the shifter.

It took even less time to arrive at the office than he assumed. He pulled out his camera and hid it under the seat before heading in. The halls were quiet, as the rest of the forensics team was at work.

David followed protocol, meticulously performing his job duties. He liked a few of the images he selected for his report, but the urge to develop his batch from another camera became unsettling. Once all the photos were processed and documented, he scanned the lab to find out what the rest of the team was doing. Having Natalie around made the team's work life easier, and most of them had already left after Mike's approval. Even Mike was about to wrap up and advised David that he could head home.

His fingers tingled again as he headed back to his car. He didn't spare a second, jumping into the driver's seat, yanking his small camera out from beneath the passenger side, and holding it like a trophy.

"And now, precious, let's get you home."

Chapter Fourteen

The car ride was silent and uncomfortable as we kept quiet throughout the drive. The more I reflected on what had transpired over the past hour, the less I felt inclined to eat anything. However, as we pulled up to the diner, I inhaled the sweet aroma of pumpkin spice. My stomach gurgled, and I figured one small piece wouldn't hurt.

Dr. Lance held open the door, and as soon as I stepped inside, an even more mesmerizing array of aromas hit my nose. I floated toward the counter, where dozens of pies, pastries, and breads awaited eager consumption. A few people sat quietly in booths, enjoying their early bird specials, but the breakfast rush hadn't begun yet.

"Good morning, welcome to Trudy's," a voice called from a few tables over. "Help yourself to any table."

I chose a table in the corner, as far from the other guests as possible. If I have to discuss my breakdown, I probably should keep it out of earshot of ordinary folk.

"What can I get you two this morning?" the young girl approached our table and asked, holding out her notebook and ready to take our order.

She isn't Trudy, who stood behind the counter talking to a couple, but this girl resembles the owner, perhaps a granddaughter. I found it amusing that she dyed the tips of her hair bright orange to match her nail polish!

"I'll take a coffee, please, black. And for you?" Lance looked over at me while I perused the menu on the table.

“I scanned the front side, turned it over, and quickly examined the back. “I'll just have one of your early bird breakfasts, please- scrambled eggs and white toast. Oh, and some orange juice.”

"All right, coming right up," she said, scribbling on her pad.

I turned my gaze to the beautiful-looking pies behind the glass windows. “I should 've asked for the pie, smothered in whipped cream.”

Dr. Lance smirked. "I assume that's a childhood favorite of yours?"

And it begins.

"Not so much from my childhood but more from my twenties.

"Really? Why's that?" he asked, clearly trying to foster some form of exchange.

He’s going to analyze how I eat my food. Okay then.

"I don't know. The older I got, the more indulgent I became. It wasn't like I ate like this as a kid. Is there some psychological explanation behind my liking a lot of whipped cream on my pie?"

He laughed a little but maintained a solid demeanor. "No, no, I'm just trying to break the ice. Maybe we can do this differently."

"How so?" I asked, glancing around at the other guests.

"Well, for starters, there will be no pen and pad. It will be just you and me conversing over food."

"Sounds good to me, as soon as I finish eating."

The young lady served us our coffee and juice, smiled, informed us the food would be out shortly, and asked

Lance if he was sure he didn't want anything to eat. He nodded and made do with his coffee.

"I need to use the restroom," I said, slipping out of the booth. After two thermoses of coffee, I couldn't hold my stretched bladder.

"I'll be right here," he said.

I headed for the restroom, walking past the numerous pies and regretting my decision not to have a slice. I reached the back where the men's and women's restrooms were tucked away. The bathroom door felt heavy as I pushed it open, but I was greeted with a strong lemon scent and shiny floors. Trudy didn't mess around when it came to cleanliness in her restaurant.

Once my bladder felt relieved, I went to the sink and admired the cute décor. What I couldn't admire was my reflection. This is by far the worst I've ever seen myself. How the hell am I supposed to convince Lance I'm fine when a drugged zombie could show me up? I snorted a disgusted laugh, splashed water on my face, and concluded that any attempt to fix my appearance was useless. When I got back to the table, the young lady walked out with my plate.

"Here you go," she said, handing me my plate as I plopped back into the booth.

I reached for the ketchup and covered just about everything. I spooned eggs onto my toast, took a large bite, and captured Lance's eye.

"What?"

"Sorry, I don't mean to stare. It's just that Julian told me you were upset," he said, taking only a tiny sip of his coffee. I was half expecting him to raise his pinky finger.

“I was,” I said, quickly chewing and swallowing my food. “But I still got to eat.”

I ate in peace for a few minutes, savoring each bite of food, and I almost forgot the horror scene I left behind.

"Well, that was excellent coffee, and by how quickly you tackled that plate, I gather you enjoyed your breakfast." Lance pushed his cup off to the side. His change in posture told me he was ready to begin our session.

I swallowed my last bite, sipped the last of my orange juice, and wiped my mouth.

"So, what did you want to talk about?" I asked.

"I would like you to tell me what happened out there. Julian is more concerned about you than ever. I heard it in his voice when he called me. He didn't explain, but I gathered things went downhill for you."

"I'm not sure what happened." My tone came off more secure than it should have.

"Julian told me you were upset. Natalie. You can talk to me. He wouldn’t have called me if he didn’t think I could help. Tell me what happened."

I rubbed my hands over my eyes, realizing I was tired again. Perhaps the sleeping pills were what caused the profiling to go awry.

"I realized for the first time how good those pills you prescribed are.” I stopped, realizing I was about to throw myself under the bus if I mentioned I had taken more than prescribed. “I was finally fast asleep but was awakened a few hours later and coerced to profile a triple homicide."

"That couldn't have been good for obvious reasons. Did Julian know?"

The more I spoke, the more I convinced myself that what happened earlier was a side effect of too many sleep pills. "I tried telling Julian I couldn't work on a case, but it didn't matter. He insisted I load up on caffeine and do what I had to do.

"I can understand how frustrating that would be, especially when working in a sleep-deprived state." He shook his head. "Because you were in no shape to work, he should have kept you out of this one."

The young waitress walked up from behind and poured more coffee into his cup. He was a little too slow to turn down the refill, and merely waited as the waitress filled his cup, pouring in the remainder she had in her pot in a drawn-out display of friendly service.

“Okay, thank you. That will be all for me,” he smiled.

“Sure thing,” she replied, moving to the following table.

Lance reached for the cup to sip his second round, but then he became aware: "How are you feeling now? You must be exhausted."

I couldn't suppress my yawn. "I didn't want to have this talk right now. I wanted to go home and crawl back into bed. But Julian insisted I had to be there."

"Well, I'm sorry to keep you from rest, although maybe addressing this might help you rest better later." He took another sip and set the cup down. "There may be a silver lining in what happened."

"I'm not following," I squinted my eyes at him.

"Ask yourself what was so different about this profiling. Why those boys? Why now?"

I contemplated my response. "Imagine watching a movie and seeing the characters act out their parts, but you fast forward a little. That's what happens to the victim. In his last memories, I perceive his actions as if he were performing them. The body contorts to the motions of the action. This boy went through the motions, showing me what happened, but I came out of it at the moment when the bullet had gone into his back. His reaction is what I left him at, and it showed on his face after I pulled out."

He nodded in agreement. His eyes wandered, attempting to piece together what I had said.

"You're saying you left him when he got shot in the back? I guess I don't understand the rest?"

I let out a sigh. "I know the boy's deceased, but what if there's more to death than that? Movies often depict that when people die, they wear the same clothes they wore when they passed away. What if he's stuck like that? What if his pain follows him?"

His mouth opened as if understanding dawned on him. "Oh, you think you left him tortured, as if he has to spend eternity reliving his death."

"Precisely," I said, relieved he was starting to understand. "I've never seen what happens after they die. They cease into darkness, but what if I changed all that this time? That's why I was so upset?"

Lance sat up properly in his seat. "Natalie, I wish I had an answer on what happens after death, but there's no proven textbook on the subject. Although I believe there is more beyond this world, I can't say for certain what that is. You are a kind-hearted person. You only want to help, and because of that, I can't imagine you would have a gift such as yours if it were only to punish you."

His sincerity oozed, and I appreciated what he was saying for once. "Thank you, but I don't think I could continue calling this a gift," I said, thinking about the victims from my dreams.

"You have it for a reason. I believe you are serving your life purpose," he smiled at me. "Which reminds me, what about the rest of your family? Does anyone else exhibit psychic gifts?"

"Not that I'm aware of, and this doesn't seem like something they could have hidden. I would know. I tried. When I couldn't hide my ability, I tried to find out if other people could do what I could. I remember trying to test my sister to determine if she was like me, but it only scared her."

"How did you do that?" he asked.

"I would usually connect with dead animals and have her try to copy me. I had her touch me when I did it, believing she could see what I could, but nothing worked. She would run off and get me in trouble with my grandparents."

"What happened after that? Your grandparents had to have known there was something different about you."

"I think it scared them at first. They wanted to make sure there wasn't anything wrong with me, so they took me to different doctors, wanting a second and then a third opinion."

I glanced at the man sitting across from me, contemplating the root of my deep mistrust of doctors. “Initially, several doctors hooked me up to machines, connecting wires to my chest and head. When they found nothing wrong, they referred me to others.” I gave him a pointed look. “Those doctors interrogated me and pressured my grandparents to put me on antipsychotics. They tried filling my grandparents’ heads with lies and bad opinions."

He shook his head, knowing what their diagnosis had been back then. "Let me guess, you were doing it all for attention after your brother's death."

"Pretty much. If it wasn't for that, I was trying to avoid school. I didn't have many friends, after all." Annoyance built up inside me. "For years, I lived with people believing I was a liar or a freak show. I tried to prove to my grandparents that I wasn't lying. I found a dead bird in the backyard, brought it into the house, and tried to demonstrate it to my grandfather."

He smirked. "I bet he panicked."

"Quite the opposite. My grandfather got angry with me and told me never to do it again. He took the bird and buried it in the backyard. I tried to plead with him, but then my grandmother sat me down and explained what would happen if other people learned what I could do. She told me bad things could happen to me. People might tease or ridicule me. And then some would exploit me."

"I understand. Your grandparents accepted your psychic ability but wanted to protect you, so they kept it a secret."

"Exactly. The problem was that it became an obsession—even a need. Every time something died around me, I felt this strong pull. The more I did it, the less scared I became.

His facial expression softened. "And here you are, working in law enforcement and solving cases. When you're not profiling, how do you spend your free time? Do you try to have a normal life without me sounding rude?"

"Yes. I love food, as you can tell," I said, nodding toward the empty plate." I also love music, movies, reading, and writing. Everything else about me is normal."

He gave me the kind smile he had shown earlier. "And your relationship with your sister? How is that going?"

"It is what it is with her," I sighed. "Her son, Kyle, is the sweetest boy." I glowed, picturing my nephew, who had just turned five.

"Do you spend time with him?"

"No," I responded, annoyed that he was about to enter a more sensitive topic.

"Why not?"

I breathed, realizing I could not shift the conversation elsewhere. " Because of my sister. We didn't grow up close, especially after my profiling exercises with her. She was afraid of me and never understood me. After Kyle was born, she was scared to leave me alone with him. She never asked me to babysit or anything."

"It must have been hard dealing with your sister, judging you."

"People judged me my whole life; at least with my sister, she tried to be cautious for her son's sake. I can't blame her. I would, too."

"But have you tried talking things out with her? Tell her you wouldn't hurt him or do anything she wouldn't want you to do?"

"Yes. Nicole pretended things were fine, but I knew better. She was afraid I couldn't control it."

He nodded. "I understand that part, but you're older now, more aware of your ability. Do you still feel the pull?"

"Not as much. I found a way to incorporate it into a job and do what I could to make it work. Kind of like a ghost whisperer."

He snickered. "Something like that."

His tone, body position, and overall relaxed state were unfamiliar to me. He is more intimidating when he has a pad and a pen. As I regarded him, an urgent question sprang to mind, and I voiced it. "Do you think I'm insane?"

His gaze met mine over the rim of his raised mug. Setting it down, he wrapped his hands around the cup and paused for a moment before responding. "You realize this is the most you have ever said to me. I learned a lot about you, and I may have drawn a natural conclusion, " he answered in confidence.

"And what is that natural conclusion?" I asked. "I want to know what you think, and I'm not looking for your textbook analysis of me."

He set his mug aside and entwined his fingers. "It's hard to determine what is going on inside that mind of yours when you don't talk to me. That is, after all, what I'm here for. If you opened up more like this, I could say that Natalie Rhine has the most unorthodox trait I've ever encountered as a psychiatrist, which makes her the most interesting person I have ever had the pleasure of getting to know." He rested. Looking at me, he took a few moments to gather his words. "No. I don't think you are insane."

"Do you believe I have control of it?" I asked, gripping the napkin.

"I believe you can if you let someone help you through the experience. Although you're unique in my book, you're not superwoman," he said, smiling kindly. "And that is my honest opinion. I don't believe what you do for a living is insane, per se. Psychic mediums have converted the most skeptical individuals into believers with their findings. I am concerned about your emotional well-being after experiencing people getting murdered. It's hard not to be. I choke up just watching those ASPCA commercials."

I figured the cozy atmosphere was working its magic as he relaxed and rested his arms on the table. He almost seemed relieved to get that off his chest. "So, I admit, I have a hard time believing you can keep it all together. I think you need to step back and experience life apart from death."

I struggled to wrap my mind around his answer. He said he didn't believe I was insane, but he also hinted that he thought I was. "I assumed that was what I was doing?" I arched my brow at him, confused by his response.

"Well, for starters, try to patch things up with your sister or convince her that you are not Frankenstein's prodigy. Speak to her as you would to me now. And by all means, be open and honest."

"That's easier said than done. You already forgot that Nicole grew up with me. She witnessed firsthand what I can do."

He nodded. "Yes, but that doesn't mean you're a bad person for it. Prove to her that you have a total grasp on your ability and make her believe you have no intention of bringing it around her or your nephew. Things could go well for you all with a little assurance."

I released the napkin and smoothed it out. I wish I could do the same with my life. I wanted a relationship with my sister and nephew. I wanted my family back. Kyle was a fresh start to normalcy. He never judged me, feared me, or denied me. When I came by, we always had fun, but a wall between my sister and me kept me away, and I wanted that to come down.

"Natalie. She's your family; she has lost a brother and her parents as well. From your expression, I can tell you want to connect with her, and something suggests it's not your sister putting up a stop sign when you're nearby."

"What do you mean?" I almost whispered.

"You said you didn't have many friends, and your parents and grandparents made it hard to accept your gift. They punished you for who you are, and you became accustomed to rejection."

I kept my eyes on the white napkin, still trying to soften the creases. I pressed hard at the corners, fighting against the lump in my throat and the tears in my eyes.

"Natalie. Look at me. I've said this before. Allow yourself more time enjoying the people and hobbies you love. You owe yourself that."

I blinked a few times to focus while a dark voice chanted in my head: What's the point? They don't want you. I stopped imagining the future long ago. The past consumed my life like a black hole. Even living in the present was hard.

I wouldn't know how to exist in the here and now- to have family outings or find a man to settle down with and start my own family. I convinced myself I couldn't have these things or didn't want them. But that was far from the truth. Deep down, I was afraid to love again. I was scared to lose another person I cared for because everyone I've ever told "I love you" has either passed away or rejected me.

"I will," I said with determination.

Dr. Lance's eyes were warm and empathetic. I needed to give him a chance, too. He was here to help. I smiled back at him. So, he preferred his office to be neat, orderly, and outdated. What was so wrong with that?

"Well, then, I think we had a breakthrough. I feel better about this," he said, motioning for the waitress.

I texted Julian to let him know I was ready for him, and Lance kindly offered to pay for the check. When Julian's black charger pulled into the parking lot, I waved at the owner and stepped out into the calm and refreshing morning air. I was surprisingly chipper, even surprised that I may have removed a massive weight off my shoulders. Turns out, Lance wasn't the only one feeling good about this chat.

"Thanks for bringing me here, allowing me to indulge and divulge. I think it helped this time," I said.

"This time?" Lance let out a small laugh. “I'll take whatever I can, and it was nice to get out of the office." He waved his hand toward the diner. "You know, I drive past here and never stop in. I think I've hit a discovery," he said, waving goodbye before getting into his car and driving away.

Julian got out of his car and came around to open the door for me, throwing a wave toward Lance's direction. "Did you have a nice talk?"

I slipped into the passenger seat and pulled my seatbelt over me. "For once, my time with him wasn't horrible. The food may have had something to do with it." His car had that masculine leather smell, which I rather enjoyed, but the weather trumped the interior of his car, so I rolled down the window and lay back. We didn't say much during the drive to my house, nor did he ask me for details about my chat, but that was Julian. He'd come in hot and then dust his shoulder like nothing happened.

I was grateful for the quiet. We were both exhausted and had a long night, and I was still feeling a happy buzz. Lance helped me consider a few things that I hadn't given any worth to. I have to stop believing that rejection was my only outcome. Am I a freak? Sure. Unorthodox, as Lance mentioned, but he said I'm interesting. I can live with that. I may be a bit sarcastic and stubborn, but I'm interesting.

I tipped my head toward the open window, catching the wind against my cheeks, and saw myself smiling in the sideview mirror.

Hello stranger.

Chapter Fifteen

After Julian dropped me off at my house, I went to bed and slept most of the day. I woke up a little after six p.m. and decided to soak in the bath, which would be good for me. I set up my tub caddy with a raunchy romance novel, a candle, and some wine. The hot water soothed parts of my body I didn't realize needed soothing.

I read up to the first ten chapters until the water cooled. When I stepped out, it felt like a wall of cold air hit my damp skin, making me scramble to dry off and slip into my lounge pants and oversized shirt. As I fixed my hair in the mirror, I reenacted some scenes from the novel.

"How dare you kiss me, you disgusting oaf!" With my brush in hand, I thrust out my arm, fighting off my imaginary nemesis. Of course, he had to be sexy, strong, loved by all, but despised by me. Wasn't that how those novels always went? And who would play my forbidden nemesis turned lover? I could only imagine one man: tall, gray-eyed, and fit.

I ogled the man posing on the cover—My Viking Lord. I laughed; I couldn't imagine Julian dressed like that, and if I were being honest, I would have made it much easier for Julian to win me over than the snotty princess in the novel.

I picked up my wine glass, tucked the book under my arm, and sauntered toward the living room. It wasn't too cold in my house, but the novel put me in a mood, so I lit a fire for ambiance and curled up on my couch, grabbing a thin fleece blanket to throw over me.

For once, I didn't finish the entire glass of wine as I placed it on my side table and shuffled on to the next chapter of the novel. I barely made it through the first paragraph as the firelight pulled my attention, and the flames danced. My eyes shifted to the photographs on my fireplace mantel—the only proof I had of another life.

I smiled at the picture of my grandparents holding their great-grandson on the day of his birth. My sister sat in the middle of them, exhausted yet happy. A short-lived romance turned into a lifelong commitment for her, but it didn't matter. Kyle was never looked at as a mistake. He turned all our worlds around and gave us something to look forward to. It was the happiest time of my life, and the only time I could remember experiencing true joy.

I skimmed the other photographs. My parents, brother, and I stood next to Santa Claus. It was the last Christmas before my brother died. There was also a picture of Nicole sitting in a barrel full of pumpkins when she was a toddler. And lastly, Kyle, posing with his new bike, which I bought him for his birthday. Four moments were all I had of the happy times in my life. All the other memories were a giant blur of loss and rejection.

A knock sounded at my door, pulling my thoughts away from the past.

"Natalie, it's me," Julian's voice came through softly.

My skin tingled at the sound of his voice. My stubborn side still wanted to be angry with him for his earlier actions, but I couldn't compel my feet to stay put. I jumped from the couch and rechecked my hair in a mirror before unlocking the deadbolt. Julian stood looking at me. Seeing his tousled hair and dress shirt pulled out, I guessed he had a long day at work.

"Hey," we both said. We stared at each other briefly before Julian stretched out his arms, and I accepted, moving in for the embrace.

My head rested comfortably against him as I inhaled traces of cologne on his dress shirt. His chin rested on the top of my head as he rocked me back and forth—a motion I enjoyed all too well.

"I'm sorry," I muttered into his chest.

"Sorry for what?" he asked as if nothing had gone wrong earlier.

"For the way I acted."

Julian ran his fingers through my hair. "Natalie, I'm the one who should be sorry. I didn't listen when you told me you couldn't do it, and look what happened. I feel like such an ass."

I wanted to give him a big I-told-you-so, but thought better of it.

"I'm fine now. Admittedly, I lost it a little, but I discussed my issues with Dr. Lance, had breakfast, and here I am." I used my arms to make a sudden 'ta-da' gesture.

Julian gestured, "Can I come in? It's been a long day."

I moved aside as he walked past me to my couch. He removed his dress coat and plopped onto the cushion. Relief flooded his face as if it were his first time sitting. He stretched his arms, lay his head back, and took a long breath.

I couldn't decide whether to sit next to him or stand a few feet away. I wanted his closeness, but my persistent side wanted him to know I was doing fine. I hovered.

He exhaled again, keeping his head back and his eyes shut. "Regardless, I shouldn't have pushed you. I had no right. I am sorry."

Only Julian would be the kind of person to say sorry but still make it seem like his word was the last on the subject. He was the type of guy who would apologize rather than ask for my permission.

I bit my lip. "I can't be mad at you for calling me back when it was a group of kids. I probably would have been pissed at you if you hadn't." I had no idea what else to say to him.

Julian looked me over, moving his head from left to right, mimicking my swaying. "Am I making you uncomfortable?" he asked.

I froze. Was he? I didn't realize I was doing it.

"Come here," he asked, tapping the seat beside him.

I moved over to the couch, pulled my legs in, and sat curled up next to him.

"No, I'm not uncomfortable with you; I didn't want you to worry about me. As I said, things went well between Lance and me earlier. I felt like I was able to get a lot off my chest."

"I'm glad to hear that, but Lance didn't hesitate to give me a chewing out earlier. Deep down, I know he's right. I often tend to be selfish with your gift, and I'm sorry for that." He glanced at me with regret but managed a smile.

The bumps on my skin rose from his closeness. "I don't believe you are taking advantage of me, not in a bad way. There is nothing wrong with wanting a murder case solved and getting the criminal behind bars-"

"After what happened earlier, I think it would be best if you took a break," he said.

My brow furrowed. "We already talked about this."

"No. We didn't," he breathed out. Something in the way he spoke made my stomach do a little dance.

"What kind of break?"

"An indefinite one," he said with a pause.

I straightened, searching for a sign that told me he wasn't serious. "What are you saying? I'm fired!"

"No. Not fired. But… I can't have you around solving the cases."

He straightened up initially, then leaned his elbows on his knees, focused ahead rather than on me. "I've never witnessed such pain on your face before, and I can't tolerate seeing it again. It would be wise for you to distance yourself from the department."

I couldn't believe what I was hearing. Julian wanted me to leave. I sprang off the couch, needing more than just a few inches of space between us.

"I have one bad episode, and suddenly you want to give up on me?" The hurt in my voice was raw and unfiltered. Julian, the one person who had always accepted me and recognized the good I could do, was pushing me away, urging me to abandon the very thing I excelled at.

Julian's voice was steady, his concern palpable. "I'm not giving up on you, Natalie. I'm trying to help you start anew, to live a life that's yours."

I threw my arms up. "I am living my life. What I do is a job, Julian. Like you, we all have a career that pays the bills and gives us some purpose in life."

Julian's eyes narrowed. They screamed in disappointment. "You've done enough. You need to grasp reality before you lose your sanity."

"Where is this coming from? You never had an issue with me working cases. You said it yourself: you were always selfish with my gift, and now, suddenly, you feel I need a grasp on reality?" I turned away, not wanting him to see the tears welling in my eyes.

Julian stood up. "For Christ's sake, Natalie, it's glaringly obvious to me now that this job has put too much stress on you, and it's all my fault. It's time for you to find something else, something that isn't going to tear you apart from the inside. That's all I want for you."

I turned so fast I almost lost my balance. "That's all you want!" You apologized for being selfish when you walked through my door, yet you still stand here talking about your wants regarding me. What about what I want?"

I threw my hands up in confusion, baffled by the sudden turn of events. "This is my problem. This is why I can't just express what's on my mind. In the end, it wouldn't matter what I say. Either you or Lance would still consider me unstable. Not to mention, you both want to control me. Lance wants to dictate how I'm supposed to feel while you tell me how to live."

The expression on Julian's face fell. "I tell you that I think it's best to take time for yourself, and that's what you come up with... control? It's not like that, and you know it." His voice turned confrontational. He reached for my arm, but I pulled away and signaled for him to keep his distance. When he made no further movements, I shut my eyes and focused on calming the chaos in my head.

I walked away from him and sat back on my couch, curling my legs up to my chest. "My whole life, I never felt like I owned a minute of it. My family forced me to keep things hidden. They were terrified of what would happen if the truth were discovered. But then I met you and thought, here's someone who accepts me for who I am and doesn't consider me a freak.

Julian raised an eyebrow. "Before you accuse me of anything, believe me when I say I've always accepted you."

I interrupted him. "Only when it was convenient for you." I jumped up and dashed into the kitchen, seeking any escape from him.

He followed behind me with arms raised in defense. "Why is it so bad that I suggest you take a little time away from work and have fun in life?"

"At what point did you suggest taking a little time? You said, and I quote, 'indefinite'!"

"OK, fine. Then I suggest you take some time off from work." I cringed when his breath brushed against the side of my neck. "I know you better than most, Natalie," Julian said as he rubbed my shoulders.

I couldn't help but tense at his touch. Now, he made me uncomfortable. "I'm not ready to leave," I breathed out.

His mouth moved close to my ear. "I'm not trying to control you, but I witnessed something today. I don't know how to describe it except to say it wasn't you." He turned me around to face him, cupping the sides of my face with his hands. "I have always cared for you. The years we have worked together have drawn me closer to you. Tonight, I realized how much. All I'm asking is that you give yourself some time."

"That's what I was doing before you called me and pulled me back in. I'm not trying to blame you, Julian, but there are times when you're the one who pushes it too far."

A horrible knot filled my belly, knowing that what I just said would be something I was sure to regret.

Julian pulled away. "And that's what I'm saying. It's my fault what's happening to you. I'm obsessed with solving cases and having answers when I want them. Most of all, I admit I'm obsessed with you, and it's not a healthy obsession either. I'm killing you."

Julian ran his hand through his hair and rubbed his eyes. "I think I'm trying to say I must stop needing you. I'm now making a real promise to back off. I need to let my department return to work the old-fashioned way so they don't lose any more respect for me, and you don't lose any more of yourself."

He turned to me with pleading eyes. I could hear the voice inside my head urging me to speak up, insisting I was fine, but my mouth wouldn't open. I understood what he was conveying. He wanted to stop working with me and end what we had, convinced that was the only way to prevent him from needing me.

"Just think about it over the next few days," he said. He turned away and walked out, leaving me paralyzed in my silence. I dug my fingers into the edge of my counter, fighting the urge to hurl something across the room, and allowed my emotions to flow freely from my eyes.

A couple of minutes later, his car pulled away. I pulled away from the counter, dove toward my front door, turned the deadbolt, and fell back against it. Why do I ruin everything? Why do I make everyone want to leave?

I went over to the front room window and stared out into the empty driveway. Some of me hoped Julian would come back, but the driveway sat empty, leaving me overwhelmed with guilt. If someone were to walk by, I would look like a hostage begging to be freed, which wouldn't be far from the truth.

Chapter Sixteen

I rose at 5 a.m. the following Saturday with an overwhelming desire to deep clean my house, hoping it would distract me from my inner turmoil. What Julian said still bothered me. I did as he said, I thought about it, and I still didn't like it.

Indefinitely. Why not a week or two or a month at most? Why do I need to leave my job indefinitely? The word squeaked with every stroke I made as I scrubbed every surface and organized every drawer and cabinet. I then tackled some small projects that had built up over the months. Once I finished those tasks, I decided to create a comprehensive to-do list and managed to check off quite a few tasks, unsure where all my energy was coming from.

With the house cleaned and organized, I channeled some energy elsewhere. The temperature had dropped to the mid-seventies. There was a comfortable breeze, and the sun was out, making it a perfect day to head outside. I mowed the lawn and tended to most of the small garden areas I had neglected over the summer. I finished my seasonal cleanup in the garage, then settled down in my rocking chair on the back patio and allowed myself a few moments of rest.

By the time my energy had diminished, it was almost noon. I checked my phone to ensure I hadn't missed any calls from Julian and was surprised that I hadn't received a single call or text from him all week.

I'm fine. This is fine. I need time away from work, and after that last episode, I need time away from him. I repeated this to myself, telling myself that this change is necessary. My mind believed it, but my heart wasn't convinced.

I caught a whiff of something awful and sniffed the air around me, then acknowledged the smell was coming from me. Covered in sweat, dirt, grass clippings, and dust from the garage, I headed for the shower. Once dressed, I decided to swing by the grocery store and pick up a few items for dinner. Instead of heading home, I drove to my sister's house. Now would be a good time to share the news with her. If there was anyone who could convince me to stay away, it was her.

I beeped my horn as I pulled into her driveway. Kyle was out front shooting hoops, and I almost melted from his big smile as he watched me pull in.

He shrieked as he dove into me and hugged me, "Mom! Aunt Natalie's here!"

I snatched him up and hugged him right back. "Oh, how I've missed you!"

"Where've you been? How come you haven't been over?" he asked.

I messed up his hair and wrapped my arm around his neck, pulling him toward the house. "I'm sorry, kid. It has been crazy busy with work. But I have some news to tell you and your mom."

The front door opened, and Nicole paused before greeting me. "Hello there, I wasn't expecting you," she said.

I was taken aback by how radiant she was. She was modeling a white dress accented by a mauve cardigan, and the color blended well with her skin and hair. She came down the porch steps and offered me a light hug.

Surprised, but I wasn't about to deny it. "You look great! There's something different about you," I said. A new man? Better job? Nah, definitely a new man. She's wearing a dress.

"Thanks for noticing. I've dropped a little weight and been more active lately." She pulled back and scaled me from top to bottom. "You're pretty fine yourself."

I'm sure she was trying to be nice. My job aged me twenty years, but I wouldn't worry her with details.

"So, what do we owe the pleasure of this visit?" she asked.

"Oh, I hope it's okay. I wanted to cook dinner for us all. I found some great recipes online that I want to try, but I need a couple of critics. Plus, I wanted to talk to you about something." I held my breath, waiting for her to respond.

"Of course, you can stay. Right, Mom?" Kyle intervened.

Nicole smiled down at Kyle, who gave her a thrilled nod, then back at me. "Of course. We would love to have you."

The tension eased from my body

as a considerable weight lifted off my shoulders. I asked Kyle to help me with the groceries. We both grabbed a bag and went inside. I began boiling water, chopping vegetables, and sautéing them in oil.

"Aunt Natalie, guess what?" Kyle asked.

"What? No wait, let me guess, you're kicking butt in school?"

Kyle gave me his signature shrug, but shook his head.

"You found the Batcave and are now Batman's sidekick?"

This put a big smile on Kyle's face, but he shook his head again.

"Okay, I give up, what?"

"Mom is taking me to buy a Halloween costume, and I wanted to ask if you are coming trick-or-treating with us."

I raised my brows. "Oh, that's right. Halloween is just around the corner. So, what are you going to be for Halloween this year?"

Kyle jumped with excitement. "This time, I want to be the Joker. I'll have green hair and all that makeup on my face. The Halloween store has a Joker outfit that's purple and green. It's going to be awesome!"

I smiled. It felt good to be here with Kyle and listen to him. I tried to stifle a laugh when I watched Nicole stir the pasta, then pull a spaghetti string and toss it on the wall.

Kyle watched her as well, and we both burst out laughing. "Are you serious? You still do that?" I asked her.

She turned and gave me her typical shrug. Like mother, like son.

After dinner, Kyle and I went to the backyard. We tossed his baseball around, and then we headed to his room. He was both excited and serious at the same time. "I got the Batcave, the Batmobile, and his plane. There are still a few toys I want to get." He ran around his room, showing me his entire toy collection and the pictures he drew. My eyes spotted a picture taped to his wall of three people: him, his mother, and me. Kyle never met his father, a deadbeat who showed no interest in children. His loss.

"I love that picture, Kyle!" I said, pointing.

He stopped what he was doing and ran over to where the picture was hanging, pointing at each person. "I drew this a long time ago. It's of you, me, and mommy."

"I see that. Well, I think it's great!" I winked.

Things felt different. It had been a while since I felt relaxed inside these walls. With my sister's upbeat mood and Kyle's overexcitement, I finally felt at home. I don't know what look I had just then, but as if Kyle could read my mind, he dropped whatever toy he had in his hand and dove onto me, forcing me into a bear hug.

"I have missed you, Aunt Natalie. I wish you would come by a lot more."

I held him for what felt like an eternity. It had been too long since I hugged this boy, too long since I visited this house and spent time with him and my sister. That all needed to change.

"I believe now is the perfect moment to share my exciting news with you and your mom." I gently nudged him back so I could meet his gaze. "I hope you'll be as thrilled about it as I am."

Kyle leapt up. "Well, come on, then, and let's talk to Mommy." He used all his strength to pull me off his bed.

"Puuullll," I said, pretending I required all his help. He managed to pull me up, but with such force that we both fell to the floor laughing. Once we had exhausted all of our giggles, we returned to the kitchen, where Nicole finished wiping the table.

"You aren't supposed to clean up. I would have done all that. After all, I am the one who showed up and made the mess," I said.

Nicole waved me off. "Oh goodness, no, it's fine. Besides, that was a great meal, so it was worth any mess made."

Kyle took a couple of steps next to me and placed his hand in mine. "What do you want to tell us?" he asked, waving my arm back and forth.

I breathed and said, "Well, Julian and I talked." I walked over to the table and sat down, bringing Kyle with me and placing him on my lap. "It was decided that I am going to take some time away from work, which made me think. With my extra time off, I hoped to come over more often and spend time with both of you.

I feel like I've missed so much and don't want to miss out anymore."

I held my breath, hoping my news was something Nicole wanted to hear. Some time had passed since we last spoke, and our discussions rarely ended on a positive note.

"Was it a mutual decision?" she asked.

I smirked. Nicole knew what Julian could be like based on how often I gabbed about him, and I frequently touched on his stubbornness several times in one sitting. That, of course, is before we start arguing, and I would haul off, upset.

"Yes and no. It was more Julian telling me to step away from the job and my arguments against it, but after considering what he said, I guess I can't argue with him."

Nicole nodded but kept her gaze fixed on mine. "Well, then, all I can say is good. I agree with Julian. That line of work is creepy, dealing with dead people, so you should leave it behind."

I had a feeling she would say that. She was still uncomfortable with my job, but I didn't want to make a big deal out of it. I wanted to make amends and reunite with my family, and this was the first step toward achieving that goal.

"So, are you okay with seeing me around more often?" I sucked in my breath again, reeling with anticipation. She had no poker face; her expressions revealed she was game.

She nodded and smiled at me—a sisterly smile that was neither judgmental nor faked, but genuine and sincere. "That would be nice."

"Yeah!" Kyle shouted. "You can come over all the time and play." He slid off my lap, spinning with excitement. "Aunt Natalie, we can go for bike rides, play baseball, and build a fort in the woods." Kyle stretched out his hand and, using his fingers, counted all the different activities we could do together.

Nicole turned to Kyle. "Sweetie, can Mommy talk to Aunt Natalie for a minute?"

Kyle scrunched his face at her. He still had more playdates to discuss.

"Please? "Nicole asked him again.

"Okay, fine," he said, walking into the living room. Once Kyle was out of the room, Nicole stood, moved to the fridge, pulled out two beers, and handed one to me before returning to the table.

"Natalie, I've been thinking a lot about you, and I wanted to let you know I'm sorry for how life has been between us as we grew up. I'm sorry I was such a difficult person."

Her apology was unexpected, and tears filled my eyes without warning. "That's alright," I whispered to her. "I came here tonight to bare my soul. I wanted to apologize to you for everything I put you through."

"No, it's not alright. It was hard for both of us growing up, losing family members left and right. But it was worse for you. Seeing how everyone treated you. How I treated you. I made you out to be some monster, and here it was, I the whole time. It must have been horrible."

I saw the shame in her eyes and wanted to reach out and hold my little sister. I scrunched my face up, suddenly aware that the timing was odd. "Did a psychiatrist reach out to you?"

Nicole's eyes met mine. "What? No. I'm just saying, I was a total ass and I want you to know how sorry I am."

I cocked back my head, convinced I had it all figured out. "Okay, who's the guy?"

Nicole shuffled in her seat. "There's no guy. I'm being serious right now, so let me get this out."

I raised my hand, cutting her off. "Nicole, I know I wasn't easy to be around. You were just a baby and lost the chance to get to know your older brother, and I doubt you remember Mom and Dad. I had to be a better sister, and I failed. Not a day goes by that I don't regret my actions. I miss you terribly. I miss my little sister."

“I miss you, too.”

I couldn't keep my composure any longer, and my eyes filled with tears again. But we both stood up, and tears of joy accompanied our shared hug.

At some point, Kyle walked back in and watched us. He moved in to join the hug, and when I peered down at his handsome little face, he winked. I smiled so hard that I felt it down in my soul. We were going to be a family again. For once, I had something to hope for.

"So, there's no guy?"

Nicole smirked. "I can't with you."

Chapter Seventeen

I woke up the next day sensing a confident change in the air. The morning was gloomy, and storm warnings were scrolling across my sister's television screen, but it felt like rays of sunshine were bursting from my body, and I was ready to start my day with a positive mindset.

I stayed the night at Nicole's in my old bedroom. This used to be our grandparents' house, a place we both cherished. We decided it was best for Nicole to keep the house, as she needed the space for her growing, adventurous young boy. Given the state of the economy, being a single mom, she couldn’t afford a new home.

Kyle woke me up by jumping on the bed, and I wrestled with him before getting up to make breakfast for the three of us.

Do you want to join us for Sunday Mass? Nicole asked.

I perked up. "Absolutely. I haven’t been to church in a long time. Besides, I should give thanks for the blessings that have come back into my life."

We attended the Sunday service led by a new pastor. Nicole mentioned he joined the church a few years ago and felt he was a breath of fresh air compared to the previous one. I was disappointed. The last pastor had guided my family through baptisms, Sunday school, and funerals. It was unfortunate that we were unable to listen to him deliver his sermon.

When the service was over, I pulled out my cell phone to check for missed messages. Still, nothing. At this point, I just wanted someone from work to get in touch with me. I prayed that Julian wasn't upset with me, but I knew him well enough to know that wasn't the case. He could never stay mad at me for too long, even when I managed to cross the line with him. I reminded myself to let it go. This was my time with my family, and I wanted to cherish every minute.

I sighed and dropped my phone into my purse. Nicole and Kyle were talking with the pastor, and she nodded in my direction. The pastor smiled at me and waved before turning back to her. I shrank a bit and offered him an awkward smile. I had not attended church in years. I wasn't sure if that was something people frowned upon around here.

After church, the three of us went for brunch. Luckily, the weatherman had it wrong. The storm passed us, so we took advantage of the day and visited a hibachi grill. Kyle was captivated by the cook's grilling performance and caught a piece of shrimp in his mouth when the chef flicked it at him. I ended up getting hit on the forehead with mine. I think Nicole's piece of shrimp landed in her hair somewhere. Either way, we all laughed, enjoyed our meal, and topped the night with ice cream.

By the next day, I was back home and looking around for things to do. Monday should be a back-to-work day, not sitting home wondering if I still have a job. The concern had set in hard, with no single message from Julian, Jeff, Mike, or anyone else at the office. My worst fears were coming true—they didn't need me. They were probably celebrating that I was out of the office. Maybe word had spread that Julian asked me to leave. Perhaps someone had even gone above his head and persuaded him to release me.

I wanted to find out what was happening and seek a good source—someone who knew everything. I pulled out my cell and called Dr. Lance's office. He would open a time slot for me without question. Clara answered the phone on the fourth ring, her sweet voice coming through almost like a whisper.

"Good morning, Baltimore Psychiatric. How may I help you?" she said.

"Good morning, Mrs. Rice. This is Natalie Rhine. Is there any way I could meet with Dr. Lance today?"

I could hear her smile. "Oh, hello, Natalie. Let me check his schedule for today."

I listened to her chair squeak and the papers shuffle. "Well, he is quite busy today, dear. I'm afraid it won't be a good day," she said before a voice interrupted.

"Who is that? Is that Natalie? Of course, today is a good day. Tell her to come in whenever she pleases," Lance ordered.

I could tell Mrs. Rice was shrinking into her chair. Lance made her uncomfortable, but she complied and told me to come on in.

"Thank you," I said and disconnected the call. Why does he have to be so hard on her? She should be home, enjoying retirement, not sitting at that worn-out desk.

I had a lot to discuss, and I wanted to report on my sister and how we reconciled. Mostly, I wanted to know if I was missed. Someone had to have said something. Yes, there's the patient-doctor confidentiality issue, but I'm not inquiring about the emotions of the people he treats; I'm just curious about what everyone has been doing. Does that count?

Over the past few days, I've been considering Julian's request to leave the department. Leaving was out of the question, but I would consider taking extended leave, enjoying a few vacations with my family, and returning in three months. I couldn't imagine Julian arguing against my proposition.

When I arrived at Lance's office, Mrs. Rice appeared out of sorts. She rushed around as quickly as her fragile, old legs would allow, carrying files back and forth at Lance's demand.

"Is everything okay?" I asked her after she urged me to take a seat.

"Yes, dear, just busy, busy, busy," she said with a kind smile.

"Clara, how many times do I have to tell you… Last week! I need the ones from last week!" Lance yelled from behind his door.

"Oh dear, sorry, I have those right here."

"Where they need to be is in front of me," he responded.

I raised my brow. He was in a foul mood today. I almost told Mrs. Rice I would return another day, but Lance heard me in the waiting room and called for me to enter his office.

"Take a seat," he commanded more than invited. He was sitting at his desk, shuffling through papers. "Sorry for the mess," he said, scribbling something on a notepad. He straightened his desk and walked to the door.

"Clara, I need you to look this up for me." He handed her the note, closed the door, and walked over to his usual chair. "Sorry. It's been a crazy morning.

"I see that… you're running your secretary ragged," I said, implying his poor treatment.

He scoffed. I figured he had nothing nice to say about Mrs. Rice, so I changed the subject.

"I took your advice and enjoyed my weekend. I reconnected with my family and had a heart-to-heart with my sister."

"And how did that go?" he asked.

"Better than expected. I feel good that our relationship will only improve."

"Well, that's good to hear." He smiled and grabbed his notebook. "Tell me, are you feeling any better about that last profiling, or does the boy still plague you?"

I almost forgot all about my last profiling until he mentioned it. I was so focused on Julian and my sister that for a moment, I forgot about the previous cases. It also occurred to me that I didn't have any bad dreams in the past few days, either. "I guess I'm okay. Now that I think about it, I may have overreacted between our conversation and my one with Julian."

He squinted at me in confusion. "Did you talk about something else?"

"Julian visited me later that evening, after you and I talked. We argued about him wanting me to take an indefinite leave of absence."

Lance's brows rose. "Really? Why?"

"That's what I asked. Julian believes he has contributed to my stress by putting me in difficult situations. Even though that's my job, he's suddenly had a change of heart." I stretched back in the chair. "What I can't figure out is why now? I've been doing this for a few years."

"Perhaps that's why. He's finally realizing that he's always calling you in on cases, and it's too much for you to handle. Of course, I may have had something to do with that, in case he hasn't said anything."

"Yeah, he mentioned something about you chewing him out. If it had anything to do with bringing me on while on those pills, thanks for that." I threw him an appreciative smile.

He nodded. "Julian is brilliant, but that wasn't one of his smartest decisions. Who knows what could have happened while you had a sleeping pill in your system?"

Pills. But I kept that to myself.

"So he's finally encouraging you to take time off, is he? It's about time he and I were on the same page."

"What! I thought you hated it when Julian called the shots?"

He shrugged. "Don't get me wrong, I certainly do, but common sense tells me you are not finding a peaceful release with these criminal cases as you used to."

I furrowed my brow. I hate it when he's right.

"When you talked with him, did you tell him I should leave indefinitely?"

He averted his eyes but shook his head. "Nope, that was all him."

"Have you spoken to Julian in the past couple of days?" Now would be a better time than ever to ask him what he knows.

"I have not. I'm sure we both decided that you should be left alone."

The muscles in my body went from an exciting tension to crumpled mush. "Oh."

"Was I supposed to talk to him?" he asked.

I looked up at him. "No, but it's not like him to not speak to me, even to ask how I'm doing. I haven't heard from him in days. I can't help but feel concerned."

"Ah. Got it." Lance's face softened. "Natalie, it's nothing personal. You need time away from work, and he's giving it to you.

"I just hope I will have a job to return to. Julian was adamant about my leaving, and I just couldn't. Not indefinitely."

"I have the impression that the argument went badly?"

"It wasn't what I expected."

"How so?" He leaned forward, causing the notebook to slide between his hip and the chair. For once, I was grateful it wasn't getting any extra pen marks.

I had to consider that Lance knew about our relationship, but I don't believe he was aware of the whole story, and there was no reason he needed to know.

"Well, he caught me off guard. I thought I would end up getting fired, and I may have had a temper. You and I know my job is the only link that defines my identity. Without it, I would be this crazy person who plays with dead things."

Dr. Lance furrowed his brow at me, returning my gaze. "Minus the last part, I believe it helps address that burning question you've pondered about why you can do what you do." He appeared more relaxed than usual, despite sitting in that overused chair.

He drummed his fingers on the chair's arms and peered out the window. "You know what I can't understand?" he asked.

"What?" I replied, shaking my head at him.

"You have no problem jumping in and facing one of the biggest, if not the absolute worst, fears people have; yet when it comes to something as simple as talking to Julian, you run and hide."

"Who said I was hiding?" I retorted, annoyed.

He raised an eyebrow at me.

I exhaled and slumped back into the chair. "Julian's a scary man. What can I say?" I had no counter for him. Sometimes Julian intimidated me as a boss, but my romantic feelings and the fear of disappointing him kept me at bay. I didn't hide; it felt more like running and crying.

He crossed his legs but kept his arms resting on the armrests. He wore his psychiatrist's demeanor. This was no laid-back Dr. Lance like at the diner; he was all business.

"I'm glad you found a way to improve your relationship with your sister. That's a great first step toward a new and better you. However, when it comes to Julian, I can only offer so much advice, and my current recommendation is that you approach him and reach a compromise, just as you did with your sister. Julian is easy to persuade if you present a strong, valid argument."

"I hope so. I planned to meet with Julian today to let him know my decision."

Lance's brow peaked. "Really? And what decision is that?"

"Well, it will be impossible to keep me away, but this mini vacation was necessary. More days off like this will be appreciated in the future. I feel much better already, so if Julian is willing, I could use an extended vacation and return to work after a few months."

He nodded in agreement. "Sounds like a good plan. I can't see any reason Julian would argue against it, assuming you hold up your end of the deal and get the rest you need."

"Pinkie swear," I assured him.

"So, my little homework assignment was successful, then, huh?" he asked.

I allowed him this moment of gloating. For once, I gave Lance credit for being right. I need to stop being afraid of the people in my life: my sister, Kyle, and Julian.

"It was a much-deserved, much-needed time off. I got to spend some time with my family. I've compiled a lengthy list of things to do during my vacation." I realized how much I wanted to be in their lives, to watch my nephew grow up. I also wanted to reconnect with my sister. It's unfortunate that I know so little about her, and it's time that changes.

"I'm glad to hear this new determination in your voice." His watch beeped, and he pressed a button to silence it; then he stood from his chair. "The only thing left for you now is to talk to Julian and close this chapter in your book. The two of you will probably work something out." He raised his arms and gestured for me to go toward the door. "Now, I hate to rush things, but today has been busy, and bringing you in was a tight squeeze on the schedule."

"That's fine. I just wanted to check in with you; nothing big. Just an update here and there." I turned to the door, intending to work it out with Julian. I realized my vacation would not include any appointments with Lance. No emotional responses from my work meant nothing to discuss with my psychiatrist. "Thanks for the help," I said, moving toward the door.

"Natalie, just because you are not working doesn't mean my door isn't open to you. You are always welcome to come and talk."

I opened the door and paused for a moment. "I'll consider that," I responded. This man is starting to know me too well, even reading my mind.

Mrs. Rice looked up from her typewriter and smiled. "Good day, dear," she said.

I smiled back. "Good day indeed."

Chapter Eighteen

I drove from Dr. Lance's office to work. When I arrived, the department was buzzing with energy. Personnel were hustling behind every door and at every desk, making calls, searching for files, using databases, and doing what law enforcement should do: investigate. The department felt alive, but it highlighted my absence.

A few confused expressions greeted me as I walked past cubicles, and the energy in the room shifted.

"I thought the boss sent her packing," someone whispered.

I turned my head toward the voice and regretted it. A couple of officers shot annoyed glares at me, exchanging words.

My hands clenched as I walked past them, relieved I had bitten off all my nails the night before; otherwise, they would have torn into my skin. I was about to turn and give them a piece of my mind when Jeff popped up next to me.

"Nat, you won't believe…oh, hey guys. What's going on?" He looked past the two officers and gave me a devious wink, then diverted back to them. "So get this…" Jeff raised his arm to touch the shoulder of one of the officers, and a sharp buzz ran through the air. The officer jumped, and I took that as my cue to step closer.

"What the hell was that?" the officer screeched, finding me in his face with a shrewd smile.

"Natalie! Did you forget to eat today?" Jeff brushed past him, hiding the hand buzzer in his pocket, and tapped me on the shoulder. He lowered his voice to a noticeable whisper. "What did I tell you about eating your coworkers? Not cool!"

"Sorry," I peered back at the officers. "I missed breakfast." I ground the words out through clenched teeth.

The off-centered cop straightened but held an uneasy expression on his face.

"See, she's sorry," Jeff urged. "Okay, so we need to take care of that little problem of yours." He raised his arm to encourage me to walk away. "Thanks for understanding, guys. Teamwork!" He shouted over his shoulder as we both walked off.

Jeff escorted me within a few feet of Julian's office door and pretended to polish his fingers along his shirt.

"Thanks for the save. Appreciate it," I smiled, then leaned in. "And that's still my favorite prank by the way."

He popped his chest. "Yeah, yeah, what can I say. Always the hero. Rescuing damsels in distress and all that. And let's be honest. I don't think that will ever get old."

I tried to give another smile, but I knew he saw through me.

"Don't let those schmucks get to you. They're still rookies." He winked and strolled off in the other direction.

I glanced back at the cubicle farm of desks and uniforms. Some people stared, but most continued to work. I suddenly felt less motivated to discuss my leave with Julian. Except for Jeff, it was clear my coworkers didn't want me around.

I turned my back on it all and forced myself to shrug it off. Too damn bad if they didn't want me here. I belonged, whether they liked it or not. I approached Julian’s door, knocked, and listened as he uttered a low "come in." I let out a breath and walked in.

"Hey," I said, closing the door behind me.

Julian slouched against the desk as his right hand drummed the paperwork sprawled about his desk.

"Guessing a big case?" I asked.

He rubbed his forehead, then his eyes, and used both hands to rub his face to snap out of his fog.

"I hope you had a better night than I did," he said. "There was a woman discovered dead in her car.”

He immediately raised a hand to ward off any reaction from me. “Now, before you say anything, it appears to be a mugging, but it’s nothing the team can't handle."

His last line told me he was sticking to his word and keeping me away from cases.

"I'm sure they'll do what's necessary." I didn't argue. I walked over to his desk and sat in the hot seat. "This is probably a bad time, but I want to talk to you about the other night." I straightened my fingers, realizing my hands were still clenched from earlier, and I had to wiggle out the soreness.

Julian shuffled all the paperwork on his desk and stuffed it in a folder. "I was about to head down and speak with Mike, but I can spare a few minutes for you."

"I will try to make it brief, then." My body stiffened. "I cannot leave the department. I just can't. It's all I have. I don't have any work experience anywhere else. So, I’m willing to compromise."

Julian sat quietly in his chair. He had more than a five o'clock shadow, and his clothes appeared worn. His hair had also seen better days. He seemed as vulnerable as I felt. I was almost ashamed of the smile I pressed myself to conceal. Julian had been reminded of what it's like not to have me around. Score one for me.

"What kind of compromise?" he asked.

I pretended to ponder. "A short-term leave."

Silence filled the room for what felt like an eternity. Julian stood up, walked over to the chairs in the corner, pulled one next to mine, and sat down, facing me. He took my hand and cupped it in his.

"I did a lot of thinking. I wouldn't be where I am without you, and neither would this department-"

"Which is why I'm willing to compromise," I interjected.

Julian dropped his head in defeat. "I'm still listening. What do you have in mind?" he asked.

"A long vacation…maybe a month…"

"Six." He quickly responded.

"Two, and I can be back to start the new year. Final offer."

He smirked. "You're giving me an ultimatum?"

"Please, Julian. I can't leave my job. It's a crazy one, but it's mine. I'm begging you."

Julian raised a brow and gave me a sly smile. "I can get behind the begging," he winked.

He let out a long breath. "Fine. We'll start with a couple of months, and then we'll reconsider bringing you back to ensure you are ready." He steered his gaze to meet mine. I would have shrunk into my chair if I weren't so captivated by their color. After a brief pause, he softened his expression, released my hand, and sat back.

"Don't take offense, but they're going crazy out there. It finally occurred to me how much I have been taking advantage of you when I realized the sizable workloads I took from them," he said, pointing toward the door.

I peeked through the frosted glass of his office door. Shadows moved in the distance, but didn't hover. "I may have noticed the case files scattered over desks."

I let out a slight gasp as an idea struck me. "What if you call me in for the more challenging cases- those with no evidence, no suspects, no resolution?"

Julian stood and pushed the chair back into the corner. "No."

"But those are the cases you would need me for. And since you have such a strong team of investigators, I doubt you would call me in as often. I'm guessing at least one or two cases a month." I dawdled for a moment, considering if that was too ambitious. His team was proficient, but I wasn't sure they were as capable as I thought. I had never seen them in action without my assistance. All I knew was that they would initiate the case, and I would take over. I never worked directly alongside any of his detectives.

Julian walked back to his desk and gave me a stern look. "I said no."

I dropped my shoulders, ready to plead my case, but he reached for his keys and the paperwork file and headed for the door.

"Wait, so that's it? You release me for two months, and I'm out just like that?" I dashed for the door before he could.

"I said fine, didn't I? You're the one who suggested two months, and I accepted. What did I miss?" His voice was even-keeled.

"Fine?" I asked, surprised by his quick response. I wasn't sure what to say. The deal was made. I'm taking a two-month vacation away from what I have known for years. Did he want me out for that long? It's only been a week, and he already looks like he's about to drop.

I sank against the door. "I went through this discussion repeatedly in my head, and I expected to have a few days to prepare for an extended vacation that you were supposed to argue against. I wasn't ready to walk into my boss's office, exchange a few words, and give in after a few minutes. At least let me leave with a bang and help with this new case."

"Natalie, I'm not going to tell you again." He pulled me from the door and moved me out of his way to open it.

"Two months. No last-minute cases. No on-calls. Two months. That's the deal," his voice was adamant.

I gave him my best doe eyes. "Okay, so not to be a pain in the ass."

"Too late," Julian interjected.

I sneered at him. "I may have suggested two months, but I don't want to go that long. I'll go stir crazy if I'm not busy."

He closed the door, raised his arm above my head and rested it against the wall, and moved in within inches of my face.

"For the record, it will be the longest two months. However, I must admit that everyone needs this. You need to get back to normal as much as possible. I need to reorganize my department," he said, turning toward the window, "and they need to work. It's as simple as that."

"All right." My stomach tightened. What if, in these two months, he realized he didn't need me and decided to cut me off the payroll? The little voice inside me circled, squawking insults and what-ifs in my head. "Any other commands before I leave?"

"Take care of yourself," he said, giving a playful brush under my chin.

I stood there, captivated, my gaze locked onto him. How does he do that? One moment, I felt the tight grip of anxiety curling in my chest. Yet somehow that weight shifted like a tiny flame sparking to life. I fought against the urge to show weakness, determined not to come off like a defeated, spoiled girl.

"Fine, then I'll clean up my desk and go."

Julian pulled away, but just as he was about to open the door again, he hesitated. "Natalie, would you like to have dinner with me again tonight?"

The fire inside me burned in a whole new way. A spark shot through me, causing my body to tingle from the inside out. When I lifted my eyes toward Julian, he winked.

"Okay," I said with a playful shrug as I left his office. I didn't glance back at him. I didn't have to.

I fluttered back to my desk, receiving looks as if I were raiding the evidence room. Julian always managed to change the conversation and was better at surprises than I was.

I slowed as I neared my desk and spotted Jeff studying his monitor, at least to the unsuspecting eye, but I knew his tricks too well. Those fake glasses never fooled me. I closed in behind him, moving close to his ear, and in my best impression of Julian's voice, I roared, "Detective!"

I expected him to jump, but I never imagined he would leap out of his chair and dive into the giant plant beside his desk. At this point, I paid no mind to whoever was watching me; suppressing my laughter would have caused significant stomach pains I wasn't willing to endure.

"Wow. Good job, Detective. You got them. That tree won't be lurking around here anymore." I didn't bother trying to hold back. I skimmed the office to see if anyone else witnessed his takedown, but I was the only one. Oh well. I laughed so hard my stomach hurt. He bared his teeth in a playful growl, fixed the plant, and settled back into his chair.

"I was having a much-needed snooze." There wasn't any anger in his voice. He could never get mad at me; he knew he deserved that. He was the king of scaring me, sneaking up behind me during the early or late hours. He would either bark like a dog or jab me in the side, making me jump out of my skin. After a few minutes, he laughed and added a few more jokes at his own expense. Our shared laughter made me realize I wouldn't be doing this for a while, and then all the laughter ceased.

Jeff plopped back into his chair. "So, how did your talk with Julian go? Nosey minds need to know."

"He wants me to take a vacation."

"Huh? Oh, is that all? Julian came up to me the other day and ripped my head off when he ordered me to stay away from you."

My smile faded. "What do you mean, ordered you?"

"Exactly what I just said. At first, I wondered if this was a jealous boyfriend thing? But then, a rumor got around that you had a rough case and lost it, or something like that."

I sank into my chair, aware that those few days were just the beginning.

Jeff furrowed his brow. "Wow. If you could see the look on your face right now. You didn't even catch my jealous boyfriend comment. What happened there?"

He seemed shocked when I told him about my departure for a couple of months, but he insisted that once I was gone, the department would realize how much they had taken for granted with me around.

"At least I would want you back. I love the work-life balance I have when you're around," he said.

That brought a smile to my face. Jeff always knew how to lift my spirits.

"And he's not my boyfriend!" He assured him.

"Uh-huh, sure," he smirked.

I tossed a paper clip at him, and he deflected it.

"So what are you going to do on your time off?"

"I don't know yet. Probably spend time with my sister and nephew. Get some stuff done around my house. Nothing big."

"You have no idea how much I loth you right now," Jeff cocked his head toward his desk drawer, insinuating that a certain cutout was about to make a familiar appearance.

"What did I do?" I asked, confused.

"Are you kidding? First, and I say this with the utmost love and respect for you. Your corpse-loving self gets to take a long vacation away from this place. And second, it will drive Haley crazy, sitting in this drawer with no one to talk to. You're selfish!"

"I didn't want to leave. He's not giving me much choice."

"Oh no. A forced vacation. However, will you manage?" He didn't even attempt to hide the sarcasm.

"Knock it off. I'm upset over it. It's a vacation for you because you are a good detective and can count on a job when you return. I, on the other hand, am incredibly paranoid and convinced he'll realize I'm not needed and shut the door on me. We are not the same."

"Ha. Yeah, no kidding. You eat dead people!" Jeff raised his voice as another officer walked by. The young woman recoiled and sped up her pace.

"So funny." I snarled at Jeff. I yelled after her, "I don't eat dead people," but that only drew more attention.

I growled as I organized the few items on my desk. Then, I moved to the window and dusted the fake plant I had sitting on the ledge.

"At least this should be here when I get back. I don't have to worry about it dying."

"So, Natalie," Jeff called, raising his voice enough to be heard across the room. "How long will you be working for the CIA? That sounds like an intense case you'll be dealing with."

I paused, confused about what he was referring to.

"What are you talking about?"

Jeff gave a few sporadic winks. "Ah crap, it's top secret, isn't it?"

I turned and spotted several faces watching me as I cleaned my desk.

"Oh, about two months," I said, picking up on Jeff's cues. "There are too many important people involved in this one, so yeah, it's supposed to be kept on the down low.

We heard whispers coming from different corners of the office.

Jeff leaned closer to me. "There's no reason not to fuel the desire to have you back sooner. If people around here start regarding you as a national sensation, they'll never want to let you go," he winked.

I gave Jeff a smug smile and checked the clock.

"How about some lunch?" I asked.

Jeff tipped a bit to the side, shooting me a devious grin. "Are you buying?"

I let out another growl in his direction. "I'm the one who's going to be unemployed for two months."

Jeff pursed his lips. "So, is that a yes?"

I let out a muffled laugh and sank back into my chair. "I suppose."

Jeff opened his top drawer, pulled out his Haley Joel prop, and held it to his face.

"Can I come too?" he asked, raising his voice to sound childish.

I let off a scowl louder than I intended. "Hell no."

I glanced back at Julian's office, realizing how much I would miss his pacing and hand gestures behind the window. My mood dropped again as I recognized that my time here was ending.

"Hey, you're doing it again," Jeff said.

"Doing what?

"I can tell just by looking at you that you think your job here is over. Don't be so dramatic. It's just a couple of months! I wish I could have a few months," he reassured me.

"I know I'm being dramatic, but I don't need a vacation—at least not for that long. I feel like the department is dismissing me as the crazy person due to a lack of funds and space."

"That's not it, and you know it. Now cheer up, or I'm bringing this guy with us." Jeff waved his prop at me.

"Oh no, please don't." I smiled back at him.

Jeff slumped his shoulders in protest and gazed at his cutout. "Sorry, kid. I tried." Then, he tossed it back into his drawer.

Chapter Nineteen

The lunch and Jeff's amusing company helped relieve some of the stress. Jeff's part took a lot of work to convince me that my time away was for the best. It wasn't that I disagreed; I just prayed it would only be two months.

Jeff drove and drilled simultaneously: "Repeat after me. No more dawdling, no more self-doubt, no more fearing the worst. I will only have positive thoughts and enjoy the time off."

"Yeah, yeah. I got it." I had the window cracked open, allowing a cool breeze to blow through my hair. "Still going to be weird, being out of work for two months."

Jeff scuffed. "I can't. I just can't with you," he said, shaking his head.

When we got back to the station, everyone was busy. Good for them, I suppose. Detective work happened long before me, and as much as I hated to admit it, it could very well go on without me. My only fault was wanting to be a part of it.

I made a quick stop at Mike's office, wished him a temporary goodbye, and waved to his team. Mike wished me well, and a look on his face made my heart sink. He would never admit it, but his smile told me he was relieved I was going out on leave. His team will even conduct some in-depth casework for once, utilizing all his gadgets and toys and bringing science back into the game.

I returned to my desk and took in its emptiness. What did I need to clear out? Now that I think of it, why did I need a desk anyway?

My only personal item was a photograph of Kyle, and for a few moments, I felt a sense of hope. I ran my finger over his picture before putting it in my satchel.

"I need to make a pitstop. Don't leave yet," Jeff ordered, pushing his chair out and heading toward the restrooms.

"Yes, sir!" I dropped back into my chair and studied the activities around me. I spotted Tony walking by with a guy in handcuffs as he escorted him to the interrogation room. "Busy, busy, busy," I whispered to myself.

The phone on my desk rang, and I flinched, more out of surprise than anything, as if it was the first time it had ever rung. I reached over to pick it up.

"Natalie Rhine," I answered.

At first, there was no response, but I could hear someone breathing on the other end. When the person spoke up, I wasn't expecting a frantic, sorrow-stricken voice to scream at me through the earpiece.

"I need you to help me. I need you to help my wife." A male voice cried in my ear.

My body tightened. I glanced over at Julian's office, but he was still gone. "Tell me what happened." Dread seeped through me. I didn't want to deny helping anyone, but I was under Julian's orders to leave the cases to the department.

"Someone killed her. Shot her. She was picking up...," the man said between sobs as his voice trailed off. I waited for him to catch his breath. "The police are already investigating, and they claim it appears to be a random mugging, but how the hell are they going to solve this? Please, I need your help."

I heard him take deep breaths and force the words out, trying to stay in control. This must be the case that kept Julian up last night.

"Sir. I am sorry. I can't say that enough, but I assure you, the department doesn't give up, and we have the best team-"

"No. The department has you. That makes them the best team; don't lie to me."

I closed my eyes and gripped the phone. "I'm sorry about what happened. The captain himself is working on this case."

I didn't doubt Julian and his team's ability to solve murders, but random murders are more challenging. Utilizing standard investigative resources would require a significant amount of time to generate leads.

"Why weren't you on the scene? You were supposed to be there?" His voice was so cold and full of despair.

My heart sped up. If it were up to me, I would have been there. I could have seen what happened, and the forensic team would have investigated all the details I provided.

But it wasn't up to me. I peered back at Julian's office. Why did I have to answer the phone?

"I'm sorry. I can't help you. The department placed me on leave. I can't work on the case."

"Do it anyway. Please, I'm begging you. My wife didn't deserve to die. She was a good woman. I know you can do this, please. I'm begging you," he cried. "Help me. Help us."

I pulled the phone away from my ear and squeezed the receiver between my hands. I couldn't—I couldn't—Julian would freak out and fire me.

I raised the phone back to my ear. "The department will work hard to find your wife's killer. Have faith that whoever it was will be brought to justice, and your wife can rest in peace." I uttered my apology and slammed the phone on the base before he could say anything else.

"Damn you, Julian," I muttered. My hands shook, and I leapt out of my chair and paced between my desk and Jeff's.

"What's wrong? You all right?" Jeff said, racing toward me.

My words came out muffled. "I believe the husband from last night's murder case just called me. He demanded that I work on the case. I can't, Jeff. I want to, but I can't. Julian will kill me." I looked up at him, needing assurance that I had made the right decision.

Jeff's face dropped, but then he offered a reassuring nod. "Don't worry about it. We can handle this. He's upset," he said, grabbing hold of my hands.

"I should have left when I had the chance." I pulled my hair off my face. How did this man know to call me?

"Jeff, is there something about this new case that I should know?" I asked him.

Jeff turned his head to the left toward Julian's office. For a moment, I thought he would give in and tell me, but he sided against me. "This is not your responsibility," he said, consoling me as best he could. "You can't solve them all. If Julian insists you can't be a part of this, then walk away."

"But I can help, Jeff. When it's all said and done, I will work it out in my head, but I can help!" I begged.

"Look, I get it. You have a heart of gold, Natalie. I don't blame you for wanting to help." Jeff moved to his desk and sat down in his seat. "I wish there were something I could do, but there isn't."

My stomach twisted into a dozen knots. Walking away from the cases was more complicated than I thought. For the first time, I realized that my ability was a gift, not a curse. I could give this poor husband closure. Exasperated and annoyed, I ran my fingers through my hair.

"Can you at least tell me if they have any leads?" I asked.

Jeff let out a breath, "Nothing yet. Mike is still running any DNA pulls." His face reflected the sadness I felt. "I'm sorry, Natalie. I wish you could help."

I walked to the window, desperate for something to grab my attention, but my mind reeled from that call. Julian wasn't the only one who was addicted to my profiling. I was addicted to it as well. But what could I do?

Jeff came behind me and tapped my shoulder, "You need to leave, forget everything that happened. But remember, I will be sitting here, counting the days until your return."

I turned toward Jeff. "Don't go replacing me. I will be heartbroken," I responded.

He returned to his desk, opened the drawer, and pulled out my least favorite of his props: "Haley and I will have to find someone else to torment for a while."

"You should retire him. I don't think anyone else will appreciate your sense of humor like I do," I smirked.

"Well, there won't be anyone quite like you. It would be impossible to replace you. I'll miss you, psycho," he said, giving me a goofy smile.

"I'll miss you, too, weirdo." I grabbed my satchel and headed for the elevator. As I pressed the down button, I sensed Jeff closing in on me. When I turned, Haley Joel Osment stood with his hands outstretched. I put my bag down and hugged him again. No one else would understand how challenging the next two months would be.

Chapter Twenty

My first week on vacation was a testament to my personal growth. I transformed my house, adding a fresh coat of paint and a new garden in the backyard. I even indulged in some crafting projects I discovered online. I pushed the fear of joblessness to the back of my mind, and I began to grasp the essence of Dr. Lance's philosophy on life.

Julian kept to his word to give me the time I needed. He even helped me take my mind off work by taking me on a few dates. Dating was never easy for me. Any dating opportunities I had were short-lived, and that's if I managed to capture a man's attention. Most of the guys I dated managed to stick around up to the three-month mark. There was something about me that didn't scream marriage material, and it was back to the drawing board for me. After a while, I grew tired of not being good enough, even in the romance department, and swore off dating altogether. That is, until I laid eyes on Julian.

It was nice to finally experience what it was like to spend time with a man I found myself attracted to. When our dates were over, we allowed ourselves some cuddle time, and I even drew up the courage to go in for the kiss. It was awkward because I practically nose-dived into him, but he gave me a cute laugh, cupped my chin, and had me curling my toes like a schoolgirl.

As far as my sister, my relationship with Nicole was on the mend. We were back to sharing stories and discussing the men in our lives, just like sisters should. Despite past concerns, we agreed that Kyle was happy to have me around, and we all missed each other. I shared my growth journey with her, and she responded with renewed hope for our relationship, inviting me to spend the weekend with her and Kyle.

Friday afternoon rush hour was one of those quirks in life that I couldn't stand but had no choice but to deal with. My car idled on the thruway at a dead stop, two exits before my turnoff. I turned the radio to an 80s pop station and drummed my fingers against the wheel, fighting the impatience that was brewing within me.

I shifted slightly in my seat to catch a glimpse of what was causing the holdup. Everyone in the far-left lane had their blinkers on, trying to move into the right lane. Brake lights taunted me every 20 seconds as they lit up and disappeared, only to announce the small opportunity to creep up a couple of feet and then entirely stop again. It took over forty minutes to pass another exit.

"C'mon," I yelled over the radio. I checked the clock and groaned. I was late.

Just ahead, police have cleared one part of the road for vehicles to pass through. Sure enough, two cars that looked like they were playing a game of chicken collided, missing their front ends, and their airbags were deployed. I moseyed on at a snail's pace, stuck behind onlookers who wanted to get a good look.

"Move, dammit!" I didn't care that I was coming up on police officers, but I withheld any urge to beep my horn. The last thing I needed was to get pulled over for road rage.

Once I cleared the accident area, the rest of the Thruway traffic wasn't as bad. It was still busy, and some drivers insisted they had to go five miles under the speed limit while staying in the passing lane. I was grateful to see the sign to my exit and barreled off, taking the corners faster than I probably should have.

I hope Nicole hasn't started dinner yet. I wanted to enjoy cooking together like we used to. Kyle would be home from school, and I could spend time helping him with his homework or playing outside with him.

I finally got a few blocks from my sister's street when another line of vehicles clogged the road. I heard sirens coming up from behind. "What in the world is going on today? Doesn't anyone know how to drive?" Up ahead, the police were all turning down the same road I was heading. Julian's car caught my attention. Mike and his CSI crew followed him. A crazed knot filled my stomach.

My cell phone caught me off guard when it blared out the Michael Meyers/Halloween ringtone. Jeff downloaded it into my phone as another one of his jokes, but it did amuse me.

Nicole's name flashed on my caller ID.

I answered. "Hey, Nic."

"Natalie."

"I'm late, I'm sorry. First, there was an accident on seventy, but I'm just up the road. What is going on down there? A ton of squad cars pulled down the street before me."

"Natalie," my sister said again. The tone of her voice hit me like bricks.

"What's going on? Are you all right?"

"No. I can't breathe," Nicole said, sobbing into the phone.

"Tell me, Nikki, what's wrong?" Panic raced through my system, setting my heart rate in overdrive. Where was Julian going?

"I can't say it, let alone believe it," she said, pausing.

I held my breath. The sound of all the sirens exploded through my head.

"Natalie, he's dead." The words barely escaped her mouth when she started to scream out her cries. "He's dead. My boy's dead."

My foot pressed the gas pedal unintentionally as my mind tried to grasp the words I just heard. The road and cars in front of me felt like they stretched out for miles and miles as my head started to sway.

"Natalie, say something! I can't handle this, please."

I blinked. I steered the car to the shoulder and slammed my brakes. "How can you say that to me…I mean, Kyle can't be. He just-"

"I don't know what happened." Nicole sobbed. "He went outside to play while I was getting dinner started. I noticed he wasn't in the backyard, so I called and called for him, but he didn't answer." She cried, continuing between breaths. "I checked out front, then looked around the woods, but I couldn't find him anywhere."

Hearing the grief in Nicole's voice made me remember the moment my mother went through the same ordeal as she looked for my brother, and then her reaction when she found him face down in the pool, stuck under the pool cover.

I didn't wait for Nicole to continue. I slammed down on the gas pedal and skidded back on the road. Her street was within eyesight. Cars blocked me from getting by, so I drove over the sidewalk and across lawns.

"I'm coming," I said, feeling the painful lump in my throat.

Her voice kept on, delirious of my words, "Chris and his daughter heard me screaming for Kyle, so they came out to help look. I heard Alexis scream." Nicole bawled out. "I went running and found Kyle lying on the ground. He wasn't moving, and blood was all over his head!"

"Hang on, I'm coming," I said, warding off the tears stinging my eyes. Not Kyle. Not him. Please, dear God, make this a bad dream.

I sped past officers waving and yelling at me to stop, but my foot didn't let up from the gas pedal. I don't remember putting my car in park; I drove across the lawn, jumped out, and ran to the backyard. People were everywhere, and I barreled past several more officers to get to Nicole. She uttered a muffled cry and reached for me as I fell into her and hugged her as tightly as possible while scanning the woods. Officers and forensics moved through the trees about fifty feet away. A few more officers gathered around a sectioned-off area.

Mike was kneeling while Julian stood next to him. Both were studying what lay before them.

Nicole sobbed, "Natalie! I want my boy!"

I pulled from her arms and held her head in my hands. "I need to see him," I told her, leaving her on the ground. Two officers stayed with her, trying to console my sister.

I darted into the woods where Julian and Mike were standing. As I came upon them, my eyes caught the shape of Kyle's little body slumped among branches and rocks.

"Kyle!" I screamed, seeing his lifeless little body lying only a few feet away.

Julian turned and caught me when I ran up. "No, Natalie!"

"Let me go," I demanded and tried to pull out of his grasp, but Julian kept a firm hold of my arms and kept me at bay from Kyle's body.

"He can't be dead, Julian, he can't." I sobbed. He held me tight, and my tears blurred my vision.

Julian leaned into me as I screamed into his sleeve, not believing any of this was real. I tried to convince myself that he was only hurt and that I would kiss his pain away, but Kyle's body didn't move. Forensics hovered over him, taking photographs and measurements. My tear-soaked eyes roamed over him, his face lying sideways, covered in dirt and blood.

"Get away from him!" I tried to yell through my sobs. "Stop taking pictures!" I tried again to pull away from Julian's hold.

Julian put his arm around my torso and dragged me away from Mike and his team. "Natalie, you can't be here." He tried to carry me, but I fought him on it and collapsed to the ground, not more than ten feet away.

I tried to hold my breath, watching for some movement from Kyle, just like I did when I was five years old, when the paramedics worked to revive my brother. I concentrated on his body to watch for signs of breathing. Nothing in this world could convince me he was dead. Not my Kyle.

I mimicked the words I said thirty years ago, "Wake up. Wake up!" But there was no movement in his chest, no fluttering behind his eyes. He was gone.

His fingers still dug into the ground beneath him. His body was contorted. His sight brought on an onset of pain in my stomach, so fierce that I could vomit.

"Mike," I cried out.

Mike looked at me. "We don't know anything yet, Natalie," he said softly.

Julian rocked me in his arms. Shock set in, and all I could do was stare at Kyle's lifeless body, trying to make sense of it.

"Natalie!" my sister's voice cried out. She ran out of the house against the police officer's protest and ran toward me. "You need to help him. You need to find out what happened!" she demanded.

"No. I can't. Not Kyle!" I spoke over Julian's shoulder. My words weren't audible even to the closest ear. The dread piled up inside me.

My sister's screams were the same as my mother's. Her anguish reverberated in my head. I squeezed my hands to my ears to block the sound that was tearing me apart and buried my face in Julian. The traumatized inner child had surfaced and taken over. I was reenacting every moment as I did with my brother's drowning.

"You have to. Natalie, help him!" she screamed, pulling my arms and forcing me away from Julian's hold.

"Natalie, let the team do their job. You can't do this," Julian yelled. I could hear the plea in his voice.

My lungs burned with every glance I made toward Kyle. I wanted to summon any means to remove all the air inside of me and put it into him. I would give my life to him. I would gladly take his place if it meant bringing him back.

My muscles ached. The voice in my head screamed for me to go to him, open his mind, and dig inside for answers, but it was my sister's child—I would have to feel the fear and pain of my sister's child. I couldn't breathe through my sobs.

I looked around and caught everyone staring at me. My sister was on the ground, crying and pleading for help. The forensic team was afraid to move toward the body, and the officers stayed off to the side. Nobody moved.

"Let's go inside, Natalie." Julian's voice commanded me to stand.

"No. My sister is right. We need to know what happened. I must know," I said, looking up at Julian's. "You will not keep me from this."

Julian drew back, reading my face. "Natalie-"

"I'm doing it!" I said for the last time.

I pulled away from Julian and crawled toward Kyle. Mike and his team backed away. When I reached Kyle, the tears came out in full force. I didn't care about the rules. I put my hand against his cheek and stroked his cold skin, brushing away the dirt. Mike attempted to speak up in protest.

"Go away! All of you, go away!" I demanded. They looked at me in disbelief, unsure of what to do. Julian motioned for the forensic team and the officers to distance themselves. He and my sister remained close by.

I studied Kyle's face. He was so beautiful and so innocent. After my brother, I swore I would never connect with a child again. The pain, confusion, and fear of death were terrifying and more consuming in a child's mind. Experiencing a child die was the cruelest of all experiences life could throw at me, but I needed to do this. It was Kyle—my Kyle. I swallowed back a sob, trying to work its way out.

"I have to do this," I cried out, not caring if I was trying to convince them or myself.

"I have to," I said again, leaning close to Kyle's ear. The overwhelming sensation of guilt seeped through me. His poor little body will have to endure this trauma again.

Taking a deep, hard breath, I looked at his angelic face once more before lowering myself down next to him.

I calmed my mind and stared blankly at the sky above, wishing I could tear the world around me apart. The sky had grayed, and the trees shuddered in the breeze as if Mother Nature wept with me.

"I'm sorry," I whispered, closing my eyes as I prepared to enter his mind.

The winds swept around me, and I could hear the trees rustling, but no voices. No voice dared to speak, as if I were a magician performing a death-defying act. I would show all of them what they longed to witness. I didn't care anymore what anyone thought of me. They were all about to discover who and what I am.

Chapter Twenty-One

Focus. I struggled to breathe, overwhelmed by a numbness enveloping me. Time and again, I had approached death, but this time it demanded my presence, forcing me to break a promise: no more children, especially after losing Nathan.

Death felt like mist rising from the damp ground on a humid morning, chilling my veins as my personal hell closed in. My fingertips twitched involuntarily as I met his lifeless eyes, reflecting sorrow I could hardly bear. In that moment, I felt a fierce urge to fight, to pull myself back from the brink of despair. *No! Keep going.*

"Show me! Show me everything!" I whispered to him as I sank into the trance, and then I felt it—the pull. It didn't come with its usual intensity, coercing me to follow like a carrot on a string. It was weak and gentle as Kyle's soul called to me, leading me into his memories. Then, his voice registered as I found myself inside his mind.

"Batman, the trees are growing bigger. Poison Ivy must be behind it."

"I think you're right, Robin. It's Poison Ivy's work. Don't let the trees get you." He responded in his best Batman voice.

Kyle started thrashing around, portraying two of his favorite heroes. "It's too late, Batman. The trees have my arms and legs. I can't move!"

"Don't worry, Robin. I'll save you!"

Kyle's energy grew in intensity as the potential for danger, followed by a dramatic rescue, projected from his vivid imagination. His spirit was as alive as a five-year-old could muster. His creativity surged as he fought to free his crime-fighting partner from the all-powerful tree branches hanging around his head and shoulders. Kyle thrashed his body, pretending to fight against the dead trees, and bammed and poww'd his way from them.

"I've got you, Robin; you're safe now," he said. A smile of victory crept across his face as he took notice of his reflection in the patio window. Kyle was pleased with himself. He saved his friend and stood proud like a true hero.

A shadow flickered among the trees, its dark form briefly reflected in the glass of the window. He turned sharply to investigate the dense forest behind him, but the trees stood still. When he glanced back at the window, he pushed aside his unease and resumed his heroic stance, chest out and chin held high.

However, a sudden, violent swaying of a nearby tree caught his attention, its leaves rustling wildly. The sound of crunching leaves mingled with the sharp cracks of snapping twigs, echoing through the still air. It was clear that something-or someone—stirred just beyond the line of sight, raising the hairs on the back of his neck.

"Hello?" he yelled, eyeing the bush. He glanced back at the house and followed his mother, walking into the kitchen.

"Maybe it's Poison Ivy back for more," he murmured softly, casting a wary glance at the dense thicket behind him. Kyle stood at the edge of the yard, contemplating the challenge ahead. Before him loomed a three-foot wall of slick, dark mud—a barrier that separated the yard from the mysterious unknown of the woods.

Beyond the mud wall, a steep, rugged path sloped upward, tangled with roots and uneven rocks. Huge, jagged stones the size of boulders jutted out, and Kyle could see thorny bushes lining the trail, their sharp branches ready to snag his clothes or skin. He weighed his options, knowing he had to tread carefully.

It didn't look that scary. It was just a bunch of trees. There's nothing scary about trees. Unless Poison Ivy is commanding them?

"Should we go after her?"

"No, Robin," Kyle said, returning to his Batman voice. "We stand to fight another day."

"But what if Poison Ivy turns the whole woods against us? We must go in there and stop her, Batman," the caped sidekick responded.

He saw his mom standing at the kitchen sink. I could feel his need to protect her. "You're right, Robin. We must keep Mom safe. Let's stop her for good!" He declared, looking back to make sure she wasn't looking.

He ran about a hundred feet into the woods, jumping over rocks and fallen trees. Then he heard it again, the woods rang out in a synchronous tune of whisps and cracks.

He stopped. "Is someone there?" Listening to any noise, he walked forward, deeper into the woods. His body tensed at the thought that he had never gone this far before, and something told him to turn back.

"I think we chased her away, Batman," he said. He took one more step, and a twig snapped under his shoe. He halted, startled by the sound, and was sure his superhero best friend was right.

He turned and retraced his steps, but then a sudden jolt sent him crashing to the ground. Something struck him violently in the back of the head. As he struggled to regain his footing, he quickly glanced back to uncover the source of the attack.

"Hey! Who did that?" he exclaimed, rubbing his head and wincing at the painful lump forming just above his neck. He glanced down and saw the large rock that had rolled to his feet. Grabbing it tightly, he scanned the woods for the person responsible.

No one was in sight. Trembling from the shock, he noticed blood on his fingers after wiping at the wound. Mom needs to see this. He pressed his trembling hand against the swollen lump on his neck, wincing with each movement as he slowly made his way toward the familiar silhouette of his house. The roof, with its worn shingles, came into view, but just as he took a few labored steps, a sharp, agonizing blow hit him from behind, sending him crashing to the ground once more.

His hands and chin burned from the impact of hitting the ground, the rough earth scraping against his skin. Without warning, something slammed into his back with a bone-jarring force. For a moment, he imagined it might be a bear—its massive weight pressing down on him. Panic surged as he instinctively dug his feet into the earth, desperate to flee. But another crushing kick landed, stealing the breath from his lungs and leaving him gasping. The only sound that pierced the silence was the desperate escape of his own torment—no growling or snarling of a wild animal echoed around him.

Tears blinded his eyes as he turned to glance at what was behind him, but a kick to the back of his head caused a cracking sound in his neck. He struggled to breathe as his attacker kept on and on. A mixture of blood and saliva pooled out of his mouth as he choked to breathe. The kicking didn't stop- another, then another, forcing his head and face into the mud and stones beneath him.

"Mommy," he pried out, his voice inaudible to his ears. A shoe stepped into his line of sight and hovered over the side of his face before delivering its final blow. Blackness seized him.

My eyes opened in sheer panic. "No!" I screeched out as my body jerked back to consciousness. I took in a hard breath as if I had inhaled water.

"What happened?" A voice yelled.

My hands whipped around, looking to grab onto something. The air was still trying to enter my lungs but wouldn't release from them, and I went through the shock of my body believing it was dying.

"Natalie! You're all right. You're back here with us!" A familiar voice said to me as two hands pulled me toward him.

My sister's voice begged through the air. "Natalie, what happened?"

"Kyle," I bellowed, catching my breath and gripping Julian.

"Calm yourself and try to take slower breaths," Julian's voice demanded.

A stammered cry escaped my throat as I tried to scream out. I had a death grip on Julian's arm as I tried to pull myself up, but he held me down with his weight.

"No. Stay down, and try to calm yourself first," he ordered.

"Kyle! Oh, dear God, why Kyle?"

Tears blinded my eyes as I cried long and hard in Julian's arms. No one made any further requests to ask me what happened. The pale stares of onlookers turned away, consumed by the emotion of what they had witnessed.

"Someone killed him!" I cried out in intense sobs. "Someone killed him!"

The screams of my sister echoed through the trees.

"No. Ma'am, you can't."

"Not my boy!" Nicole cried out as she tried to run toward Kyle's body.

"Take her inside," Julian commanded.

Nicole protested as three police officers restrained her. "Who killed my boy?" She demanded and kicked at them as they carried her into the house.

I lay in Julian's arms, crying uncontrollably. "I couldn't see him. He attacked Kyle from behind." I said, pleading for it all to stop. My body was in the worst state of agony it had ever felt. The fear, panic, and torment Kyle endured were unbearable.

"How could someone do that to him, Julian? How could he hurt him?" I begged for an answer.

"I don't know," he said, pulling me into him and petting my head. "Whoever it was, we'll find 'em."

My eyes locked onto Kyle's body. "No. I will find him. I swear on Kyle's life that I will hunt him down, and when I do, no justice system will stop me from taking my revenge," I declared, my sobs silenced.

"Natalie, pull yourself together. You can't get any more involved in this," Julian insisted firmly. "Leave this to us, we will find him. I won't allow this to go unanswered."

My eyes surveyed the people standing around, unable to make eye contact with me. "They're not enough."

I broke away from Julian and took one last look at Kyle's poor, battered body. He was just an innocent, beautiful, happy boy. The same age as my brother when his life was suddenly taken from him. Was this a curse on my family? Anger boiled inside of me. I could hear my sister screaming and crying from inside the house.

My senses were on high alert, absorbing every detail—the hushed whispers carried on the wind. The cool breeze tousled my hair, and the earthy scent of the woods wrapped around me, but the most jarring was the unmistakable smell of Kyle's blood.

I looked down at my dirt and blood-covered hands. I squeezed them shut to absorb the piece of life that I loved so much. More than ever, I had to harness my anger, as I clawed into my skin and vowed to destroy the man who did this to him. He will learn about me. He will know I am looking for him. He will know I will find him, and then he will know Kyle's pain. The monster everyone believes I am is now set free, and I'm coming for him.

I let out a cry that erupted through the sky. The woods became alive with eyes and ears everywhere. The fear and agony of every victim overpowered my body as if their souls powered through me.

Kyle's final moments were now intertwined in the circle of those that lingered inside my head. I could feel the weight of his pain from the injustice that had befallen him. I vowed that whoever was responsible for this atrocity would not escape unscathed; their soul, like Kyle's, would also become bound to mine.

Chapter Twenty-Two

David monitored Natalie from afar as she stood still over the boy's body. There was no doubt in his mind; her scream was raw with torment, anger, and madness. He recognized that pain.

"All right, everyone. I think we have everything we need for now," Mike said, instructing the team to clear away so the coroner could step in and do his job.

David hid his camera from sight as he saw the boy's body being carried out of the woods toward the van that awaited his transport.

"David!" Mike asked, walking up toward him. "What on earth are you doing here. You're on grievance leave, are you not?"

"Yeah, but I heard what happened. I feel awful. There's been too much death."

David kept his voice soft and sincere, expecting his boss to focus solely on his profound concern. He no longer cared about Natalie or life in general. His wife's case remained open, as he expected it would. With her burial scheduled for next week, his mind was filled with desperation for closure.

Mike patted him on the shoulder. "I know my boy. I know. And a child, no less- it's not easy for anyone. But David, you should create some distance between yourself and all this. I can't imagine that this is helping your grief."

"I'm here as a friend. That's all," he lied.

"Well, that's noble of you. However, I don't think Natalie will be open to extra attention right now, so you should go and ensure you take care of yourself."

David nodded, and Mike trailed off toward his car, stopping briefly to speak with Julian. He scanned the area as the crowd slowly dispersed.

A few officers were walking in and out of the house, most likely keeping an eye on the boy's mother. Then he trailed Julian as he escorted Natalie away.

Natalie. He couldn't take his eyes off her. She emerged so defeated and broken--screaming about not seeing the killer, and he couldn't determine what was tearing her apart more inside- the death of her nephew, or the inability to solve what happened. He guessed that even a psychic as skilled as she couldn't have all the answers.

As the wind grew stronger, he zipped up his jacket with his camera tucked inside and walked out of the woods toward his car. After he got in, he turned on the engine and sat there staring at the house's windows. The darkness behind each window made him ponder the life that had been taken from this home.

All she could muster was a scream. Disappointing.

He shifted his gear into drive and pulled away. Usually, he would head to the lab to fulfill his duties, but as Mike mentioned, he was supposed to be on grievance. This time, he didn't need to fret about trivial work details. This time, he could go straight to his house and develop the latest photos for his collection.

It was just past ten when he walked into his house. This was the usual time for him and his wife to start turning off the lights and head to bed. Not feeling remotely tired, given his state of depression, he descended into the basement.

His workroom was off to the right, and as he entered the doorway to turn on the light, faces stared back at him from every direction. They all shared one thing in common: those hauntingly incredible eyes whenever Natalie profiled the dead.

What a telltale day, he thought, as he eyed the small curio cabinet in the corner of the dark room. He pulled a bottle of bourbon and a glass from the shelf, then plopped down on a stool and looked over the photographs scattered across the table. Pictures of Natalie were spread out along the work surface, and some still hung from the drying line.

His eyes scanned the museum of photography, then his face twisted as a hollow burning seared his belly. He swallowed down a gulp and caught sight of a photograph hanging on the far wall. The image showcased a pair of striking eyes that seemed to shimmer with life. The image drew him in closer as he felt an undeniable connection to the emotion captured in that moment.

"Why wouldn't she help us? All I wanted was to find closure."

He reached for the only photo that wasn't of Natalie. This one was encased in an oak picture frame - his 'Brown-Eyed Girl'. Had he known he would lose his wife, he would have spent every waking minute showing her how much he loved her.

Loud sobs filled the quiet room as he pressed his lips to the photograph. Tear streaks marked the protective glass as he wiped them away and gazed at the picture. He never imagined succumbing to such emptiness. Like many marriages, theirs was not ideal, but they always found a way to make things work.

He glanced at the other photographs of Natalie scattered across the table. Perhaps she could have seen the killer's face if his wife had taken a closer look at him. All he sought was her help. She was the only person who could provide him with better insight into what had transpired or even who might have done it. A description of his wife's killer…anything. No fingerprints. No DNA. How the hell is he supposed to cope with that?

Anger overpowered the regret. He set the photograph of his wife on the table and stared at it for a moment. "But she didn't help. She didn't do a damn thing!"

He seized the photos, consumed by intense hatred, tore them from their hangers, shredded them into pieces, and then hurled the stool against the wall. The crashing and banging of metal reverberated through the room as he searched for anything he could destroy.

In seconds, he turned the entire room upside down. Shredded photographs and shattered glass were scattered across the floor. David used his shirt sleeve to wipe his eyes and mouth, then gripped the bottle of bourbon. He wrapped his lips around the bottle and chugged more of its contents.

"If she thinks she's feeling it now, just wait. Natalie has no idea about the pain that awaits her," he said, reaching for the photo of his wife. He backed against the wall behind him and slid to the floor, holding his eyes fixed on the picture. A torn piece of a photograph of haunting white eyes stared back at him.

He laughed, lifting the bottle as if proposing a toast. "My condolences, Ms. Rhine. Welcome to my world."

Chapter Twenty-Three

"Natalie, where are you? No one has seen or heard from you in two days. If you don't call me back, I'll send out a search team for you!"

Julian slammed his cell phone onto his desk and fell back into his chair. His palms were sweaty, and his left eye kept twitching as he rubbed it for the third time in less than an hour.

"Still haven't found her yet?"

Julian looked up to see Dr. Lance leaning against the door.

"Jesus, Josh, how do you always do that?" Julian asked, rubbing at his twitching eye again.

"Do what?"

"Sneak up on people."

Lance shrugged. "I didn't realize I was sneaking up on you. My apologies. I wanted to know if there were any updates on Natalie." He gave Julian a speculative glance, noting Julian's rapid eye twitching as he stepped inside the office and closed the door behind him. "Not sleeping, are we?"

"What? Oh yeah, it's been a crazy few days. I don't know where Natalie is. I'm also handling her nephew's case, and we're still piecing together another one." Julian sighed. "It's during times like these that I hate my job."

Lance monitored Julian as he stood and paced around his office. He straightened up and took a seat.

"You are not the only one who has dealt with all of this. My schedule was booked for the entire morning with people discussing what they had witnessed on the scene. Can you believe people are calling her a witch? They're no longer convinced she's human. They're terrified of her now," Lance said.

"What do you mean?" Julian snapped at him.

"Julian, I think you know what I'm talking about.

Julian studied the psychiatrist for a few moments. Skin ridges rippled across the doctor's forehead, and a concerned stare met his gaze.

Lance crossed his legs and folded his hands in front of him. "Those who witnessed Ms. Rhine's skill the other evening are afraid she might be dangerous. Most of the department has heard she can perform unnatural things, but many had never seen it and relied only on rumors. However, now more people can prove those rumors true, and many in the department are worried about her. Julian, we both know she isn't okay after what happened to her nephew."

"All right, Joshua, I don't need to hear your 'I told you so' ranting. Give her a break, will you? Some sick bastard beat her nephew to death," Julian said, removing his suit jacket. "He was just a kid. She reacted in a way anyone would."

"Well, based on what I heard, she didn't," he replied.

"What do you mean by what you heard?" Julian asked. "Those sharing their sides of the story judge Natalie's capabilities. Since day one, most of the staff have never felt comfortable around her. You know all too well what this office can be like. Hell, you hear all the stories they tell. As a doctor, I would assume you understand the difference between opinion and fact," Julian said, raising his voice.

"I'm not saying Natalie isn't entitled to feel grief over losing her nephew; I agree that everyone has always kept their distance from her due to fear and misunderstanding." Dr. Lance stretched his fingers, cramped from hours of notetaking. "What I'm primarily concerned about is that she promised to kill the person who did it, and her insistence that you won't be able to stop her. She mentioned in a few sessions that she always keeps her promises. I fear she may do just that regarding finding her nephew's killer."

"If I recall, said she would get her revenge." Julian corrected him.

Lance rolled his eyes. "Apologies. Semantics."

He ran his fingers through his hair and turned away. He reached for the nearest chair and hurled it across the office. "So, what are you suggesting? We lock her up in a loony bin and let God sort out her mind?"

Lance ducked and leapt from his seat, looking astonished. "You must accept that Natalie needs much more help than I could ever provide. I hate to say it, but I now believe she should be under supervision for her safety and ours."

Julian glared with fury in his eyes. He maintained eye contact as he returned to his chair and took a seat.

"I won't confine her to a mental hospital. She's not insane, Joshua. She's just experiencing immense loss right now," Julian responded.

Julian didn't want to admit that he feared what Natalie might do. The look in her eyes, her promise, and her scream convinced him she meant every word. At that moment, all he wanted in the world was to find her, talk to her, and ensure she was all right.

Lance approached Julian's desk, leaning on it. "I understand your concern for her. I have a soft spot for her as well, but I must consider this from a medical perspective. Natalie can't think clearly right now, and she's wandering the streets. What if she harms someone or even herself? I've worked with her for months, and I know it's there, just beneath the surface. She had to profile her nephew, witnessing what he experienced. It's not just grief she's dealing with, Julian; that's vengeance. She needs to be found and placed under surveillance."

Julian raised his hands to his head, trying to squeeze out the stress of the last week. "I intend to find her. I will speak with her, and if anyone attempts to do anything without my consent, they will encounter something even more intense than Natalie's current state of mind," Julian said.

"Good. In that case, I suggest setting up security at Natalie's sister's place and her house."

Julian raised an eyebrow. "You're kidding me? I did already?"

"I apologize; I want to assist you as much as possible," the psychiatrist responded, noticing Julian's glare. "On that note, I will return to my office; I'm sure others are waiting for me. Good luck, Julian. I hope you find her," Dr. Lance added, backing toward the office door.

Julian reached for his phone. He had to find Natalie. His heart couldn't accept the idea of locking her up in a mental hospital, but the psychiatrist was right about one thing: she had experienced more than any person can handle. If anything, he would try to keep her under house arrest for the time being until he figured out what to do next. That way, he can keep a close eye on her. Regardless of the psychiatrist's professional opinion, he couldn't bring himself to believe that Natalie was dangerous.

Julian glared at the paperwork scattered around his desk and angrily shoved it aside.

Where the hell are you?

Chapter Twenty-Four

I settled back into Kyle's bed, my eyes wandering across the walls that were a captivating collage of his creativity. The surfaces were adorned with an eclectic mix of his school artwork, each piece bursting with color, that danced alongside vivid photos and larger-than-life posters of Batman and his notorious foes. On the surfaces below the drawings, his desk sat, covered in crayon and marker smudges, where a bright, young artist brought his colorful creations to life.

The floor was a mini landscape of scattered Matchbox cars, with a bright orange hot rod sitting in the center of the fortress of cars. I smiled to myself, that would have been the car I'd have picked as well.

My gaze slowly drifted to the weathered dresser that once belonged to my brother. On its surface lay a framed photograph capturing a joyful moment: Kyle beaming with pride as he sat atop his shiny new bike. I vividly recall that day when I took him to the store. We brainstormed ideas for his birthday wish list, but the instant he spotted the sleek, black Batman bike adorned with bold yellow accents, his eyes lit up with pure delight. In that moment, we both knew without saying a word what his birthday gift would be.

"Oh my God, Aunt Nat, check this out! This bike is incredible!" Kyle exclaimed, his voice charged with pure excitement as he leaped onto the bike, turning into his favorite superhero.

"Wow, now that's cool!" I said. Nicole drilled me about over-spoiling him, but the aunt in me couldn't help it. However, we did agree we were only there to look around and get ideas. I dreaded the moment I had to tell him that he'd need to wait until his birthday to receive it.

"Of course it's cool! It's Batman!" he said, reaching for the water bottle featuring the Batman symbol attached to the mainframe.

"And it has a water bottle. What more could you ask for?"

"Super thrusters and missiles firing from the side," he quickly added, his imagination soaring beyond the bike's design limits.

"Oh, right. What was I thinking? What's a Batman bike without heavy armor?" I slapped my head against my forehead.

"Can I have it?" he asked just as I began to wander around. I froze and pursed my lips, not having time to think about how to deliver the bad news to him.

"Well, buddy, you know we're just here for some ideas for your upcoming birthday," I reminded him, hoping he would understand. I couldn't help but recall my childhood when my mother took my brother and me to the toy store for our birthday shopping. I always left with a new toy and wanted the same for Kyle.

"I mean, can I have it for my birthday? You know... when it's my birthday?" he said, getting off the bike and acting like that was his plan.

I was relieved, but knew he wanted to leave the store with the bike. "Well, I'll make a deal with you. There are three things I need you to do for me, and if you do them, perhaps you might discover a certain bike sitting in the driveway on your birthday."

"Ok, what?" he asked with a let's-make-a-deal face.

"Well, first, you must promise to help your mother with the housework. She's been working more hours and is exhausted when she gets home. The last thing she should do is pick up all your toys," I said.

"Ok. Deal. Clean up toys. What's next?"

"Second, your mom would appreciate it if you told her how beautiful she is more often. I don't think she hears that enough from you." I snapped my fingers to get Kyle's attention off the bike and back on me.

"I tell her that she's pretty," he said, flashing me his charmingly boyish grin.

"Oh. When was the last time you told your mom she was pretty?"

Kyle bit his lower lip while he contemplated my question. His eyes roamed around him, searching for an answer.

"Anyways, tell her more. Moms love that stuff," I said, beating him to the punch.

"Alright. Fine. You have one more thing," he said, staring down at the bike as if it were about to become a done deal.

"Well, this last one is a biggie," I said as I checked out an adult bike that caught my eye. I surveyed the bike before swinging my leg over it and settling into the seat. Grabbing the handlebars, I imagined what it would be like to ride the bike with Kyle around the park.

"Well. I'm waiting," Kyle said, sitting on the Batman bike again.

"I want you to go bike riding with me whenever I ask," I insisted, smiling. I looked down at my nephew. From his smile, I knew we had a deal.

My eyes shifted away from the photograph as if a photographer were gradually zooming out. Kyle's smile, bright and almost magnetic, seemed to reach out beyond the frame, drawing my gaze involuntarily. Yet, amidst that infectious grin, a haunting echo of his voice resonated in my mind, fragile and pleading, whispering, "Mommy."

Nicole's voice interrupted my thoughts. "I can't bring myself to clean anything up, let alone walk in here. I would somehow lose him."

I turned my gaze toward my sister, who was slumped against the doorframe, her posture weary and defeated. On the surface, her face appeared scorched from too much sun, but I knew better. Swollen cheeks and bloodshot eyes were the result of endless crying. I could see the pain she put herself through, blaming herself for not keeping a better eye on her son, or not doing a better job keeping him from the woods; whatever torment she placed on herself, convincing her that it wasn't her fault would be pointless.

Her hair was a tangled mess, and coffee stains lingered on her white cotton shirt, which I guessed had been worn for the last couple of days. She hadn't attempted to shower or even change her clothes. She was nothing more than a dead vessel. A soulless woman doomed to live the remainder of her life without the one person who gave her reason to live.

"Natalie, for the love of God, say something!" Nicole's voice urged, though with a softened tone.

"What do you want me to say?" I responded.

I lay in Kyle's bed, hands folded, admiring the wall of pictures. "Kyle's dead. Somebody killed him, and I couldn't see who it was. I couldn't even help my own nephew. So many cases solved, but the one that matters most, I…"

A headache surfaced as my blood burned inside me. I couldn't recall a time when I was so engulfed by anger, heartbreak, and overwhelming loss. I experienced unrelenting loneliness when my brother died, and again when I lost my parents, and then my grandparents. But this. This pain was unfamiliar to me--malicious, vengeful, lethal.

Nicole used her eyeliner-stained shirtsleeves to wipe her eyes. She attempted to stifle her next few sobs and looked back at me. "What are you going to do? Your whole department is searching for you. I had to lie to Julian; he's afraid you might do something crazy."

I peered at Kyle's school photograph. "I'm going to find out who killed Kyle. Julian will try to stop me. They all will. Tell them you haven't seen me."

"That's what I've been doing," Nicole said, wrapping her arms around herself, seeking solace. "Please find him, Natalie. Don't let that bastard get away with what he did to my son."

Nicole stood in the doorway, her plea resonated throughout the room. "I just don't understand why him? I need answers, Natalie. Please."

My eyes locked onto hers. "I don't know, but I will figure it out. You have my word."

I stood, walked to the doorway, and embraced my sister. It was the only physical comfort I could offer her. Then, I strode down the stairs and out the back door. I made my way into the woods to where it all happened. Crime scene tape surrounded the entire twenty-foot section where Kyle was found dead.

The attack consumed my thoughts, each agonizing moment playing on a relentless loop in my mind, like a haunting replay that refused to fade. I concentrated on the sharp, punishing blows that rained down on his back, trying to discern if his attacker had uttered any sounds during the chaos. Lowering myself to the ground, I positioned my body as if I were experiencing the assault again, every detail flooding back with vivid clarity. The memory of Kyle's ordeal weighed heavily on my heart, causing the anger to surge within me like a storm ready to erupt.

"He wouldn't stop hitting him," I repeated over and over, pressing my forehead against the cold ground. "He was just a child!"

As I pressed my fingernails into the ground beneath me, I fought to maintain my focus, my mind racing back to each brutal assault. What about the attacker? What did Kyle witness in those chaotic moments? "His shoe," I murmured under my breath, the words escaping like a faint breath of wind. I strained to visualize the shoe, recalling every detail in vivid clarity: it was black, laced down the front, its shape unassuming yet somehow ominous, and it appeared to be of average size, a perfect fit for someone trying to blend into the crowd.

I mimicked his movements as my fingers ripped at the mud around me. The memory of the black shoe stole my concentration as I belted out muffled screams into the solid ground, lifting then smashing my face into the dirt. The physical sting did not come, though I wanted it to. Any pain would have been better than this. My body was numb, but my mind begged for mercy.

I got up and hurled myself at the trees and nearby bushes. I ripped and punched anything that obstructed my path. A thick tree branch lay close by. I picked it up and slammed it down into the spot where the attacker had stood, imagining his head bursting open from the impact of the branch.

The woods stood still, and the air grew heavy. The sky was overcast with thick gray clouds as the sound of distant thunder charged in. I backed against a tree, still gripping the branch. Large holes marked the spot where my nephew's murder occurred; broken twigs, leaves, and shrubs now covered the entire scene.

What have I done? Caution tape was strung all over, newly created potholes, broken branches-- I examined my destruction, wanting to scream again for ruining the crime scene. I didn't see his killer. I don't know what to do! My mind went into panic mode. If Julian didn't kill me for wrecking a crime scene, my determination to find Kyle's killer would.

"Think dammit!"

I re-examined Kyle's memories to ensure I hadn't overlooked anything. Kyle heard cracks and rustling in the bushes, but I found nothing while walking around the area. No footprints matched the shoe, and nothing appeared disturbed or out of the ordinary.

There was nothing more to pursue here. I needed to head to the station and talk to Mike to learn whether his team had made any discoveries—if he was willing to share, that is. Nicole had warned me about a patrol car stationed at the street corner, keeping a vigilant watch. I knew Julian dispatched police to monitor my whereabouts. If I didn't have enough to deal with, there would be a tiresome number of roadblocks I'd have to push through.

I ran back to the house.

Nicole remained silent. She sat at the kitchen table with a fresh cup of coffee, allowing it to grow cold as she gazed out the window into the woods.

There was nothing more I could do to console her. I had a mission. The first challenge would be to avoid the police, who were most likely hiding on the corners or sitting on the sides of the road.

"I need to borrow Grandpa's truck," I told her as I ran to the cabinet where she kept her keys. I grabbed the keys and turned to look at her. An ache tore through my insides at the sight of her like this.

I dropped my head, squeezing the keys in my palm. I pulled open the door leading to the garage and paused, "I'm not going to stop. I'll find out who did this."

I didn't sense any movement from Nicole, her eyes remained fixed on the woods sitting outside the window.

I pushed on, flicked on the garage light, and admired the old blue Ford truck sitting alone, unused, calling me to let it out. The windows were squared, which wouldn't do much to conceal me during the drive. It had a single row for sitting, with a white top and a flatbed for hauling. It was the perfect grand-daddy vehicle. Now, I just needed to make myself look like my grandfather.

Nicole kept my grandfather's fishing collection in remembrance of him. Reels, hats, nets, and waterproof overalls lined an entire wall. I grabbed multiple reels and nets, threw them in the flatbed, and made sure they dangled over the side. Then, I grabbed the biggest hat and hopped into the truck.

Its old engine roared to life, and I was relieved that there was enough gas to get me where I wanted to go. I was about to leave the truck and press the garage opener when I saw Nicole standing in the doorway. Her blank, heartbroken eyes blinked away a tear as she pushed the button. I couldn't smile, but my eyes gave her a final reassurance as I drove the truck out of the garage and down the driveway.

A patrol car was waiting at the end of the road, sitting in a park-and-ride lot. There was only one way out, and the other side of the road led to a dead end. At least Julian was being courteous to keep the police out of sight for my sister's sake.

I pulled my grandfather's hat down over my head to appear as the most relaxed man on his way to catch a few bass. I tapped on the door, pretending to listen to music, and drove past him. He looked up for a brief moment, then dropped his head back down to whatever he was sitting in front of him. The police weren't looking for an old Ford pickup truck. They were waiting for a cream-colored Jeep Wrangler or Nicole's white Lexus. It was too easy.

Turning onto the main road, I pressed the gas and sped off toward the thruway. Police cars were stationed off to the side of the road at every few markers, as I figured they'd be, so I made it a point to maintain my speed and keep on with the old man profile.

You would think I was a wanted felon, and the whole world was out to get me. I was almost humbled.

Chapter Twenty-Five

When I arrived at the station, there were more uniformed personnel on duty than usual. Gaining entry would be more challenging than I thought. I left the truck in a populated area and walked the rest of the way to the station, doing my best to remain unseen.

Walking through the front door was clearly out of the question. A few officers guarded the employee entrance, making it unavailable. The point of entry was limited as I assessed every inch of the building.

I hurried around back and spotted the loading dock. A delivery truck was backing into it, and two men got out, wearing uniforms with the logo of Commercial Office Services. One opened the back door of their truck while the other banged on the garage door. A maintenance man stepped out from behind the door, accompanied by an officer. After a brief conversation, both delivery workers began their tasks. One pushed a large cart and headed inside, while the other unloaded a load of carpets from the truck.

The maintenance man propped a door jamb to keep the door open, then returned inside. He sat at a desk and ate a sandwich while the officer accompanying him stood at a table, facing away from the door, looking down at a clipboard.

This was going to be my only chance. I dashed to the delivery truck, grabbed a handful of carpets from the edge, and hoisted them over my head to shield my face. I slipped through the door, carefully avoiding any attention from the officer.

As I navigated down the hall, I unexpectedly collided with someone.

"Oh, thank you! I didn’t realize I had some extra help," the deliveryman said, lifting the carpets off me.

His surprised expression revealed his realization that I was a woman, causing a nervous twitch. "Of course! Happy to assist," I replied, passing him the rugs while keeping a watchful eye on the guard. Still no reaction from him. So far, I was in the clear.

I cautiously approached the empty staircase and descended to the dimly lit basement. As several figures drifted by, their footsteps echoed against the concrete walls. Seizing the moment, I slipped into a narrow hallway and managed to get two-thirds of the way down when I heard footsteps rounding the corner. I ducked into a nearby supply closet, terrified that I didn’t move fast enough. My heart raced, pounding like a trapped bird desperate to escape. In the darkness, I held my breath, trying to calm my nerves. Suddenly, a familiar voice floated through the hallway, snapping me back to the moment.

"I don't know what you expect me to do, Josh. I'm in a difficult situation here. Natalie is likely going through a tough time right now," Julian said.

"I understand, as I’ve said already, but you must put aside your emotions for the girl and follow protocol, Julian. Wait, let's talk in here," the psychiatrist said, guiding Julian into an interrogation room a few doors down.

Julian. My heart ached for him, but he was the last person I wanted to be around. And why was Dr. Lance here?

I wanted to hear what they were saying and decided that forensics would have to wait a few more minutes. I crept out of the closet and into the observation room on the other side. I sneaked in and closed the door behind me, then approached the table of monitors and turned on the primary monitor to listen in on their conversation. Julian was leaning against the table while Dr. Lance moved about. Their voices revealed that neither saw eye to eye with the other.

"You don't even know where she is," Lance said. He moved to the wall and leaned against it, cleaning his glasses with the hem of his usual sleeveless sweater.

Julian crossed his arms. "I told you I would find her, and then we can take it from there. However, I don't want to rush into any orders to lock her up so that you can sink your claws into her."

"Julian, why are you convinced I'm trying to use her?"

"Aren't you? Natalie was convinced you would write her off as a mental case and lock her away."

Lance was taken aback. "I take offense to that. Moreover, she and I have made significant progress over the past few weeks. I want to think she can trust me now , and I hate to remind you, but I don't think she is the one whose opinion you should be considering now."

Julian's forced nod indicated that he agreed with Lance.

Lance finished cleaning his glasses and put them back on. "I'm simply stating that she needs a psychiatric evaluation to ensure she doesn't do anything reckless. She won't leave this case to those assigned to her nephew's murder. She's stubborn, and I'm sure she's determined to find out who's behind it. I can talk to her." He moved to the other side of the table and took a seat. "If anything, I know her well enough to listen and can help," he said matter-of-factly.

He made a valid point. I was stubborn and, above all, determined. But what can Lance do to help? I dropped my head and gritted my teeth. Did he think I could talk my way out of my emotions?

I turned my gaze back to the two men and watched Julian closely for any sign of emotion on his face. His duty as Captain ranked higher on the priority scale than any feelings he might have had for me.

"Alright. Once we locate Natalie, I'll call you," he said. "She is still a valued member of this office. You can sit down and talk with her, but if I find out that you are pressuring her too much, I will intervene and take her somewhere else!"

Dr. Lance raised his hands in defense. "Agreed. No pushing, just talking, as I always do."

"Bullshit," Julian said, casting one last glance before exiting the room.

Lance blinked hard at Julian after the second insult he received, but remained seated, drumming his fingers on the table. He tilted his head back and exhaled before getting up and walking out.

A tear rolled down my cheek. I wanted Julian to do more for me, but now he is willing to hand me over and prevent me from doing the one thing I need to do. Instead, he prefers to subject me to the sermons of a psychiatrist about how my mind works. I swallowed hard as a lump formed in my throat, gave myself a shake to alleviate the disappointment searing through my body.

Regardless of what Julian or Lance said, I wasn't about to stop now. "Stubborn. You haven't seen stubborn." I slipped back out into the hall and navigated the precinct's basement floor. My destination was the last room on the right, its glass doors emblazoned with the title "Trace Evidence Unit" and "Michael Cannon, Forensic Director" listed beneath. Peering through the glass, I spotted the short, middle-aged man in a lab coat. The very man that I was seeking.

"Hi, Mike," I greeted as I strolled into the lab like any other day.

He raised his gaze from the desk, where an oversized microscope rested, and eyeballed me with mild confusion.

"Natalie! Where have you been? We've all been looking for you."

He swiveled in his chair to face me, his oversized lab coat trailing on the floor. Despite his stocky build, his intellect was towering. Over the years, his stature had diminished because of his dedication to his work. His hunched back was a result of his unwavering commitment.

I waved and smiled, "Oh yeah, well, I'm as fine as can be. I had to leave for a few days to gather myself." I moved over to a stool and sat down. Mike critiqued my every move.

I raised my hands, noticing his concern. "Don't worry; Julian had a field day with me. I wasn't avoiding anyone. My cell phone fell between my car seats, and I couldn't find it. I wasn't purposely avoiding anyone." I checked around the lab to figure out what he was working on. "Besides, I just needed time to grieve." I lowered my voice, hoping Mike's empathy would outweigh his attention to detail.

"I understand that, but from what I heard, you had many people on edge looking for you," he replied, walking over to me and giving me a quick hug.

"Yeah, I know. I was talking to Julian in the hall, and Lance too, and we decided I should stay here and keep out of trouble." I assumed that if Julian had walked the basement halls, he would've stopped to speak with Mike. "I think he figured that if I didn't get in your way, I would be safe and sound down here for now. He'll be back in a bit, once he unloads Lance."

"Uh-huh," he said, placing his hands in his coat pocket. He assessed me, scrutinizing my physique from head to toe.

So much for empathy.

"Well, I'm not sure there's anything you can help with while you wait," Mike said, turning his back as he walked back to his chair. He sank into it, causing it to emit a screech that made my teeth clench.

"Have you found anything yet?" I asked, maintaining my steady voice.

He regarded me for a few seconds with a quizzical look. It was his signature look, yet I held my demeanor steady.

"This has to be hard on you?" The corners of his mouth twitched in an attempt to offer a smile, but none came.

"I'm doing my best to get through this." I turned away from him, not wanting him to read my intentions. "I want to help. Maybe I can offer insight into what you've found so far?" I added.

"Well, you might not like what I'm about to tell you," he said as he got up from his chair and walked to another table. He reached for the top stack of files wrapped in a rubber band, turned to face me, and gave me a sardonic look.

I shrugged. "Then just tell me what you found out. I understand the forensic process- time and patience- something I have no choice but to possess," I adjusted myself in the chair, exhibiting my readiness and willingness to help.

"We have no prints, blood, skin, or bodily fluids except for that of your nephews. The attacker was careful. We did find shoe prints—a man's size ten- but his shoes had no markings on the bottom to identify their brand. Unfortunately, we haven't found anything beyond what you provided us. I'm so sorry, Natalie, but we are still on top of this."

Mike towered over me, even given his short stature. He looked down at me with his pressed lips, scrutinizing my presence. "I must be frank, Natalie. You should never have performed that profiling until we were finished. You corrupted the scene."

If I corrupted it, then you certainly don't want to see my recent handiwork. I widened my eyes in dismay. "Mike, this is my nephew we're talking about. You would have acted the same way if you were in my position. Plus, I can discover things far faster than you and your forensics team, no offense," I added, shrinking down from his unimpressed stare.

His voice was soft but stern. "But I'm not you. I follow the rules. I do things the way they should be done. We arrive first, and then you come in afterwards. What if you did discover the killer? How could we hold the murderer accountable if we can't use any evidence we find because you already made it inadmissible in court?"

My body tensed as I discerned the look on his face and recalled the damage I had caused earlier. He will never work with me again after he sees the scene now. I lowered my eyes. Shame, guilt, and regret weighed on my mind.

"Well, there's no reversing any of that now," I said.

He let out a long sigh. "I'm aware of that." He removed the rubber band, opened the first file, and scanned through the notes stapled to the flaps. "We took images of any possible paths the attacker might take to get to that location, as well as the house and yard; anything we deemed questionable. They are all in here," he said, closing the file and turning his back to me.

"Mike."

He turned.

"Can I please review what you have?"

Mike's jaw clenched as he hesitated. "We still have plenty to work with; I assure you of that. But Natalie, this case is too close to you. I say this with the utmost professionalism: I can't have you meddling with this anymore."

I tried to understand Mike's viewpoint on the subject. This was his area of expertise, not mine. It was a long shot to expect him to share crime scene photos of a victim who was my own family. At this point, all I could do was plead for mercy.

I took a deep breath, calming my nerves. I understood that projecting an overly professional demeanor would come across as inauthentic to him, and I had to avoid being excessively emotional, as that could push him away. I was composed, and it was crucial for him to see that I was in control.

“Mike, your notes may spark something I overlooked. I promise I won’t mess anything else up. You could still use my help.”

Mike's blank face examined me before he passed me the files and returned to his workstation. "Why do I get the feeling I'm going to regret this?"

I placed the file in front of me, counted to ten, and reviewed its contents. I read several pages of Mike's detailed notes, but nothing jumped out at me. It was all observations, witness statements, and Nicole's accounts of the day's events. I moved on to the following folder, which held all the photographs. The first picture was of Kyle's beaten body. I squeezed my eyes shut and set off a scream in my head that I was sure the director heard.

I shot a frustrated glare at Mike, seated with his back turned to me, oblivious to the storm of emotions boiling inside me. I fought to contain the anger rising within, committed not to let him see the effect he had on me.

Keep going.

I flipped through the large stack of photos. Each one was harder to look at than the one before. Some were close-ups of Kyle's face and body, while others were taken from a distance, showing the surrounding area. My eyes captured every picture as I compared each photo to a memory. I focused on every detail and recalled every moment from arriving at the scene to Kyle's profiling. My stomach twisted in knots as I envisioned the attack, matching each mark on his body.

My foot trembled in an irregular rhythm, keeping pace with the torrent of thoughts racing through my mind like a movie projector. I clenched my hands to stave off the throbbing. "Is this everything?"

Mike kept his eyes fixed on the lens of the microscope. "Yes, Ma'am. I told you that you wouldn't like it."

I dropped my face into my hands. I wanted to take that microscope and throw it through the glass door. I closed my eyes and counted deep breaths. I knew it wasn't his fault, but his self-righteous tone made me want to sew his mouth shut and slowly pluck away the tender threads.

I reviewed the file again, flipping through the photos one by one. I slowed my pace, taking inventory and comparing every detail to that dreadful time. My foot tapped in slow beats as I replayed Kyle's attack, kick by kick. Then I turned my thoughts to what I had seen before and after profiling him. My foot stopped.

"Something is missing," I said too low for Mike to hear.

I started again, shuffling through each picture and comparing what I knew to the images before me- replaying every moment, every voice, every person, and every object.

Something was missing, I told myself again. My foot restarted, pounding so violently that the chair trembled.

"Mike? Who was working at the scene?" I asked.

He pulled away from his microscope and turned to face me sideways.

"Hmm? I was there, of course. Michelle was taking samples, while Ryan took measurements. Julian tried to assist whenever he could. And then the photographer." He stood from his chair and jotted something down with a pen he pulled from his lab coat.

I remembered the faces of the people and assigned each of them to their respective tasks, indicating where each was standing.

"Don't you mean photographers?" I asked, shifting my gaze back to the photographs.

"No, there was only one, Erin," he said.

"I know Erin was there, but I also saw David," I said, flipping through them again.

"Yes, he was there, against my better judgment, but he wasn't working. He wanted to offer his support." The director looked up from his clipboard and turned toward me. "Don't worry, Natalie, he wasn't being nosy; he was just a coworker showing concern for you, as we all were," he offered with a warm smile.

"But I remember seeing him take pictures," I said almost under my breath. "Where's his collection?" I asked, sifting through the entire file.

He appeared shocked. "No, he wasn't. I didn't see him with a camera. What are you looking for?" he asked, his annoyance evident.

"How do you determine who took which photo?" I asked.

"We label the photographer's ID at the bottom of each photo," he said, pointing to the credentials in the bottom right corner of the photograph.

"These aren't all of them," I said, confused.

"Natalie, of course they are. The department requires that all information be recorded and kept on file. David wasn't on the scene working, and he wouldn't withhold any photographs; he knows it's against policy," he replied, masking his annoyance at anyone questioning his department's standards.

"I saw David taking pictures in my direction right after I profiled Kyle. Those pictures aren't here." I drummed my fingers on the pile, making direct eye contact with Mike.

Mike walked over to a workstation with a computer and nudged the mouse to wake up the monitors. "Are you sure he was taking pictures of you? That seems unlikely."

"Yes, I'm certain. I recognize a camera when I see one."

Mike slammed his hands on the desk and sprang from his chair. "Oh, come now, Natalie. That sounds ridiculous. David is excellent at his job and wouldn't jeopardize his work, especially now that it's all he has left." He snatched the file from me, dropped it on the workstation beside him, and turned back toward me.

"What do you mean, 'all he has left'?" I asked, giving him a look that could burn through his forehead.

He peered back at me with the same glare. If he suspected that someone was challenging how he managed his crew, he would put them in their place.

"Not that you need to know this, but he is also struggling. His wife was killed in an attempted carjacking. We're still investigating that case, too," he added, turning his back on me. "It was one of the first cases that we handled since you left."

"His wife?"

"Yes, his wife. My heart goes out to that poor man." He adjusted his lab coat and took a seat. "I'm sorry, but I have a thousand things to do, and you're interrupting my concentration."

I recoiled as the realization hit me like a bag of rocks. His wife.

Mike turned toward me. "I'm sorry I didn't have more, but I have everything we can get. Regardless of what Julian said, I must ask you to leave so I can work." His face wore a solemn expression as he gestured for me to leave.

I was about to ask more about David when Mike's desk phone rang; the sound echoed in my mind as another memory emerged- the frantic phone call from two weeks ago and the panicked voice on the other end. David's. Everything from that moment made sense now- how the man knew about me. It felt like a bubble burst inside my head as I wondered if the two murders were connected. There was no question: David was hiding something.

He walked over to his desk to grab the phone. I was about to slip out when I spotted a pile of files at the end of the table labeled “Complete." Inside were notes and photographs from past profiling work. Most of these were cases in which I was involved. I sifted through the images and found one with David’s credentials listed on it. I swiped it and dashed out of the lab while he was distracted. I heard him speaking into the receiver as the heavy glass door closed behind me.

"Yes, she's here now," he said to the voice on the other end. His voice faded as I quickened my pace down the hallway, tension building in my body again. My time at the precinct was up, and I had to find a place to hide that had a computer.

I ducked into the stairwell as loud footsteps rumbled around the corner. Taking the stairs two at a time, I reached the ground level and found a small, unoccupied office with a computer. I hurried over to the desk and tapped a few keys to wake up the PC. I pulled up the database, but the login box appeared before I could enter David's information. I entered my credentials, and a pop-up appeared, informing me that my passcode was locked. Of course, Julian would have put a password lock on my security code.

I pushed aside the frustration as Jeff's face flashed in my mind. I typed 5-9-1-9-8-0. He always talked about the release date of his favorite movie, Friday the 13th, which also contributed to my phone ringtone. The main page of the database opened, and I navigated through the system to find David's address. I wrote it down on a Post-it note and closed the page. Now, I need to sneak out of here.

I moved to the door and cracked it open. Personnel were rushing up and down the hall. How the hell am I going to get out of here?

I rummaged through the cabinets and drawers, unsure of what I was looking for. In the corner shelf, I spotted a few file boxes and a hoodie featuring a Baltimore Ravens logo.

Why not. It worked before. Please let this work again.

I pulled the hood over my head, opened the door, and hauled the file boxes to shield my face. I swerved to avoid the oncoming rush of people. No one tried to slow down and brushed past me without a second glance.

I made my way to the other side of the building, where the courtrooms were located. I set the boxes on the floor next to a table showcasing community event flyers. A group of three young people emerged from one of the courtrooms. Hearing them loudly complain about a fine, I moseyed up to them and blended in. When we reached the main entrance with security, I raised both hands, pretending to scratch my head, concealing my face as I walked out of the building.

I sprinted toward my grandfather's truck. My hands trembled as I attempted to insert the key into the lock. "Come on, come on." Adrenaline coursed through my body, driven by the fear of getting caught. When the lock clicked, I jumped in, inserted the key into the ignition, and navigated out of the parking lot while keeping the hood over my head. I tapped my cell phone to open Google Maps and entered David's address.

1738 Old Springs Road

The progress swirled around in a circle as it analyzed routes. Twelve minutes. I made a sharp right turn onto a side street and pressed the gas pedal.

I carefully scanned my surroundings, feeling a slight flutter of anxiety as I made sure no one was following me. I adjusted my grip on the steering wheel and caught my reflection in the rearview mirror— a mix of determination and apprehension looked back at me, a stark reminder of my objective.

David's face suddenly appeared in my mind. What are you hiding?

Chapter Twenty-Six

"Well? Where is she?" Julian demanded as he burst through the glass door of the forensics lab, with a few officers following him.

Mike was sitting at his computer desk when he stood and said, "I'm sorry, Julian. She just left."

"What do you mean she just left? Why on earth would you let her go?" Julian raised his voice.

"She told me that you knew she was down here and that you had agreed to keep her at the office. She didn't provide me with a reason to doubt her."

"Are you kidding me?"

"No, I'm not. Natalie always came down to visit and ask about cases, so her behavior wasn't unusual," he said, ready to raise an argument. Julian observed Mike's expression. Both men acted surprised that someone outsmarted Mike.

Julian slammed his fist against a filing cabinet. "Dammit, Mike. We've been searching for her for days. I'm worried she might do something reckless." He skimmed the lab. "What did she want?"

"To understand what we discovered about her nephew's murder, of course. I informed her that we are still investigating and have gathered as much information as possible. She then tested my patience by insisting that some photos were missing from the case file." Mike walked over to his desk and picked up the file.

"Did she say what photos she was talking about?"

"She insisted that she had seen one of my photographers taking pictures of her and wanted to know where they were. But I told her that David wasn't working; he was only there to offer support. She insisted she had seen him with a camera, and it was his photographs that she was inquiring about. Julian, I'm sorry. I believed she cooperated with everyone and that all was settled."

"You have a better sense of character." Julian sifted through the photographs in the case file. He dropped it next to Mike, placing his hands on his hips, aggravated and ready to throw something. His eyes traced over Mike's cluttered table and noticed a file out of order.

"What's this?" Julian asked, reaching for the file.

Mike squinted at the file in Julian's hands. "That's another case, but we've already solved that one. It just needs to be filed."

Julian flipped through the file, observing the photographs. "Fifteen's missing," Julian remarked. "Any idea why?"

Mike snatched the file back and rifled through the pictures. "Blast that girl. She must have taken it!" He examined the other photos, all of which were organized by the date they were taken. "Honestly, Julian, I have no idea why she picked that one. It's the same as these, just from a closer angle."

Julian snatched the file back and paused to contemplate the pictures. "What the hell is going on in that head of hers?"

"I know Natalie is experiencing a tremendous heartache right now, but I can't believe David would jeopardize his career for this case by withholding information," he said.

Julian stopped on one of David's photos. "You're telling me that she insisted he is hiding something related to this case?" he asked, thumbing through David's employee ID information.

"No, not that one specifically that your holding. Again, she believes David is hiding pictures he may have taken from her nephew's case" the Director replied.

"So David didn't perform any work on her nephew's?"

"No. He's on leave."

"Julian ran his thumb along another photograph submitted by David. "Someone look up this number," Julian said, holding it up to show David's ID. An officer noted the name and number before walking to a computer. He entered the number into the computer's database, and moments later, a photograph of a dark-haired man in his mid-thirties appeared on the screen.

"David Christie, Old Springs Road," the officer reported.

"I bet that's where she's headed. Barrett, notify whoever is closest to his address to go there immediately," Julian said over his shoulder as he ran out of the room.

A few officers followed him, prepared to assist. "No. I need you all to stay put. The last thing I want is to attract too much commotion that might scare her off."

Julian stepped into the elevator and pressed the button for the ground floor.

"This is something I need to handle." As the elevator door closed in the officers' faces, confusion, fear, and uncertainty flowed through his mind as he considered his next move. "She better not do anything stupid!" he grumbled to himself.

Chapter Twenty-Seven

I slowed the truck as I made a right turn onto Old Springs Road. I drove along a scenic, tree-lined street adorned with porch swings, basketball nets, and cars parked at the side. My keen observation skills indicated that this was a safe and pleasant neighborhood, except for a potential killer.

I spotted the number 1738 engraved on a boulder in front of a white ranch home with black awnings. I stopped and surveyed the house to see if there were any signs of David being home. No cars were in the carport or driveway, nor parked in front of his house. The front windows had closed blinds, and the landscaping appeared to have been untouched for weeks. The house emanated a sense of hopelessness.

David's voice echoed in my memory: "What if it were someone you loved?

So, help me, if you killed my nephew, you would be joining your wife!

I didn't notice the car approaching from behind, and I flinched when the driver honked her horn at me. I checked my rearview mirror, hoping it wasn't David, then moved the truck to the side, parking a few houses away from his home.

My heart raced a mile a minute. What on earth was I doing here? I turned my gaze to the rearview mirror.

Getting answers.

A flicker of movement captured my eye in the rearview mirror. I ducked as two police cruisers pulled up in front of David's house. I peeked out the window and watched as two officers exited their vehicles and approached David's door. One rang the doorbell while the other circled. When there was no answer, the officer who rang the doorbell communicated something over his walkie-talkie while the other remained nearby.

Julian figured it out again. I had half a mind to jump out of the truck and run up to them, screaming "murderer," but I knew they weren't there to talk to David. They were there looking for me.

A few minutes passed as I stayed out of view. The officers returned to their cars and departed, leaving me to collapse back into the seat, cursing the headache that throbbed in my head.

I had no plans or idea what to say or do if I encountered David. Logic was absent, and here I was, evading the police left and right while running toward someone who might be dangerous.

"I suppose I can eliminate undercover cop as a career option," I grunted in disgust, pulling myself up with the steering wheel.

A dark blue Dodge Avenger pulled up minutes later, entered David's driveway, and parked under the carport. My body froze. I could make out the outline of the driver, but he didn't get out of the car. He sat there, leaving his car running.

Is that you, David?

I attempted to focus on the face in the car mirrors, but couldn't discern much.

When the driver turned off the car and opened the door, I recognized the man I had often seen during several of my profiling sessions. I had never noticed him before, but now that I had studied him, I gathered that he was about six feet tall, with medium-dark hair and a lean build. He wore black khakis and a thin black leather jacket. My eyes darted to his shoes, but I couldn't make them out clearly.

A young boy walked past his driveway and waved at him. "Hey, Mr. Dave," the boy said. He sauntered, waiting for David to wave back, but David ignored the boy.

He walked toward the front door, passing by his overstuffed mailbox, shuffled through his keys, unlocked the door, and entered his home. I slipped out of the truck and ran across the street, moving along the side of his house while checking for any neighbors who might have seen me.

I ran up to a window above eye level and peeked inside. I couldn't make out anything besides my reflection. Not wanting to risk him spotting me, I hurried around to the back of the house and discovered a basement window open. Squatting close to the ground, I opened the narrow window wider. With enough space to slip in, I removed my jacket and squeezed inside.

The basement was spacious and clean. In one corner, there was a laundry area, while another corner was designated for tools. Next to the stairs leading up to the main level, a door concealed a small room.

Trying hard to steady my breathing, I strained to listen for any sounds over the loud beating of my own heart. Running water and the clanking of a kitchen drawer reverberated through the thin layer of flooring. I flinched at the sound of a ringtone and raised my head toward the ceiling as footsteps creaked across the floor.

"Hello," said the man upstairs.

I took a moment to breathe and calm my nerves. "Easy. Easy. You can do this," I whispered to myself.

I was unsure of my next move, and assessed the door, curiosity taking over. I tried to listen to the muffled conversation coming from above as I turned the doorknob, tensing when the door let out a faint creaking noise. Pausing for a moment, I listened to the voice overhead. I couldn't make out any words, but I sensed he was still on the phone.

I turned the doorknob, and the door opened with a slight jerk. I slipped into a dark room, quietly shutting the door, and moved my hand along the wall for a light switch.

Finding a double switch, I flipped on the first one, and a red light illuminated a small room. A long, narrow table stretched out, covered with metal pans. Torn photographs were scattered across the room and the floor. I took a step, flinching at the cracking sound beneath my feet, and looked down to meet my reflection staring back up. I bent down and picked up the picture, furrowing my brow as I tried to focus on the image using the red light.

It was an image of me, but I couldn't remember when the photo was taken or where I was at the time. I knew I wasn't wearing that outfit the day I found Kyle. There were other pictures of me strewn about. Grabbing each one, I examined various poses of me—different outfits and places—all familiar, yet I was still trying to place each one. Then I realized—these were all other cases. Why did he have all of this?

More images sprawled over the table, and others were dangling from a drying rod. The few hanging on the line were the ones I had been searching for. The ones from

Kyle's profiling. He had taken a few while I was in connection mode, and then came out of it. He had one where Julian was holding me, then another was a close-up of my face, pained and grieving- someone who had just experienced the worst loss of her life.

I swallowed as a wave of nausea rose in the back of my throat. He possessed a collection.

"You sick bastard."

I shuffled through the pictures and found horrible photographs of a woman slumped over the steering wheel with her back covered in blood, many from different angles. I paused to catch my breath, unaware of when I had lost it. My heart was beating harder than before.

I pulled away from the photographs and searched the room for more answers—several months of profiling cases- the teenage girl, the executive, the nurse, Sherry Sweeney. I grazed a finger over her photo, reliving a familiar, painful twinge behind my eyes.

I clutched the table for support, fighting against the wave of dizziness that washed over me. Victims and their tragic deaths surged through my mind, overwhelming my senses. My eyes darted between the pictures in front of me —the woman in the car, my nephew —images pounding through my memory like a snare drum. I fell to the floor and crawled away from the table.

My eyes scanned the room and settled on a picture frame on the floor beside me. A brown-eyed, brunette woman smiled back at me. I focused on the photo, absorbing its calming effects.

"That was my wife," a voice said from behind me.

I shot up from the floor and rushed to the other side of the room, turning to face David, who stood in the doorway. He eyed the frame in my hand, his jaw clenching and fingers twitching. He assessed my presence before stepping towards me. I tried to step back, but the table blocked my way.

"She was beautiful, wasn't she? I swear it was love at first sight when I laid eyes on her back in college. She used to give me this look, raising her eyebrows. It would get me every time," he said, reaching out an expectant hand for the frame.

I handed him the frame and eased to the side, out of his direct path. I tried to scan for an escape without revealing my movements. David walked to the shelf and carefully replaced the frame. He stood gazing at the woman in the photo, brushing his thumb across it as if still searching for the warmth of her skin.

"She's dead, you know," he said. “Mike said she was in the wrong place at the wrong time.”

He turned to face me, that same cold stare across his face.

"You may be wondering why I have all of this." He raised his hand and used a finger to itch the side of his face, a queer smile creeping out as he looked over the room.

"Well, I'll tell you. I enjoyed your work, as you can tell, but I admit, I did become a little obsessive," he said, taking a few steps over to the table and grabbing a couple of pictures.

I adjusted my position as I watched his movements. I didn't make a sound.

David turned and gazed in my direction, "I was astonished by what I witnessed each time I saw you. Your abilities are nothing short of incredible. I mean, you don't experience this kind of stuff every day, and believe me, I have seen some crazy things in my time, but not this," he said. He picked up a photo of me in connection mode - eyes wide, head cocked to the side.

David reached for another photo. "This was from the first time I witnessed you. I wasn't supposed to be in the room, but I heard stories and just had to see it for myself. I hid behind some furniture and enjoyed the show. Like anyone else in the room, I almost shit myself when the body moved." He let out a sound between a muffled laugh and a snort of disbelief.

I tried to steady myself as I considered my next steps. The room was too narrow for any attempt to run out; David would jump in my way the instant I moved. His eyes, which had changed from amusement as he studied the pictures, now bore a look of insufferable loss.

"You helped all these people, but you wouldn't help me? I just wanted to find out who did it. A face, a name-something, anything," he said. His voice was low and pleading.

Something behind his eyes and voice made my stomach turn, and my knees began to shake. I recognized that look and sound. I had been carrying the same look for days. Now I realize why everyone acted the way they did around me.

I swallowed hard before opening my mouth to speak. "I'm sorry I didn't agree to help you. If you've followed me this whole time, you would know what I've dealt with all these years. All the murders took a toll on my physical and emotional state. Julian feared what the profiling was doing to me, especially after profiling a triple homicide with three kids, so he removed me from further cases. I wanted to help, I swear I did, but he wouldn't let me."

David slammed his fist on the table. The room echoed as the metal tins on the table chimed from the sudden movement.

"Don't treat me like a fool. You were his prized possession, his reason for being top in the field," he yelled back.

My nephew's face caught my eye, and David turned to see which one I was looking at.

The air in the room stilled as neither of us attempted to breathe. "Did you kill him… to get revenge on me?" I asked, determined to get what I came for.

David reached for the photo. "I told you that someday you would know how it would feel to lose someone you love. It hurts, doesn't it? Enduring such unbearable heartbreak when no amount of physical pain in the world matched what you are going through on the inside. And the worst part is not knowing who did it."

He crushed the photo of my nephew in his hand and then slammed his fist onto the table. Once, then twice…

My eyes widened as he dove at me and threw me against the wall, slamming my head hard against the cement surface.

"You should have helped her, you bitch!" He screamed, spitting out his words. His hand wrapped around my neck, forcing me off my feet. I tried to kick my legs in hopes of them striking some part of his body, but his knees locked mine in place.

Whatever you do, don't panic. If you panic, you die. To get myself out of the house and socialize, I did attempt a few self-defense classes. No new friends came out of it, but I did manage to retain a few things from the class.

I seized his wrists, bearing my chin down to reduce his grip, while using my elbow to smash his arm away. With nothing working, I released my hold on his wrists and used my hands to perform an open palm strike to his ears.

The air filled my lungs as I dropped to the floor. David fell back, grabbing at the sides of his head and yelling from the explosion inside his eardrum. I kicked him hard in the shin, knocking him down to the ground and sending a second hit to his nose with my other foot.

Discombobulated, I attempted to jump over him, but he reached for my legs and pulled me to the floor. Pain ran up my arms to my body as David took his fist to my neck and back. His actions reminded me of Kyle's attack from behind. Anger coursed through my veins as a new wave of adrenaline ran through me. I recoiled before he landed another hit, caught his fist, and launched my foot to his chest.

I kicked him with every ounce of energy I had. With the memory of every kick he laid to my nephew, I returned with my own—one to his face, shoulder, and knee.

Blood spilled from his mouth and nose every time my foot made contact. Mustering up the strength, I delivered him one final kick to the ribcage before slithering away from him.

David remained where I left him on the floor, spitting out blood in between laughs. "Damn. You sure pack a punch, "he gasped through gurgled breaths.

My whole body shook uncontrollably, and I eyed the door next to him.

He forced himself to stand, pulled something from beneath his shirt, and pointed it at me. My breath caught in my throat.

"See if you can come back from this one."

My eyes widened at the gun aimed directly at my head.

The next moment unfolded like a silent movie. Julian burst into the room with his gun drawn and pointed at David. He ordered him several times to lower his weapon, but David kept his eyes focused on me and didn't move. He screamed at David, warning him that he would shoot if he didn't put the gun down.

David's eyes shifted to the gun. A crazed smile crossed his face as his hand slowly turned the gun toward himself.

"Tell me something. What do you think you'll find inside my head?"

The gun let off a sound, and I fell to the floor.

Chapter Twenty-Eight

I jerked in sheer panic, startled by the intense crack splitting through the small space of the red room as the bullet David released entered his right temple, exploding out of his left and impacting the cement wall behind him.

"Natalie!"

I pulled my arms away from my head and gazed upward to behold Julian standing over me. His chest rose and fell with each breath, and his hands trembled as he pulled me toward him. I instinctively reached around and grabbed hold of his jacket. Sobs escaped my throat, mixing with the taste of blood as I realized I was still alive.

"Shh. It's okay. I'm here. You're safe now," Julian said as he rocked me.

I glanced over Julian's shoulder at where David was sitting. His body was slumped across the floor, pierced by the bullet hole that consumed the side of his head. Nausea and dizziness crept in from witnessing a person take their own life. I was too familiar with death from those already deceased, but having to witness it as it actually happened was different and entirely too much to handle. I wanted to vomit.

Julian pulled away and held me at arm's length. "What on earth were you thinking by coming here? You should have called me first."

The disbelief from the last few minutes lingered as I searched my mind for an answer, but none materialized. My only response was to point to the photographs.

Julian squinted at my pointing gesture, and his eyes revealed the same surprise I felt upon seeing dozens of photos of me covering the floors and walls.

His eyes quickly veered from surprise to disappointment as he turned back to look at me. " You had no business coming here by yourself. You should have come to me first."

I struggled against the painful lump in my throat. "I had to. Look around, Julian. He was stalking me." I pulled away and searched through the photos, finally finding the one that mattered most. I showed him the picture of Kyle.

"He did this."

Julian snatched the picture from my hand, examined it, and then dropped it onto the floor.

"You still should have come to me. All of this could have been avoided," Julian said, glancing back at David's body.

Julian made a quick motion for me to stand, gripping my forearm and effortlessly lifting me to my feet.

"He killed Kyle!"

"You don't know that!" He quickly turned toward me, his expression was a fiery blaze that made me want to shrink away from him. "If you had let me do my job, I would have investigated this properly. But no...you had to go and..." Julian waved his hand in disgust at everything around him.

"If you don't believe me, let me profile him. He shared enough; I can glimpse his memories and know for certain."

Julian turned his entire body to face David, his brow furrowed and a shadow of concern flickering across his features. He lowered his head, as if weighing his words carefully, and then fell silent for a moment, allowing the tension to build between us. In a voice barely above a whisper, he asked, "Don't you think you've done enough?"

I focused my gaze on the center of his back. "I made a promise to Kyle."

"Did that promise include a grieving man taking his own life?"

My thoughts raced back to the murdered wife as I glimpsed her smiling face in the photograph sitting beside David's body.

"No. It didn't. I told you I would find whoever killed Kyle, but I didn't kill him, did I? David pulled the trigger, not me."

I didn't recognize the voice in my head, and the words spilled from my mouth. "Let me profile him, and all this can be over," I begged as Julian turned toward me.

"Over? You really believe that?"

The red bulb cast shadows into his eyes as he met mine—the same shadows that festered inside my head. He turned away from David and left the room, slamming the door behind him.

I gazed at the face of the lifeless man and stepped four paces closer to him. I knelt and confronted his dead stare.

"Did you kill him?"

I carefully considered David's position, paying no attention to the blood and brain matter splattered all around the area where I was hovering. That unrecognizable voice resurfaced again, telling me I didn't care. I only wanted answers that David could now give me, and I would take them all.

I looked around, grabbed a handful of intact photographs, and used them for floor cover. Lowering myself, I propped against the wall a foot from David. His head drooped to the side, resting on his shoulder. His face was mostly intact, frozen in an almost peaceful sleep. *Let's change that, shall we?* Hatred, I didn't know I possessed, flowed out of me and toward this man.

The damp basement air didn't help my concentration, but the coldness of the cement floor numbed my hands and legs. I envisioned that chill forming ice crystals throughout my body, reaching my heart. I slowed my breathing and allowed myself to release tension, synchronizing my mind to create a harmonious connection between mind and body.

The pull crept behind my eyes like a string tugging on my brain. I reached out to the other side, beckoning it to allow me in—my mind half-aware. I infused my body into David's corpse, forcing me to follow in its direction. The uncontrollable twitching spread up my arms and spine, then moved into my legs. My mind latched onto his as it detached from the chaos around me, allowing me to roam on the other side of the veil.

Visions struck like the opening of a movie as I connected with David. My blank, white eyes fixated on the dead face next to me. I tugged at its very essence. The corpse began to shake in rhythm.

Moments of bliss flashed through his memory as he recalled the joy and happiness shared with his wife. The words she had last said, along with her laughter, forced a smile, battling against the anger and grief.

He glimpsed in the rearview mirror as he turned down his street. The neighborhood he had inhabited for the past three years was a complete blur to him. There was too much vibrancy amid all this death. He tightened his grip on the steering wheel to remind himself not to slam on the accelerator and crash his car into the first happy person.

He slowed down as he pulled into his driveway, cursing the home that held many painful memories in his mind. He shifted his car into park and sat there staring aimlessly, with no desire to move. His last conversation with his wife replayed in his mind, repeating itself once more.

"Why across town?" he asked her over the phone.

"I wanted to switch things up a bit. I watched the cooking channel and wanted to experiment, but the ingredients I needed weren't available in a regular grocery store. I need a specialty store. The only one I know of is in the city," she responded.

"Will you be home when I arrive?" he asked.

"I should be. I'm going to run out right now and try to beat rush hour traffic," she said, rattling a few pots together.

"All right. Be careful. It's a bad area. Drive safely, keep your doors locked, and don't linger," he said, adjusting the phone between his chin and shoulder.

"Don't worry. I'll be fine. I'm leaving to finish this by the time you get home."

"Fine. I'll be home in a couple of hours. I love you," David said, listening to her voice echoing those words before pressing the end key on his cell phone.

A new voice cracked through his memory. His own. "No. No! Michelle!"

Getting called in to investigate what appeared to be an attempted carjacking, no one knew it was David's wife slumped against the steering wheel, until he recognized her. David shouted out his wife's name, begging to get to her. Mike held David, using all his strength to pull him away from the car and the unforgettable scene of his wife's death.

"I'm sorry, David. No one had identified her yet; I didn't know," Mike's voice echoed.

David squeezed his eyes shut until he no longer heard the director's voice. When he opened them, his knuckles were creamy white, clearly revealing his dark grayish-blue veins. He released the steering wheel and stretched his fingers, feeling the blood flow back into them. Resting his head against the seat, he waited for his mind to stop spinning.

The street vibrated with the sounds of kids from nearby neighborhoods playing as he opened the car door. He walked to the trunk, pretended not to hear the Adams' kid shouting his name, clutched his bag, and entered the house.

He set his work bag on the table in the hallway and walked into the family room. It was his first day back, and the return home was worse than expected. The house loomed with an emptiness that mirrored his heart.

He moved as if he were a psychiatric patient under medication, confused and searching for something that had seemingly vanished into thin air. He expected to see her sitting in her chair, reading a book. He breathed in the stale air, trying to sense her presence, but with each passing moment, he felt farther and farther away from his departed wife.

He left the front room and walked into the kitchen. Since he hadn't eaten anything in days, he figured he might as well try to get some food down. He first opened the refrigerator and then the freezer, surveying the contents. His phone rang as he stared at the glass storage containers, which grew mold with each passing day; he left them to sit.

He slammed the fridge door so intensely that it shook the cooking utensils above the stove.

"Yeah," he said, his voice sounding like someone on the verge of losing it to laryngitis.

"Oh, great. I'm glad I got you," a male voice said from the other end.

"Well, you reached me. Who's this?" David asked, gazing at a grocery list written in his wife's handwriting on a pad of paper left on the counter. He brushed his fingers over the dried ink, envisioning Michelle wandering the store after realizing she had left her list at home again.

"You need to be careful, David. She's missing, and there's a hunch that she's looking for you," the voice responded urgently yet calmly.

"If she wants me, I'm right…" David's words trailed off just as he detected a sound below him. He peered down at the floorboards and paused for a moment. The voice on the phone mumbled something he had missed.

David pulled the phone from his ear, tuning out the incessant nagging on the other end to focus on the sound beneath him. A smile he thought he couldn't muster again spread across his face.

"Don't you worry about me? I have everything figured out," David said, pressing the end key.

He kept his eyes on the floor and remained still, listening for other sounds. He had a hunch he knew what that sound was. A chill ran through him as he imagined her walking around in his happy place, admiring the beautiful shrine he had created in her honor.

He slipped out of the room and headed straight toward the basement. His quiet movements were effortless, given that his body was weightless and hollow from the little life that remained inside him. He paused briefly as he contemplated the cabinet drawer beside the basement door. Another smile surfaced as he opened the drawer, pulled out a gun, and tucked it into his jacket pocket. Then he moved with grace and stealth, taking the staircase down one slow, memorable step at a time.

Anticipation tingled through him as he reached the bottom of the stairs and gazed toward his darkroom, noticing the red light spilling from the crack beneath the door. With a weightless movement, he turned the knob. The red light spilled out as he surveyed the petite figure standing just a few feet before him, her back turned to him.

He spied what she was holding in her hands, and his heart skipped when he glanced at his wife's smile. He clenched his jaw, hovering in the doorway and studying her movements. His heart raced from being in her presence, but then he returned to the photo of his wife, remembering why she was there.

The torment swelled inside him as he made his presence known. I sensed the weight of each step he took around his red room, reaching for the photo, and glaring at me with intense hatred. The blame he placed on me and himself, accompanied by confusion and animosity, permeated his every thought as he gazed at the photo and then back at me.

"Did you kill him?"

He studied the images from Kyle's profiling, but his mind was blank when it came to Kyle's death. No recollections of the beating or the kicking surfaced at all—no visions of him stalking Kyle in the woods—nothing. The only memory that surfaced was his experience of capturing moments with me and Kyle through his camera lens.

He thought nothing more of Kyle as he beamed at his wife's photo. He couldn't understand why he held such an obsession toward me. Why did he focus so much on me instead of the woman he should have? He ought to have spent all his time with the love of his life rather than staying down here, developing photo after photo. He was convinced that I drew him in, controlling him in the same way I controlled those bodies.

He rushed me without hesitation. He grasped my throat and squeezed, examining my face as he envisioned the fear his wife had experienced.

An intense pop sizzled in his ears. He let go of me and covered his head. He lost his balance, and his knee crashed hard against the floor. He grabbed my left and pulled as I leaped over him, returning his attack like a crazed animal. He attacked without consciousness and took every kick I made to his body, pretending like my strength did nothing until the air whooshed out of his chest.

I expected to discover more rage in his memories, but I was surprised when flickers of amusement filled his mind as he laughed at me. It lasted only a moment when he remembered the hard metal weighing down his jacket pocket and retrieved what he had tucked inside.

Words flowed from his mouth like glue as he squeezed the cold metal in his hand, pushing himself against the wall as parts of his body throbbed. Flashbacks of precious moments with his wife rushed through his memory like leaves in a storm. He was tired of life and wanted it all to go away.

He realized someone else had entered the room and sensed the rumbling of words, but he couldn't hear anything, his ears still buzzing. It didn't matter anymore. His life didn't matter anymore. He pointed the gun at me as his eyes darted from photo to photo. He asked a series of questions – would she do that to me? Would she profile me? Make my dead body flail around? Peer into my thoughts? Learn of my suffering?

He lowered the gun away from me, smiled, and then pointed it at himself.

I pulled from David's memory after the bullet entered his body. Air left my lungs as I scrambled on the floor, struggling to breathe. I yelled out what little hope I had left.

Chapter Twenty-Nine

Julian burst through the door and dropped to my side.

"Get me a medic in here now!" he yelled over his shoulder. My eyes were still trying to regain their full sight as two people rushed into the room and knelt beside me. Warm fingers gripped my wrist as someone searched for a pulse while a light moved across my eyes. The second person attempted to place an oxygen mask over my face, but I swatted it away.

The tightening in my chest intensified, and my arms and legs thrashed as I tried to pull away. It wasn't the effects of the profiling that caused the sharp pains or the intense throbbing shooting through my head. It was everything I had learned from it.

"He didn't do it. He didn't kill Kyle."

David's body slumped awkwardly as my mind recalled every thought that had gone through his mind. No vision of killing Kyle surfaced. I studied David's eyes, peering at me from his slumped posture. He died smiling. He knew what I would do. He wanted this.

Julian leaned against the doorway, pinching at the corners of his eyes. Defeated, he dropped his head back.

"I received some unfortunate news in his wife's case. The detective assigned had reason to believe the person who killed Michelle also tried to rob a convenience store. Then, shot her in an attempted carjacking. At least that's what the original report concluded." He pulled his hands to his hips and rolled his head toward me. “A call came in later that the man matching the description of the robber was found unconscious in an alleyway. He was rushed to the hospital, where he was treated for two gunshot wounds, a few broken ribs, and a severe head injury. When the robber came out of surgery and regained consciousness, he confessed to the robbery but denied involvement in the shooting. He claimed he was assaulted and that his gun was stolen. However, he didn't remember much of the incident and couldn't identify his attacker.”

I hung on to every word he said. Painting a mental picture of the one murder scene I should have helped with, but refused.

Julian stood and stepped into the room, surveying the mess. "We thought we finally had one case solved and the bad guy captured. Turns out we did not arrest the right person for his wife's murder. Cameras from neighboring businesses caught him running from the store, away from where Michelle was parked.” He turned back toward me. “When we told David, he lost it—kept screaming at us for not letting you in on the case. I had a suspicion and did some investigating of my own. David’s family was with him, planning his wife’s funeral. They were able to verify his whereabouts when Kyle was killed."

Remorse crowded my already heavy heart. "The photos, Julian, he made me believe…"

I gazed at David's lifeless form, recognizing the grave error.

"Her vitals are normal, and her breathing is steady. It's up to her to decide whether to go to the hospital for a full evaluation," one medic said.

"Thanks, Shawn. It's not her first rodeo," Julian said, reaching for me and helping me into a sitting position.

"He was the only lead I had, Julian. He possessed photographs of Kyle's profiling. I recalled seeing him at the scene, taking pictures. Mike shared Kyle's file with me, but the pictures he took were missing from it. Something was off about him, and I suspected David was concealing something."

My desperation was no longer something worth holding onto, at least not from Julian. I broke his trust, and my actions and obsession got someone killed, just as Lance had predicted. I saw it in Julian's eyes; he was contemplating the same.

"Well, from the looks of this place, you were partly right. David was hiding something," he said, sifting through the photographs on the table.

"He said that he enjoyed watching me profile the victims and that I fascinated him."

"I know. I scolded David several times, trying to sneak peeks. I had no idea it had gone this far," he said, taking a photograph of me zoomed in. My white eyes matched the whites of a female corpse in the middle of a profile.

Moments of silence passed between us, and I eventually stood up, gripping the table to steady myself. Julian extended a hand, but I blocked it, insisting on standing on my own two feet.

“So, what now?” I asked, hoping to dispel the pounding inside my head.

"What now? Are you serious? The entire department and I have been searching for you. When I finally find you, I find him pointing a gun at your head, intending to kill you.

Now he's dead, and you're standing here asking me, 'what now?'"

"If you knew he didn't kill Kyle, why did you allow me to profile him?" I demanded.

Julian cast me a hopeless look. "Would you have believed me?"

The weight in my chest crept up on me once more. Would I? I couldn't respond to that.

"Julian. He didn't kill Kyle; I believe that now, which means-"

"Which means your obsession still led to someone's death." He didn't try to hide the hurt in his voice when he said, "I'm placing you in police custody until further notice. This will open up a massive internal investigation where you and I are concerned."

"Julian, you can't. Kyle's killer is still out there!" I said, panic seizing my lungs again as the air rushed out of my chest. I pleaded with Julian between breaths.

"Don't look at me like that. If you had come to me in the first place, none of us would be in this mess," Julian said, gesturing toward David. "He's dead, Natalie. He didn't have to die."

"He wanted to kill me, Julian, and he contemplated taking his own life. The man didn't want to continue living."

Julian shot an intense glare. "Why on earth did you have to show up here? And I'm curious: did you knock on his door and ask to come in for tea?" he asked. "Well? Did you?"

"No."

"No? Then how did you get in?"

I averted my gaze. There was no point in lying.

"Basement window."

"Wonderful," he exclaimed, raising his hands. "The charges continue to accumulate."

"If I hadn't, I would have never found all this. Regardless, Julian, something still doesn't make sense."

“Natalie! You! You are what doesn't make sense. I should have listened to Dr. Lance when I had the chance," he said, moving past me toward the door.

"But Julian-"

Julian faced me with a conflicted expression of defeat and rage. “Enough!"

His eyes fell to the floor, concealing his disappointment. "Officers! Place her under arrest."

My eyes widened. There's no way he just said that.

"No, Julian, you cannot do this!"

Two officers waiting outside cleared a path for Julian to walk past, then hurried into the room, blocking my way.

"Turn around and place your hands behind your back," one of them said.

"Julian! Please!" I cried, ignoring the command.

The nearest officer seized my arm and spun me around, applying a force I struggled against.

"I have to find him!"

The handcuffs clicked, and the cold steel wrapped around my wrists. They ushered me out of the room as Julian climbed the stairs, deliberately keeping his focus away from me.

"I'm sorry!" I yelled up at him, but it was of no use. Each officer had a firm grip on both arms and directed me up the stairs, through the house, and out the front door. Multiple patrol cars surrounded the area, and everyone stood by watching. This time, I was the monster they believed me to be.

Chapter Thirty

My body was impervious to the booking process. I didn't fight or make a sound as the officer instructed me to turn first to the left and then to the right. I was numb to the sensation of my fingers pressing against the ink pad and then onto the print card. Many faces I recognized glared as they found some reason to pass by. I saw it in their eyes, as if they had placed bets on my odds of being here.

I expected to head straight into a holding cell, but an officer escorted me to an interrogation room. Julian sat on the other side of the table, even-keeled, waiting for me. I thought I was doing a decent job holding myself together during the booking process, but seeing the disappointment behind his eyes made everything come crashing down. It didn't matter that Dr. Lance hovered in the corner.

My escort guided me to the chair across from Julian and, applying firm pressure on my shoulder, encouraged me to sit down. He then proceeded to cuff me to the table.

"There's no need for that," Julian said, raising his hand. "She's not going anywhere." With the sharp look he shot at me, I craved the isolation a holding cell would provide.

Lance shuffled over, took another chair, and brought it to my side, sitting down like my defense attorney.

"What are you doing?" Julian inquired.

"I'm just trying to ease the tension in this room. Natalie should know she has a friend," he said, smiling at me.

Julian's eyes narrowed into slits as he chided Lance. "How nice of you."

I snorted a laugh, recalling their conversation in a similar room, in which my lunacy was the main topic of discussion.

Julian refixed his gaze, and I met it with a fierce stare.

"Don't you dare give me that look. You put yourself here," Julian threw his voice across the table at me. "Why the hell couldn't you have just listened?"

I didn't answer and averted my gaze, trying to blink back the tears. I wanted to be angry. To regret ever caring about him. But another part of me hated myself for what I put him through. Why can't he understand that I was only doing it to help Kyle, to find his killer?

"So now you have nothing to say to me? No more begging, no more insisting that you have a job to do?"

I snapped my head at him. "I still have a job to do. You keep stopping me from completing it." My voice was so calm that it sent a shiver of surprise through me.

Julian glanced from Lance to me and emitted a soft grunt. "You think I'm going to let you continue this? Jesus, Natalie, what is it going to take for you to realize, you fucked up! And I can hardly believe I'm about to say this, but Lance is right; you're not in the right frame of mind. I should have listened."

"Yes, you should have!" Lance said, rapping his knuckles on the table. He quickly composed himself, realizing his outburst. "I apologize, Julian. I didn't mean to interrupt."

Julian regarded him in silence before glancing back at me.

"What a friend?" I grumbled under my breath.

"I can't undo the mess you created, Natalie. I wouldn't even know where to start." Julian sat up straight, his arms crossed. "But I can't imagine you would sit here, convinced you did nothing wrong, expecting me to let you leave to cause even more damage."

"I never said I didn't do anything," I mumbled.

Julian jerked his head at me. "What's that?"

I lowered my head but peered at him through my lashes. "I never said I didn't do anything wrong," I repeated.

The room went silent as Julian contemplated his following words.

"Let's start at the beginning. Where have you been for the past two days?" he asked, pulling the pad closer.

"I went home to get closure and have some time to think." My voice was soft, but broken. I couldn't bring myself to speak up. My confidence was diminished, but my commitment to follow up on my investigation still lingered in my mind. That little voice in my head. Telling me that I earned the right to be angry. I couldn't care less about Julian or his disappointment; about Lance and his fucking notepad filled with his bullshit opinions. Kyle was the only thing I needed to focus on—the only one who mattered now.

Lance drummed the table. From the corner of my eye, I sensed his mind reeling with the need to take notes. "Closure is always a positive goal to pursue."

"Well, it's clear you didn't get any... closure." Julian's disgusted tone drummed in my ears.

"So, you're saying you arrested the one who killed my nephew? No? Well then, I guess not."

I didn't know what else to say to him—the last few days had been a blur. I remember being at my parents' house and then sneaking into Nicole's house, but the time between them felt like little more than a gray space.

I found myself looking away, not quite ready to meet his gaze. "I almost reached out to you..." The weight of the silence in the room grew as Lance shifted in his seat.

"Why, David? Did you profile him?" Lance inquired.

I looked up at him, then at Julian. Confused. "Huh. You mean you didn't report every little detail to the doctor, as you always do? Julian, I'm shocked." I said, observing Lance's calm demeanor as he assessed me. I turned to meet his stare. " I had to."

"What were you looking for?"

Julian didn't bother lifting his pen. He already knew the answers to these questions. The muscles in his face tightened as he clenched his teeth. I figured he wanted nothing more than to leap across this table and shake the life out of me.

"I needed to know if he had killed my nephew." I gave Lance a cocky glare.

"So, it was a literal case of shooting first and asking questions later?" he mocked.

"That's a heartless thing to say right now. One of our own is dead!" Julian chimed in.

"I don't know, Julian. I warned you she would take matters into her own hands.

turn Natalie over to me for further evaluation. I'm sorry, but I have to do what I have to do, and I hope you will come to understand this."

Lance's words weighed on me, as if they were etched into my very soul. I had the urge to scream, but it was as if invisible chains held me captive, tightening around my neck and arms. Pressure settled in my lungs as I struggled to find my voice and resist the two men who were drawing closer.

Julian read the document and slammed it down on the table. His shoulders heaved, almost as if the same heavy chains were bogging him down.

My worst fear was coming true. Losing Kyle was the most painful emotional experience to endure, but now, I had to face the physical trauma of a psychiatric hospital. I imagined needles pumping debilitating drugs into me as I officially found myself on the same level as those who were insane.

"No, Julian, please. I'm begging you; you can't let him do this!" I finally got out. It was no use. An overwhelming feeling like I was going to pass out swept over me. I jerked my head, realizing one of the men was holding down my arm.

Lance approached from the side, and my eyes saw the object in his hand.

"I'm sorry, Natalie, but this is for your own good. This is only meant to help keep you calm and collected, nothing more."

I couldn't tell whether Julian or Lance said that. I was too focused on watching the needle pierce my skin. In a few quick breaths, my vision blurred, and an eerie sensation of falling washed over me.

"There, there, just let it sink in." Lance's voice was jumbled and distorted like a broken record. "You'll feel like a million bucks in no time. I promise."

I glanced back at him and caught a glimpse of his poker-faced expression as my mind and body descended into a dark abyss.

Chapter Thirty-One

As if I were rooted to the floor, incapable of any muscle movement, haunted faces loomed over me. They were all there—the victims of the past. Their features were distorted, serving as a poignant reminder of their stories and tragic endings.

"Please," I said, "I don't know what you want from me. I swear I just wanted to help you all. I'm sorry if I've done anything to keep you here or have harmed you." I did not move a muscle, but it was not because I was afraid. They hovered over me with a sense of tranquility.

"I'm sorry," I whispered again.

As I stared at their faces, I discerned something different about them. Most of them clasped their hands in front of themselves or stood at ease, hovering, as if they were protecting me from something.

"You don't have to be sorry," a small voice said.

The crowd parted, revealing a small figure.

I choked as Kyle stood before me. His appearance didn't seem tortured or afraid. With his infectious smile, he stepped forward, safe and happy.

"Kyle." My throat swelled up, and I choked out his name.

"It's all right, Aunt Natalie. You are safe here with us. They aren't mad at you."

"I tried to find the person who did this to you, Kyle, but I'm sorry I failed."

He lay down next to me and rested his head in the crook of my arm. I tried to reach for him, but my arms wouldn't budge; he lifted one for me and cuddled underneath.

"That doesn't matter now. Nana and Poppa are looking after me."

My throat swelled even more, and tears fell from my eyes at the mention of my grandparents. "They're here with you?"

"Not here, but in Heaven. I even got to meet Uncle Nathan and Grandma Rhine. Everyone is okay, and they wanted me to tell you that they are proud of you for all the good you've done." He smiled up at me, pride glowing in his eyes.

"Am I going to see them?"

"Not yet, but you will," he replied, reaching his arm across me and moving me closer.

I buried my face in his hair and cried. I wanted to stay with him and see my grandparents, mother, and brother again. I wasn't afraid of those standing over me; I was envious of them. They were here with Kyle.

"Don't cry, Aunt Natalie." He brushed his hand across my cheek. A surge of calm flowed through me, refreshing and assuring. "You're not done with your work yet. You have to do one more thing before we can be together."

I did not hesitate. "Tell me, and I'll do it. If only to be with you, I would do anything," I said.

"You have to stop him, the one who hurt me. You must, Aunt Natalie. He's a bad man."

My heart skipped a beat. "I thought that didn't matter now?"

"It's not because of what he did to me; it's because of what he did to other people and what he will do." His voice was monotone.

"Who, Kyle, tell me, who do I need to stop?"

"He doesn't realize how bad he is. He thinks that what he does is okay."

"Please, Kyle, tell me, who?"

"You must stop him, Aunt Natalie. See what you refused to see. Promise you will stop him." He raised his head, and I sensed his unwavering determination coursing through me. "Promise me you'll make it happen."

"I will do anything for you."

"Deal." He sat on his knees and smiled at me. I wanted to reach up and hold him in my arms again, to wrap myself around him and never let go.

Kyle's smile faded. "It's time, Aunt Natalie," he said, looking back at me. "You have to go now."

Sorrow surged through me, consuming my insides like birds on dead prey.

"No, Kyle, not yet. I want to stay here with you, just a little while longer." I tried hard to lift my arm, but it remained unresponsive. Helplessness flooded over me, as if I were trying to escape from something in my dreams but making no progress.

"You need to wake up now. You need to stop him so he can't hurt people anymore."

Kyle stood up and took a few steps back, blending into the crowd around us.

"No, Kyle, wait, I'm begging you, please don't go yet."

"You promised Aunt Natalie, you promised..." His voice trailed off into a whisper. The crowd parted to allow him to pass, leaving me behind. My body jerked as I called out his name. "Kyle!"

My eyelids fluttered open as I adjusted to the darkness around me.

"Ah, good, you're awake," a voice said from a few feet away.

I recognized the softness of the leather couch in Dr. Lance's office. The lights were dim, but he was scribbling something. He offered me a big smile and pushed himself away from his desk, grabbing his notebook before settling into the chair directly across from me.

"How was your rest?" he asked, making himself comfortable. He had an exciting air, like a child at a birthday party. "You were mumbling in your sleep, but I couldn't hear what you were saying, so I'm curious what you were just dreaming about?"

"Why am I here?" I said, not acknowledging his question.

"You are under my care. Why put you in a mental hospital when we can be cozy in my office? And I wasn't lying when I said you could use a friend. Julian would have insisted I take you to the mental ward, but I don't think that's the right place for you either."

"No," I said. I tried to rub my eyes, but my arms only twitched in response. "You insisted…Julian…"

"Did nothing. He did nothing. I'm sorry for how everything unfolded. I didn't want to have to administer anything, but you offered quite a bit of resistance, so I had to add something extra to the mixture. Don't worry, though; the effects will wear off soon. For now, be patient and try to remain relaxed."

I tilted my head just enough to get a full view of Lance, sitting there with his legs crossed, pretending to wait patiently, but his drumming fingers betrayed him. He couldn't wait to start writing in his notebook. Bastard.

"Is there anything I can get you before we begin?" he asked.

I shook my head at him, urging my body to respond to my will.

"Fine, then let's begin, shall we? First, Julian is aware that you will remain with me, so there's no need to worry about interruptions. I instructed that you be dropped off here instead of at the hospital. I thought it best, since he would make it all about rules. You needed time away from everything, including him, and he would interfere with our progress." He offered me a reassuring smile.

My mind drifted to Julian. He didn't even look at me as I pleaded with him. Julian would likely have me in that hospital. The way he lunged at me back in the room, he might as well be the one to tie me down to the bed and leave me to my insanity.

"A penny for your thoughts, although at this moment, I would offer you the deed to my house," he snorted with amusement.

"He didn't do anything," I found myself in agreement with him. "Julian. Didn't. Do. Anything." I whispered more to myself. "And David," I said.

"Yes. What about David?"

"He knew about David. But didn't say anything." My head was stinging from an incessant headache. The meds were wearing off, and the dizziness and nausea were kicking in.

“I’m sorry. Julian didn’t fill me in on anything about David. I had wanted to inquire, but things took a different direction. But no biggie, you can fill in all the missing pieces. So, David…”

“I can't help but wonder how he managed to get all those photos of me?"

"Photos? What kind of photos?”

"He had so many," I breathed, fighting the discomfort.

"Well, if they were photographs of you, can you blame him? He was most likely intrigued. You are a rare woman indeed. I wish you would let me in on your secret." His voice changed to a more calming, heartfelt tone.

"What I do has never been a secret."

"On the contrary, everyone knows you can communicate with the dead, but not many people have seen you do it. I never thought I would leave this office with the number of people filling my room, needing an explanation of what they saw. I never understood why people assume doctors have answers to life after death. How the hell are we supposed to know?" he snorted a laugh.

He perked as a thought wandered behind his eyes. "I have wondered whether you have the answers to life after death. I want to explore what you perceive beyond death. I know you say the victim’s memories fade away, but maybe, between you and me, we can further discuss what you may have seen, but didn’t realize you saw it, or maybe you’re just being selfish and are keeping that part to yourself. Have you ever tried hypnosis?" He spread his arms out in front of him.

My mind drifted back to Kyle. He told me he was with everyone in Heaven.

"You're mistaken about my abilities. I can't ascertain the path of the dead. I only learn what they went through before they died. I know I already told you that," I reiterated.

"So, you say, but I think there is something more. Maybe you made a pact to keep hush about what you know, fearing upsetting some delicate balance." I heard the sarcasm in his voice.

"Are you not a believer?" I asked.

"In God or Heaven?" He lifted his chin as if he were standing at a podium, about to answer the great debate. “Call me a skeptic. I'm a man of science, after all. Darwin will always be close to my heart, but that doesn't mean my curiosity doesn't question what is beyond. Although it's hard to see what one cannot, which is where you come in." he leaned forward in his chair; his face lit up with anticipation.

My stomach turned and rumbled. My body was starting to regain feeling everywhere, and I realized I hadn't eaten all day. "May I have some water, if you don't mind?" I asked.

His face dropped, and his fingers stopped twitching. "Of course," he said, letting the pen fall on the notebook. "Give me a moment.

"Take your time," I said, raining on his parade. Disappointment lingered across his features, goading me as if someone had stolen his favorite toy. He moved the notebook to the table beside him and left the office.

I took the opportunity to force myself to wake up, wiggling and stretching my fingers and toes before lifting my legs and standing up. I had to get the hell out of this office. I made a promise to Kyle. I spotted the phone on Dr. Lance's desk.

Julian may not have stopped Lance, but something about me being here didn't seem right. I would lie and tell him something terrible happened.

Lance expressed frustration about Mrs. Rice rearranging items in his waiting room, particularly noting that he couldn't find any cups or water bottles.

I willed my legs to stand, stumbled over to the desk, and managed to pick up the phone receiver and dial Julian's cell. After two rings, Julian said, "Josh, how is she?"

"Julian, something terrible has happened. Please come to Lance's office right now. Please," I said, sounding desperate through whispering pleas.

"Natalie? Why are you at Lance's office? You're supposed to be at the hospital," he asked, concern in his voice.

"Please, Julian, you need to come now." I hung up, praying my unexpected call had ignited something in Julian. Hopefully, his rage, considering that Lance undermined him…again.

I hurried back to the couch and sank into it as Lance hurried in through the door.

"Here you go, some nice refreshing H2O," he said, handing me a water bottle.

"Thanks," I muttered.

He went back to his usual chair and grabbed his notebook. "Now, where were we?" he asked, looking hopeful.

"We were talking about David and how he managed to have all those photos of my profilings?" I said, trying to steer him back to Kyle's case.

"I wouldn't know. You said Julian knew about David. So, he probably knew David was taking photographs of you. How about you ask him?"

My eyes fired an angry look. "What are you getting at?"

He dropped his hand in his notebook. "You have to admit, it makes sense. Julian is the one in charge. He calls the shots - who stays, who leaves, and so on. I can't imagine David being that slick to conceal pictures of you without Julian knowing."

"He wouldn't do that."

Dr. Lance shrugged his shoulders in defeat. "And I bet you didn't think he would agree to ship you off to a mental ward, did you? Are you sure you know him as well as you think?"

I shook my head. "No, you're twisting it all. He didn't allow…" My head was pounding now. I twisted the water bottle cap off and chugged, praying for relief. "Even if he did authorize David to be there, he wouldn't allow him to keep any of the photographs."

"Julian told me he needed you around too much. I must admit, Julian also showed a rather tremendous obsession with you. Toward your skill." He spoke to me with steady implication. "But let's not mind that right now. I'm sure you will fill in the missing pieces. For now, you are on my time, and we need to talk about you, not David, not your nephew's case, you." His voice sped up, trying to steer our conversation toward his choice. "I want to dissect the profiling in general. How do you get inside? We've discussed this occasionally, but I haven't quite grasped how you do it."

I checked the clock on the wall. The office was ten minutes from the precinct, but Julian would be here a third of the time. Just a few more minutes, I told myself. I know he'll come. What will happen when he shows up? I'll figure that out as I go.

"I don't have an answer for you. I wish I did. Death pulls me in as if it is the most natural thing to do. That's the best I can describe it." I made my voice clear and calm.

"Describe the experience. What do you mean when you say death pulls you in?"

I tensed my jaw, wanting this to end. "Like a rope tied around my waist, and something is tugging me toward it. It doesn't hurt; it's not scary or anything. It simply wants me to go toward it. That's it."

"Interesting." He scribbled in his notebook, his breathing quickening.

"I hate to interrupt again, but I need to use the restroom," I said without waiting for his response.

"Uh, well…fine, but hurry back." He said, still writing. It must have occurred to him that trying to escape was an option because he jumped up from his chair and hurried to my side when I attempted to lift myself off the couch.

I arched an eyebrow at him, feigning confusion over his abrupt movement. I needed to get him to relax, so I kept the conversation going, persuading him that his doubts about Julian were more than just baseless.

"I don't want to believe Julian would do that to me, but you make a valid point. He didn't hesitate to allow those officers to arrest me. Then this."

Lance's shoulders relaxed as he offered to help me stand. "Don't get me wrong. I have a lot of respect for him, but he's a man of power. I imagine he can have anything he wants with minimal effort."

Lance's words stung. On what side of the coin was he betting?

I trotted slowly out of the office and down the hallway toward the bathroom, ensuring I acted like I couldn't move any faster. Just as I reached the restroom door, Lance stopped.

"I'll be right here," he said.

I closed the door behind me, turned on the light, and looked around. It was just a small bathroom with no window. I sighed, unsure of my plan on getting out of here. I walked up to the mirror and examined my face. For the first time, I recognized the face staring back at me. The face in the mirror reflected Kyle's brave eyes, my grandmother's will, and Nicole's need for closure. This was not over. I made a promise.

See what you refuse to see.

I pulled back from the mirror, hearing Kyle's words echo in my ear. "See what I refuse to see."

I heard some commotion as Julian's voice echoed off the walls. I went to the door and opened it, peeking out into the hallway. Lance was back in his office, talking to Julian.

"Why the hell isn't she at the hospital? Under supervision?" Julian's roars echoed through the entire building.

Lance's office sat opposite the restroom. I just had to creep along the farthest wall and out the door.

Now is the time to move, a voice shouted in my head. My head still felt as heavy as a ton, but I moved in line with Julian's words, hoping he would mask any sound I made. I reached the main door and pulled it open. It creaked loudly, coinciding with the dilapidation in the rest of the office.

Julian called my name, but I didn't stop. I ran out the front door and discovered that Julian had left his car running, with the door wide open—typical Julian, always rushing through things.

He shouted even louder as I jumped into his car and locked the door just as he came within a few feet of me. My head spun in multiple directions as I put the car in reverse and spun the wheels against the pavement. He screamed my name again. "Natalie, get back here, dammit!"

"I'm sorry," I screamed, unaware if he heard me. I peeled away from him as Dr. Lance stood dumbfounded at his doorway.

Julian's rage and Lance's interrogation- none of that mattered to me now. I had to find Kyle's killer. I sped down a few side streets, deciding not to head straight for the thruway. Julian would assume that was where I would go. I calmed my nerves and slowed the car down, finding a driveway to ditch the car. I pulled into a 24-hour grocery store parking lot, turned off the lights, and waited.

"He's going to kill me," I said aloud, my heart beating through my chest. There was a faint sound of sirens a block away. Of course, Julian would have called for backup to catch the psycho lady.

What the hell am I doing? Think.

I spotted a couple of females smoking against the store's wall. In my frantic state, I was sure I could convince anyone to help. I quietly got out of Julian's car, snuck behind a few others to come up the side, and darted over to where they were standing.

"Excuse me. I'm sorry to bother you. I'm having the worst night ever. I locked myself out of my car, and I need to call for an Uber. I don't suppose you have a cell phone I may use?"

"Oh crap, that sucks," said a blonde-haired girl, looking homely in a red flannel and way-to-baggy pants. "Yeah, I got you." She said, handing me her phone.

"Thanks." I tapped into the internet and searched, submitting my request for a pickup. I patted around for my cards, which I usually keep in my inside pocket, but I remembered they were confiscated during booking.

"Oh shit." I handed the phone back to the girl. "Never mind. I left my wallet, phone, and whole life in my car."

"You are having a bad night."

I scuffed. "You have no idea."

The second girl, who looked like someone out of an old laundry ad—hair pulled back with a bandana; sweatshirt wrapped around her waist, and an arm sleeve of tattoos showing her love of Pokémon—asked me how far away I was to where I wanted to go.

I thought for a moment. I can't go home. The office was out of the question. *See what you refuse to see.*

"Can I use your phone again? Please." The blonde handed me her phone, and I searched for the Adams' funeral parlor. "Eight minutes…where I need to go. I have a spare key and someone to help get me back to my car."

More sirens raced up the roadway. We all turned toward the cars whizzing by. "I guess someone else is also having a bad night," I cracked. Praying they didn't put two and two together.

"Let me talk with my boss. He's a sap for helping those in need." She winked.

A few minutes later, she returned, her car keys in hand, and ushered me to follow her to her car.

"No, really, I can't ask you to drive me. I mean, I appreciate it."

"It's ok. Besides, it gets me away from having to stock shelves," she gave me a reassuring smile.

I offered no more fake arguments and followed her to her car. I gave her the address, and we exited the parking lot, entering the late evening traffic. It was so dark outside that I didn't think hiding among the numerous window decals, stuffed Pokémon characters, and other odd gadgets sprawled on her dashboard would be difficult. Those eight minutes and her random conversation about global warming, which followed after I mentioned a possible storm coming in, helped ease the panic.

The fog cleared in my head, and for once, I knew what I had to do.

Chapter Thirty-Two

"Dammit, Natalie!" Julian screamed out.

"Well, that could have gone better," Dr. Lance said snidely. He gave Julian a "I-told-you-so" side eye.

"I need to use your phone," Julian said, brushing past him without waiting for a reply. He bolted into his office, curved around his desk, and yanked the receiver from the base. Dialing the department number, he barked orders to rally anyone available to search for his vehicle. "Listen to me, Natalie Rhine needs to be apprehended, but under no circumstances is anyone to use force. Just find her and find my damn car." Anger flooded through him as the seconds passed. "Put patrols on the thruways, send a car to 35 Potomac Ave and another to 100 Southside Park, and send a car to pick me up at Dr. Lance's office on Corporate Parkway." He slammed down the phone.

"If you don't mind, I'm just going to grab something," Julian heard Lance say in the hall.

Julian paced the office, muttering to himself. He paced until he noticed Lance's notebook resting on the armrest of his chair. His eyes scanned the words written inside.

Death pulls her in. FASCINATING!

There is no afterlife —no kidding.

Lance's notations flowed down the page, one after another, like a journalist conducting a major interview.

How does it feel when life leaves the body? Do the victims convince themselves they can hold onto it? Do they plead with their cruel God while lying in their filth?

Julian's eyes skimmed over the scribbles, and he couldn't believe what he was reading. The words he used and how he wrote them did not resemble the work of a professional psychiatrist; they seemed as if a fifteen-year-old boy had doodled in his history notebook during class.

"Sorry." Dr. Lance's voice interrupted his reading. Julian looked up as Lance reentered his office and tossed the notebook aside. "What are you doing?" Lance asked him.

"That's what I'd like to ask you. What the hell is all this?" Julian lifted the notebook toward Lance.

"What? Oh, nothing. Just thoughts from others I speak with, trying to puzzle it all together, pay no mind to that," he said, playing it off.

"Joshua, why was she here? I was under the impression you would take her to the hospital, per that email."

"Yes, but then, as we were driving, I realized that the most important action now was encouraging her to speak to me. I understood how challenging it would be to get her to converse if she felt like a prisoner in a psych ward, so I decided to bring her here to make her more comfortable. Plus, I did sedate her."

Lance moved over to Julian and calmly requested his notebook, taking notice of the look Julian had given him.

Julian asked, trying to distract his attention from the notebook, "What did you manage to entice out of her?"

"Natalie did break down and cried her poor little eyes out about her nephew. She told me she couldn't take it anymore and couldn't live without him. That sort of stuff."

He moved over to his desk and locked the notebook in his drawer.

Julian eyed him. "She said that?"

"Sadly, yes. She surprised me when she just let it all out. I figured it was the sedative talking."

Julian's eyes opened wide. "What do you mean she couldn't take it anymore? Suicide? Is she talking about taking her life?"

He shrugged. "She said she wanted to end it all. As a specialist of this kind of stuff, I tend to know what 'it all' means."

"That doesn't sound like Natalie. If anything, she would be dead set more than ever to—"

"Julian, it is safe to say she has surprised you a few times tonight. Perhaps you don't know her as well as you thought you did. I'm only telling you this because you care, and I believe we need to work together for her sake. I'm risking a lot by not honoring her patient/doctor confidentiality."

"Yeah, I know, Joshua, but you can't possibly believe she intends to kill herself."

"At this point, it wouldn't surprise me. Natalie has already managed to walk herself into a situation where she has witnessed someone else do it. Perhaps she believes it's simpler than she thought. We were scratching the surface until you showed up." He glanced at Julian.

Julian paced the office. "So, out of curiosity, how did she escape your custody… if she was so sedated?" He stopped in front of him.

"Julian, I have never treated her like a wild animal. I gave her something to relax. She said she had to use the restroom. I was not about to have an accident here, so I escorted her down the hall and waited outside the door. Then you pulled in and busted through the door."

Julian tried wrapping his head around Lance's playback. He felt like someone was taking a screwdriver to his stomach. Would Natalie try to kill herself? Was she now looking to die? He didn't want to believe it.

"Did she say anything about David?" Julian asked, pacing again.

"It was just that she said something didn't add up with him. She still believes he has something to do with her nephew's case." Lance straightened himself out and stood to match Julian. "Do you think it's possible?"

"What?" Julian asked.

"Do you think she is right that David had something to do with her nephew's murder?"

Julian took a moment to ponder, then shook his head. "David? No. I don't believe he did."

"So, how do you explain all those photographs he had in that room? She told me that he had a lot of photos taken of her."

"He snuck in and watched when no one was looking," Julian said, eyeing him down. "He wouldn't be the first to show his curiosity."

"I bet he saw some spectacular sights," Lance said.

"What's that supposed to mean?" Julian stopped short.

Lance smirked and held his hand up in defense. "He must have watched her do things that entranced him."

Julian continued his pacing. Where would she go? Perhaps she returned to David's house to gather more information. He started for the phone, but a detective ran through the door.

"Captain." Detective Jeff Sands called out. "Are you all right?"

When Julian realized who it was, he hastened to get him back to the car and learn everything he knew.

"It's about time you got here. Let's go," Julian demanded. He motioned for Jeff to turn around and head back out of the office. "I'm driving," he added.

"I will just wait here for your word, then. Please keep me updated," Lance shouted over them.

As soon as Julian got in the car, he drilled Jeff for answers and slammed on the gas. "I want to know everything you and Natalie discussed, anything that might lead me to where she is."

"Honestly, sir, we don't talk much about her."

"I need more than that, Jeff. She trusts you."

Jeff let his hands fall into his lap. "I can't think of anything, sir. Honest."

Julian spun the wheels against the pavement and tore down the street, only slowing for a moment to flag the other patrols heading in his direction.

"I need you to go to David Christie's home; search his house and find out if Natalie Rhine is there. If she is, don't let her out of your sight!"

"Yes, sir." The officer said, speeding away. Julian switched the car back into gear and drove in the opposite direction.

"Where are we headed, sir?" Jeff asked, holding onto the hang bar on the side of the door.

"That depends on you," Julian responded, giving Jeff a stern look.

"I can't imagine she would go to a friend's house. She doesn't have many. Maybe she went to her grandparents' house to hide out?" Jeff said.

"I already sent patrols to her grandparents. Anyone else you can think of?"

"Her parents, but that's back in Virginia," Jeff added.

Julian peered at Jeff. "I didn't know she still had her parents' house."

"It sits abandoned. She brought it up once while looking for a realtor. I assume she was looking to unload it at one point, but now I can only assume she never got around to doing it."

"So that's what she meant when she said she went home." A new sense of worry washed over him. With Natalie already hurting from having to profile her nephew, it made sense that she would torment herself even further by returning to where she experienced her first loss. If there was one thing he learned about Natalie, it was that she was her own worst enemy.

"She wouldn't go back to her parents now. She wanted answers, none of which she would find there," Julian said, mentally crossing one place off the list.

Jeff added, "I don't understand why she is doing all this. It's not like her."

"No, but when was the last time someone murdered one of your family members. How would you act?" Julian eyed Jeff. "For the record, I don't condone anything Natalie's done thus far. She refuses to listen to orders, seriously destroyed the crime scene, and Mike is furious. Possibly encouraged a suicide. The list goes on. But I can't deny she is doing the very thing every person would do in her situation. I just wish she would cut the crap and let me do my fucking job and stop hunting down people and getting into their heads."

Julian suddenly hit the brakes and turned sharply down a side street.

"Did you think of something?" Jeff asked.

"Maybe. She was adamant about getting answers from Mike. He's got a lot of files back at the office. I wouldn't put it past her to finagle back into his lab. She has pieces to a puzzle that are missing, and if I know Natalie, she clearly won't stop until she finds more of those pieces." Julian peered into the rearview mirror and pressed the gas pedal. "She's still looking for something."

Chapter Thirty-Three

The Kia Soul rolled down the side streets like a cat on the prowl. The night seemed as if it were standing still, but I knew my adrenaline started to kick back in as we pulled up to the funeral home. Julian would be on the hunt with his henchmen, searching for me, but Kyle's voice called to me, and I followed.

See what you refused to see.

"Um. Here? A funeral home." Robin, my lovely chauffeur, asked, uncertain, and perhaps a little more curious than she should be.

"Yeah. I work here. It's my second home. I have a spare car key in my desk drawer." I said, hustling to open the door. "I appreciate your help. Makes me grateful that good people DO still exist." I played on her compassion, almost feeling sorry for taking advantage of her.

"I don't know if I could ever work at a funeral home. All those dead people."

"It's not as bad as people would think. I mean," I shrugged. "They're dead."

"Yeah, I guess," she said, sounding a bit freaked and looking ready to pull away like the first racecar trailing behind the pace car.

"Well, thanks again. I'll be fine from here. I really can't say thank you enough for your help. And please, thank your boss for me." I waved, and Robin smiled, eyed the funeral home one last time, and pulled away.

I crossed the street and entered the funeral home's parking lot. I went around the back and checked all the doors. They were all locked.

"Sorry, Adams, but you have someone I need to talk to in there." I searched and found a garden stone, which I used to shatter a small corner of a ground-floor window. I reached in, unlatched the latch, and shuffled inside.

I couldn't determine whether I was in an office or a small sitting room. I found a door and entered a long, narrow hallway with multiple French doors on both sides. I peeked into each room. Nightlights illuminated the larger rooms, helping me see if any caskets were waiting. One room had a shiny black casket with gold trim. Upon opening it, I discovered an older gentleman surrounded by navy blue satin — a father, grandfather, and veteran.

"Sorry. May you rest in peace." I shut the casket, ran back into the hallway, and checked the opposite door. In the second room, a lovely mother-of-pearl casket sat, surrounded by flowers, and a mural of pictures was displayed. I recognized the woman's face in those pictures. Michelle.

A checklist played through my mind as I reflected on what I knew. I knew David didn't kill Kyle; he was with Mike when it happened. David was on the other end of that call, begging me to help him.

See what you refused to see.

What if she saw her killer? Could they be connected? A tickle in my stomach told me that there was something there. Something begging to be seen. The pull I often experienced as I neared a body had long since eased as I helped the victims, but now, at this moment, that pull was stronger than ever, and it was coming from Michelle.

Her delicate body lay peacefully in her eternal shell. She was dressed in a pretty rose-colored dress, which accentuated a slight flush in her cheeks, or perhaps that was the result of the mortician's work. Regardless, she looked beautiful, and my heart went out to her.

Julian and Jeff drove into the station parking lot. At least Julian put the car in park, but he jumped out so quickly that Jeff had to reach across, turn off the car, and grab the keys from the ignition.

Julian darted toward the entrance door, where Tony stood swiping his employee ID to gain entry. “Hold the door!” Julian demanded.

Tony turned and recoiled out of Julian's way. “What’s going on?” Tony yelled after him.

Jeff came up from behind. “It’s Natalie, but before you ask, it’s nothing. You know how crazy things get when she does her thing.” Jeff rushed past him, gave Tony a thumbs up, and followed Julian down the hall toward the forensic lab.

“Who the hell breaks into a funeral home?” An officer turned the corner and almost collided with Julian.

“Shit. Sorry sir. Didn’t see you there.”

Julian maneuvered around him and then came to a stop. “What did you just say?”

The officer turned and uttered another apology.

“No. Before that. Something about a funeral home?”

We just received a call from a security company regarding a possible break-in at a funeral home. It’s likely a false alarm. I can’t imagine anyone being crazy enough to want to break into one of those.”

Julian darted his head toward Jeff. "Yeah, I can't imagine anyone would be crazy enough." He nodded at Jeff to return the way they came.

"You think it's her?"

"You don't?" Julian responded.

"Why a funeral home? What answers would she get there?"

"Not what, but from whom." Julian let out a low grumble. "David's wife. Her funeral is tomorrow."

Jeff paused, shaking his head in confusion. "I'm sorry, I just do not understand the point of that."

"I don't know, but I'm guessing that's what Natalie wants to discover. Let's go!!"

Chapter Thirty-Four

I studied the woman lying dead before me. Even with her grayish-white skin, she still bore a resemblance to the woman in the photographs at David's house. I envisioned her smile, and even though her body was embalmed, I could almost feel the warmth she radiated from her picture.

"I'm sorry I didn't do this sooner. I thought I was doing the right thing. But if I can, I will help you."

I inspected the room and noticed a table off to the side. I rushed to it, pulled it over, and positioned it next to Michelle's casket, eager not to waste more time.

I pulled myself to lie across it, and immediately my skin tensed against the cold wood. It was chilly inside the building, and there was no doubt the AC was jacked to help with preservation, but I wasn't expecting the table to be as cold as it was.

I followed the standard procedure of adjusting my body to fit the table, relaxing into it. The only difference was that this time, I had to tune out the chaos I had caused over the last few hours. I turned my head and discerned the delicate face next to me. Once again, I find myself apologizing to the woman whose life was taken.

"I'm sorry for what happened to you. And I'm sorry for what happened to David."

I turned away. Only a part of me felt bad about David. He seemed like a good guy, but finding all those pictures he had of me was unsettling. Discovering that obsession. I still didn't know how to process it all, and I didn't want to lie to a corpse. I readjusted and set myself back into the motions of entering the profiling.

"Are you sure you want to do that?"

I saw a tall figure slowly walking toward me, and I had to squint my eyes into the darkness as Julian's face emerged.

"Julian!" I froze, my body mimicking the dead woman next to me.

His voice was indifferent. I couldn't tell if he was angry or, worse, what his next move was.

"Where's my car?" He moved up to the table and leaned over me.

I raised on my elbows. I wanted more than anything to roll myself into the casket and seal the lid. "I left it at the FoodRite on Ontario St. It's in the parking lot."

He nodded. "Any damage?"

"Julian, I …"

"Did you damage it?" He asked again with an unnatural calmness.

"No. Of course not. I just needed to borrow it."

"Borrow it!" He laughed out. "Oh, is that what you were doing? Borrowing it?" He pushed off from the table and moved to the end of the casket, peering down at Michelle.

I remained in place. I came here for a reason, and I convinced myself that Julian would allow me to profile David; maybe he'll let me do the same with Michelle. Her murder was also still under investigation.

"You think this is going to help?" He asked, peering at me. I couldn't make out the color of his eyes. The light illuminating above Michelle's casket cast a glare that made them appear dark and sinister.

"Am I still allowed to plead my case, or will you walk me into a jail cell?" I asked, trying to steady my nerves.

The pull that Michelle's corpse was emitting grew intense. I had to discover what happened.

"After what you put me through tonight… to be honest, I have no idea what I will do with you."

Julian moved over to the front row of chairs and took a seat.

"You must be exhausted from all the chaos you've been causing?" His tone was angry and demeaning, but I knew I deserved it. I had disobeyed his orders and broken his trust. I deserved anything he threw at me.

"I am exhausted." I looked at him, and he stared back. There was no scowl or anger in his eyes. He had as much fight in him as I did.

"I never intended to cause so much trouble, but I am not sorry for my actions. I need answers. I can't let Kyle's murder go unanswered, and I need you to understand that," I said. I lifted myself off the table and stepped toward the board of pictures of Michelle's happy times. "And I owe David."

"Ah, so now you owe him. Before, it was all his fault." Julian rubbed at his nose. I couldn't help but notice how he gripped the back of the chair next to him. "For the dozenth time, I understand, but I also told you I would do everything to find out what happened," he said, aware of where my focus was, and eased his grip.

I was confused by his calmness and scrunched my face at him. "You let Lance drug me."

He dropped his arm and stood. "And for that, I will never forgive myself." He moved to where Michelle's casket was.

"You set off the security alarm by the way. You're slipping."

"Security alarm? I didn't see any security alarm." I looked around, wanting to punch myself for not considering that.

"Were you looking for one?"

"No. Who the hell puts security alarms in a funeral home?"

"Probably those who prefer not to have the bodies of their dead clients profiled by psychics," Julian smirked.

I pondered the madness of that. "I am a freak. I break into morgues and funeral homes. There's no arguing against that?"

"And on that, we can agree." Julian moved closer to me, hovering within inches of my face.

"I never wanted to upset you or disappoint you in any way. Not seeing Kyle's killer, it drove me mad. There's been so much death in my family."

He nodded in understanding. "A huge part of me is pissed off at you. But that's the cop in me. There's a whole other side that I'm grappling with." He reached and cupped his hands against each side of my face, holding me. Julian's voice resembled a lover from a romance chick flick. "I couldn't stop thinking about you for a minute when you disappeared. All I wanted was to have you by my side. When I didn't hear from you, my concern grew to anger. I wish you would confide in me."

I reached up and pulled his arms away from my face and stepped back. This will be my last chance—my Hail Mary to get the answers.

"You asked me to confide in you, okay, fine, so I will. I'm going to tell you something, and I beg you to try to believe me." I walked over to one of the chairs and sat, patting the chair next to me, hoping he'd follow.

He complied and sat next to me, adjusting his body so I had his full attention.

"When Lance drugged me, I saw Kyle. He talked to me. He made me promise to find the person who killed him. Said it would happen again, and that I needed to see what I refused to see."

I pointed toward Michelle's body. "This, Julian. I refused to help her, to see what happened. There is something inside her head that Kyle wants me to know."

"Then do what you have to do. I'm not going to stop you."

My eyes widened, then relaxed as I took in his demeanor. "You're not?" No arrests, no Lance showing up with two huge orderlies?"

"I believe you, Natalie. I am responsible for so much. Not just earlier or the last few days, but since I first met you." Julian rested his hands on each side of me, closing me in. "I swore an oath to uphold the law and solve crimes. I have broken so many rules and policies for you, but it doesn't matter now. I realized I couldn't live without you. I fell in love with you."

I blinked. My heartbeat pounded harder through my chest, but for once, not out of fear or anxiety. A sensation crept over me that I didn't recognize. He loves me.

"I tried so hard to hide it, more for your sake than mine. I was jealous when I saw how well you and Jeff got along." Julian sighed a bit.

I couldn't imagine a man of Julian's caliber jealous over me. "I had no idea your feelings went that deep. I knew we shared something more than a working relationship, but I never realized it went that far."

"Oh, but it did. When I first laid eyes on you, I thought… what is this girl doing here? I need someone with real investigative experience, not some paranormal princess."

"Thanks," I interjected.

He smiled, "But the more I got to know you, the more fascinated I was, not just what you could do, but by who you were. You were as passionate about solving cases and discovering the truth as I was. I love that about you."

His fingers brushed my cheek, then pulled me into him. He kissed me softly at first, then with more intensity. Life and death ceased to exist around us. I ran my hand through his hair and grasped his jacket with the other. We had kissed before, but nothing like this had ever happened. When he pulled away, he gazed into my eyes, brushed his thumb against my lower lip, and smiled a kind, I-give-up smile.

"You are still in a lot of heat for all the trouble you had no intention of causing, but I figure, while we are here..." He nodded toward the casket.

I cringed at the thought that Michelle Christie was lying in a casket next to us, while Julian and I were having a make-out session.

Julian snickered, "Maybe we're both freaks?" He smiled again and stood up straight. "Jeff's outside waiting. I'm going to have to send someone to grab my car. I don't suppose you have the keys."

I rummaged through my jacket pocket and pulled his car keys out, tossing them in his direction.

He caught them and turned toward the door. "You do what you must, but try not to mess anything up. I wouldn't know how to explain you to a mortician in the morning."

"Thank you, Julian. I hope this is the last time." I called out to him.

He turned to me just as he reached the doorway. "Me too."

He stepped out and closed the French doors behind him. I was smiling on the inside. My stomach fluttered, and my skin lit up as if tiny sparks roamed across it. I loved him, too. Once this was all over, I would tell him.

But until then...I returned to the table, hopped on, and lowered myself down. I focused on Michelle and hoped her memories would change everything.

I breathed in and out. The silence in the funeral home helped me quickly slip into profiling mode, and the next moment, I opened my eyes to find myself staring at a shelf full of spices.

Chapter Thirty-Five

Michelle reviewed every item on her grocery list that she had written in her mini notepad. "Green Cardamom. Got it. Kashmiri Red Chilli. Got it. Shahi Jeera?" She eyed all the spices before her but didn't spot anything labeled Shahi Jeera. A young clerk was stocking cans in a nearby aisle, and Michelle peeked around the corner. "Um, excuse me. Do you know if you have Shahi Jeera?"

The girl stacked the last can, stood up, and approached the section where Michelle was browsing. "Yeah, we have it … it's right... " she said, using her finger to scan the section. She knelt and pulled out a bag from the bottom shelf. "Down here. Shahi Jeera."

"Now, how did I miss that? I was practically staring at it… Thank you." Dropping the bag in the basket and rechecking her list, "Okay, I believe that's it."

"If you're ready to check out, I can meet you at the register." The girl waved toward the front and sauntered away. Her long, dark brown hair flowed behind her in a perfect drape down her back, almost to her waist. Her baggy, bell-bottomed jeans dragged at the ankles, the rubbing of the fabric reminding Michelle of her younger years. However, loose-fitting jeans with a pin at the ankles were more her style during that time. She squeezed her eyes shut and shook out her shoulders as the memory of her past fashion choices came and went.

When she stepped up to the counter, she unloaded the basket, and the clerk quickly scanned each item. A commotion stirred outside, grabbing both their attention, prompting them to peer out the front window. Michelle watched a couple of teens duck behind a car as a scream echoed, and a man in a black hoodie ran by waving a gun.

"Oh my God!" Michelle ducked as if something was about to come flying in through the window.

The clerk didn't appear phased, but rather annoyed, if anything. "That's the second time this week." She pulled out a paper bag and opened it. "That will be $23.38."

Michelle swiped her credit card, maintaining her focus on the event outside. "The second time you say? Doesn't that scare you?"

The clerk shrugged. "Kinda used to it. People like that run in and wave a gun, but it's usually empty. Demand money, or steal stuff, and take off. Just another day in the neighborhood."

"You need to get out of this neighborhood."

"Ha. Yeah right. That's easier said than done. Well, you have a nice day now," the clerk said, shoving the bag toward Michelle, moving from behind the counter, and heading back to her stack of boxes in the aisles.

Michelle walked to the door, peeked her head out, and saw a few people looking in the direction the man had run, which, fortunately, was opposite to where her car was parked. People were returning to their normal pace, and she seized that moment to dash for her car.

She tossed the bag of groceries into the passenger seat and slammed the door after she was seated. Not wanting to stay another second, Michelle reached for the key to put it in the ignition.

"I wouldn't do that if I were you," a male voice came from the backseat.

A gasp escaped Michelle's throat as a clicking sound shattered the stillness of the car. The noise rattled her nerves far more than her pounding heartbeat.

"Pull the key out of the ignition and throw it on the seat next to you."

Her nerves shook her entire body into overdrive, convinced that the man who had run past the window with the gun was now sitting in the seat behind her. She complied. "Please, my wallet is on the seat. Take what you want. You can even take the car. Just please don't hurt me. I didn't see anything," she pleaded.

"Shut up."

Michelle nodded, tossed the key onto the seat, and prayed it wasn't real. Tears streamed down her face as her entire body fell into a paralyzing shock.

"I have a question for you."

"What?" She breathed out.

"Do you know about his obsession…for her?"

"What… I don't know what you're talking about," her voice trembling.

"Your fucking husband. His obsession, you idiot."

"No. What are you saying?"

"It's pathetic, trying so hard to make him love you, when he's wanted another woman this whole time. And this woman…you're nothing like her. You, who's unremarkable. Pathetic."

"You. Don't. Have. To. Do. This." Michelle pleaded, trying to peer into the rearview mirror at the voice in the backseat. All she could make out was a presence; the man was tucked behind the seat, ducking out of sight.

"But I do, and…as the story goes, it's nothing personal. It's more like… a need to fulfill my obsession. She'll come. She always does."

Sharp sounds ricocheted through the car, and Michelle jerked at the sudden sting in her back. Her breath left her body like a popped inflatable. The back door opened, then shut, and as her consciousness drifted away, she glanced in the side view mirror at the figure walking away and saw his…

Chapter Thirty-Six

The loud crack of a gunshot rang out—not from behind, as if I had been shot in the back like Michelle, but from a few feet away.

"Natalie…" Julian's voice trailed off. I turned toward him as he fell to the floor.

My mouth opened as I gasped for air, experiencing the same intense suffocation as the last time I was forced out of a profiling. I lurched, and my chest heaved as if I were having a heart attack.

"Wakey. Wakey." A voice floated toward me, not so much as a demand but as a taunt.

I inched my head to the side, trying to focus on my surroundings. Darkness enveloped me as I pleaded for my body to calm down. No oxygen masks or soothing faces hovered over me to help bring me back to full consciousness, except for one face that came into view—dark hair combed to the side, glasses.

"Well, welcome back...again! My, my, I must say that was exciting." Dr. Lance hovered over me, a smile curling across his face like a kid getting off a carnival ride. The room spun like a merry-go-round as I fought back a scream from the painful adrenaline still coursing through my body. The pungent reek of death filled my nostrils.

I blinked once, then twice, and gripped the sides of the table. I was back in the funeral home again. My rubber-soled shoes made scratching sounds as I skidded both legs against the table, longing for release from the pain—my pain, Michelle's pain, possibly both.

I turned my head toward Julian's body on the floor, his blood spilled all around. "J…Ju..Jul…" I couldn't say his name. My thoughts, speech--everything was paralyzed, like I was waking from a nightmare, and my mind had no clue I had awoken.

"Are you finally coming around?" Dr. Lance moved to a chair across from Julian, who remained motionless. He sat with unnerving composure. "Take a lot of good breaths, and breathe through your mouth. You will feel better in a few minutes."

"You?" I said.

"Me," he raised his hands as if introducing himself, then clasped his hands together as if he were the winner of a high-stakes poker game and wanted to brag about it.

The dread filtered out of my system, replaced by a full onset of confusion. Julian was bleeding. I had to get up. I poured all I had into centering myself and ordering my legs and arms to respond to my command. I slid off and fell to the floor, as I kept my arms gripped to the table to steady myself. My eyes rolled back to where Lance sat. He couldn't have done this? No way in hell could he have done this?

"Having trouble?" A shadow lingered over his features, but I could swear he was smiling, perhaps even gloating.

"What the hell are you doing here?" I straightened up and eyed Julian a few feet away. I used every bit of energy and tried to walk toward him, one excruciating step at a time.

"What I've been asking for since I first met you. I want to know everything you know about death. I want to learn every little detail inside your glorious head." His entire body emerged from the subtle darkness, coming fully into view. He appeared different. His pupils were wide and black, and his sickly plastered smile spanned his face. This wasn't Lance. Not the man I've sat across from for dozens of sessions. Certainly not the same man who coaxed me into a heartfelt conversation over breakfast. No, this person in front of me was someone else.

I inched closer to Julian and winced when I noticed the faint glimmer of a gun in Lance's hand. The harsh, painful realization hit me that he had shot Julian. Why? I fell to the floor at Julian's side, panicked as time slipped away with each rasping breath. I felt across his back, checked his neck, and prayed more than I ever had in my life for a vital sign. Lance's voice came off garbled behind me as I begged for Julian to move, wake up, or do something.

"Since I was a boy, I have been intrigued by death, not just the act of dying, but by the way it takes over the mind-the fear, anger, and terror that goes through people's heads when they realize they are about to die."

He stood up from the chair and walked over to me, his steps barely making a sound on the carpeted floor. "Natalie…Natalie…" his voice drawled from behind like a hunter stalking his prey.

"Julian," my cry barely emerged as a whisper. A jolt of shock washed over me, fearing he was dead. I tried to turn him onto his back, pulling at his shoulder with all my strength. I felt a faint pulse and released a guttural sob.

“It may surprise you that I’m pretty good at shooting these things.” He waved the gun in the air. “I may have nicked something, but I think he’ll pull through.”

I ran my hand through Julian's hair and saw his blood smeared across my fingers. Tears flooded my eyes, and drops splattered onto Julian’s jacket. “Julian, open your eyes. Please open your eyes.”

"Natalie, enough of him. I said he'll be fine."

"Go to hell!" I cursed through my teeth. Once more, I found myself at the side of someone I loved. An unfathomable rage percolated inside me, unstable and ready to wreak havoc on the world around me. I can’t endure this again. “I can’t lose you,” I pleaded in Julian’s ear, praying he would hear me and open his eyes.

Lance moved closer, hunched over as if coming in for a closer look.

If I formed all my painful memories into daggers, he would have at least a dozen hurled his way. "What is wrong with you? Is that what this is all about?" Self-loathing gripped me in a terrified state. Was this my fault? Am I being punished?

"Take a seat, and I'll be happy to explain."

I ran my hand through Julian’s hair, nudging him back to consciousness and cursing myself for never learning CPR, convinced it was pointless since I showed up when it was no longer required.

"Natalie! I wouldn't suggest you try my patience." He urged, the gun pressed against my neck. I took inventory and noticed that Julian's was missing from his holster. "I want you to take a seat, and we can have a nice talk. Leave him be." Lance seized both arms and hauled me over to a chair. "There we go. That's better. Cozy." He smirked, dipping his head to the side mockingly.

I glared at him. "You are a real piece of work. I thought you two were friends?"

He looked back at Julian, nodding his head. "Not really, no; perhaps if he listened to me more, I could count him as a friend, but he was always working his angle behind my back and going against my better judgment."

I pulled my arms into my chest and applied pressure against the tightness hovering just beneath the skin. I drifted back to Michelle when she felt the sting from a gunshot wound, then moved to Julian. I experienced a similar sensation, as if a bullet had barreled through my heart. It's just an anxiety attack. I closed my eyes and locked out the darkness that covered these walls, blocking the voices howling inside me, including the one that wouldn't stop. I tried to get it together.

"You damn well know you won't get away with this. Someone had to have heard that gun go off." My eyes flew open as realization struck. Jeff. Julian said Jeff was waiting outside. Please let him still be there.

He searched around, then turned back to me. "Well, where is everyone?"

A long silence enveloped the room. Two bodies now lie in the macabre darkness of the funeral home. I wouldn't mind one of those bodies being replaced by a man dressed in a sweater vest, who would look comfortable in a plain wooden box, suited to his questionable taste in décor.

"No one's coming because no one else is here. Thanks to you and all your silly little antics, everyone on the clock is looking for you." He pointed a stiff finger at me.

Confusion and then fear fluctuated through my mind. Did he shoot Jeff? No. No, no, no!

"But you do make a good point. Perhaps this isn't the best place to have a real heart-to-heart. Well, it is, but I don't have my notes!" His voice rose as if I should be appalled by his lack of preparation. Lance waved the gun at me, gesturing for me to move.

I gave him a disgusted look. I didn't want to leave Julian, but the gun pointed a foot away didn't give me much choice. I prayed with all my heart and soul that someone would find Julian and take him to the hospital, that he'll live, and that he'll come after me and rescue me from this fucking lunatic. And I prayed Jeff was alive.

I shook my head and drew my hands to wipe away the tears. This is wrong. This is all wrong. I stepped past Lance, who waited in the doorway, keeping the gun pointed at me. A part of me almost didn't care if he shot me. I've been shot so many times; what's one more?

My soul pleaded for Julian to make any sound or twitch a finger to let me know he was fighting to survive. If I lose Julian, then, on the graves of my family, I would join him shortly, and I'll be damned if I don't take Lance with me.

Chapter Thirty-Seven

With Julian's instructions to wait, Jeff backed into a spot in the front corner of the lot, turned off the car, and dropped his head in his hands. Plagued by all the activity, he let his eyes wander and stopped at the front doors across from him. Natalie was inside doing God knows what.

He couldn't believe everything he heard about her, didn't want to believe it—breaking into David's house, causing him to kill himself. Not Natalie. He scratched at his beard and rubbed the rest of his face. Rubbed away the denial, the heartbreak. His friend was hurting, and he couldn't do anything to help her.

For so long, he witnessed the world against her. Her psychic ability never bothered him like it did with so many others. He thought it was incredible and even inspiring. Those assholes. They forced her out.

Jeff didn't have many friends either, just a small handful at most—but Natalie was someone he enjoyed seeing when he went into work. She thought he was funny and cool and understood him in a way most people couldn't. With him being a little unusual himself, his friendship with Natalie was a match made in Heaven.

He kept impatiently eyeing the door, waiting for Julian and Natalie to appear. Regardless of what has happened, this isn't the end. It can't be. The department should hold Natalie in the highest esteem for all that she has accomplished. Julian needed Natalie. It would all work itself out in the end. It had to.

"Fuck this." Jeff grabbed his keys and jumped out of the car. Slamming the door shut. He took a few steps toward the front doors, immediately thought better of it, and did a one-eighty. "Damn it!" He muttered, unsure what to do. Julian told him to wait in the car. Instead, he paced. His eyes scanned the road to the right of him, then the parlor to the left. Five steps, turn. Five steps, turn. His ADD made him count every step, causing his head to spin.

The sound of a gunshot made him stop dead in his tracks, and his training kicked in full force as he high-tailed it toward the door, drawing his gun. He spotted two figures moving quickly down the back hallway. He recognized Natalie from the back, but who was with her? He knew it wasn't Julian. The person was shorter and bald. Wait… Lance. What the fuck is he doing here?

He moved quickly, yet quietly, in through the front door. He was about to yell out when he saw what Lance aimed at Natalie. He caught his breath, as if his heart had stopped, and turned toward the direction they had come from. A pair of French doors sat ajar, and he could make out a figure on the floor. "Oh shit!" He dashed in, skidding to Julian's side, holstering his gun.

"Julian!" he yelled, shaking him. He felt a weak pulse, but there was blood everywhere. The sound of a heavy metal door opening and then slamming shut echoed through the building. Lance and Natalie must have left out the back, but his biggest priority was getting help. He reached into his jacket pocket, pulled out his cell phone, and dialed 9-1-1.

"This is Detective Sands, Baltimore PD. I need an ambulance at Adams' Funeral Home on Sycamore. Officer down. Gunshot wound. Hurry!" He dropped the phone on the floor and searched for the wound that was causing the blood flow, using his body weight to apply pressure. "Hold on, they're coming," he prayed on the slightest possibility that Julian heard him. "Fuck!"

A knot bore into his side. Lance had a fucking gun pointed at Natalie. "She's in danger, boss, I have to go after her." His mind dredged up the worst possible scenario as he stood and ran after his friend. "You just gotta hang on. I'm sorry, but I have to go after them. I'm sorry."

Jeff ran out of the parlor and down the hallway, slamming into the back door with brute strength. His heart raced as he scanned the parking lot, fearing he was too late and had lost them. The screeching of tires stole his attention, and he whipped his head as a Ford Taurus sped out of the side of the building and onto the front road.

He moved with the kind of speed he possessed back in his college days as he raced around to the front of the building. Sirens wailed as the ambulance arrived, its flashing lights casting urgent reds and blues. He gestured to the paramedics to hurry without waiting for a response. He jumped into his car and sped out of the driveway into oncoming traffic. Other drivers slammed on their brakes, honked their horns, and shouted out jumbled curses. Multiple squad cars raced past him, and he saw in his sideview mirror, as they sped into the funeral parking lot. "He'll be okay. Please dear fucking God, let him be okay."

He squinted his eyes, searching ahead, and saw the Taurus speeding through stop signs and red lights. "What the hell is going on?" he cried, putting more pressure on the gas pedal and speeding up. He followed the car, maintaining a safe distance as he searched his jacket for his cell phone. "Dammit!" He pounded his hand against the steering wheel, realizing he had left it at the funeral home.

Jeff kept a steady pace four car lengths behind Natalie. The Thruway wasn't busy, but it had just enough cars to blend in with his. He viewed Lance in the passenger seat as the sunset glared from the back window.

"That was a gun. He had a gun."

He picked up speed and cut in front of a car, wanting to move closer for a better look. He got about two cars behind when Natalie pulled off onto an exit at the last minute, causing him to brake hard. The two vehicles behind him slid into the other two lanes, hitting their horns as he maneuvered the corner and turned off onto the exit, just missing a ditch.

The exit they turned off continued for miles as the two-lane throughway wound down to a one-way road. Farms passed, and cows moved steadily, likely getting summoned back for the evening as the chase continued. He had to play it safe, or risk her life. No running up on them or forcing them to pull over. Lance could end up shooting her. He followed them, determined to find out what he was up to, then he would radio in for backup once he understood where they were going.

He trailed a few hundred paces behind and watched as she turned down a road, then disappeared. When he reached the road, he couldn't make out anything ahead of him. The sun had set, and there were no other car lights or streetlights around. It was nothing more than a dirt road. He slowed his pace, praying he wouldn't be spotted, and kept his eyes sharp toward the obscurity ahead.

Up ahead, he saw the dull flicker of a brake light and quickly pulled to the side, staying out of sight. Dr. Lance got out of the passenger side and ran to the driver's side, holding the gun pointed in Natalie's direction as she stepped out of the vehicle, holding her hands up.

"Son of a bitch." Jeff muttered to himself.

He exited his car and ducked low, watching Lance and Natalie walk toward a house. Lance didn't lower the gun once and moved ahead of Natalie to open the door, as they both stepped inside the home.

Lights lit up the inside, and he stayed down, predicting that most people, when on the run, always tended to look out the window to see if they were followed.

The front window curtain shuddered, and that bastard of a shrink's head bobbed around, searching the front of the house. He disappeared behind the curtain, and Jeff began to run.

Chapter Thirty-Eight

"Now, where were we?" Lance said, dragging up a chair close to me. "I'll make a deal with you. I'll explain my reasoning to you, and you'll share everything I need to know, without withholding any information. I can tell when you are holding back."

I surveyed the front room. This must be his home, but I was shocked by the modern furniture and decor that adorned the house—nothing compared to his worn-down office.

I reflected on Julian and prayed he would be okay. "Fine, whatever you want," I said.

He smiled that sickening smile; clearly, this whole situation amused him. "I can still remember the day Julian came to me and asked me to be your psychiatrist. When he told me what you could do," he snorted. "I thought he would be my next patient, but his details and passion when he spoke of you struck my curiosity. So, I penciled you in and have been intrigued by our sessions. You could do the very thing I have dreamed of." Lance's eyes glazed over. "My interest in you became overwhelming, and I thought… finally, I can get the answers I seek."

I cut in. "What answers? I have been trying to tell you for a long time. I don't have much to tell."

He raised a finger at me, the gun in his other hand. "I can't deny that I am intrigued by you. I don't think I have ever come across someone who fascinates me more, and believe me, I have come into contact with many people who would find you unusual or criminally insane."

"I am not insane."

"That remains to be seen, but that's not my point. I have reviewed books, lectures, and extensive research studies, and have never found anyone like you. Nothing in this world comes close to the knowledge you have floating inside your head."

"Knowledge regarding what exactly?" I asked, stalling.

He threw up his hands. "Is there a God? Life and death, of course. My personal favorite is how human emotion takes over the physical body when someone dies or performs heinous acts of murder. You've profiled both victims and killers, but it's more the killers I take a fancy to."

"And you think I can tell you all this?" I asked.

"I know you can. I have spoken to so many who committed the crime, but psychopaths always make it sound as if they are fearless, heartless, etc., etc. Boring." He laughed. Lance stood and paced the floor, caught up in his conversation. "Since I was a boy, death amazed me. I never envisioned myself as a psychiatrist, but I did have a strong fascination for science since my parents were strict religious followers. Devout Catholics."

I knew where this was going. He was about to give me his I-had-a-terrible-childhood-and-I-blame-my-parents speech. At this point, time would be my only ally while I devised a plan to escape.

"I was a good little boy—eating my vegetables, dressing in suitable outfits, and kneeling to say my prayers—

although I wasn't actually saying them; I had become a devoted Darwinist. I just never dared tell my parents."

His voice was like knives on a chalkboard, but I kept myself still as he chatted.

"Whenever they weren't around, I would perform science experiments." He laughed again, "I was that typical boy who would fry ants under a magnifying glass. Do you have any idea how powerful that makes a young boy feel? It wasn't until my late teens that I started questioning God's part in it."

"So, you fried ants when you were a kid...crazy." I accentuated the sarcasm in my voice. "Let me guess, after that, you killed a rabbit, then moved on to cats."

He seemed adrift in his world. He disregarded what I said and recounted his story.

"One day, after my latest beating, my parents both fell asleep in their bed, and I snuck in and watched them sleep. They lay there, so peaceful. Innocent even." Lance crooked his head in my direction. "But they were not innocent." He smiled, then stood up and began to move around the room.

"They had those tall glass candles, the ones with pictures of Jesus on them." He made a gesture as if he drew the candle in the air. "They loved God more than they loved me."

He moved to a cabinet and pulled out a whiskey decanter and two glasses, removed the stopper, and poured half a glass each. A mirror hung before him, and he kept glancing at it while talking to me.

"I never believed there was a God. After all the years, my parents prayed daily, devoting their entire livelihoods to a force with no real credibility." He waved the gun in his hand to accompany his words. He put the stopper back in the decanter, clenched both glasses with one hand, and turned back toward me.

"My parents required that I read the bible aloud morning, noon, and night. Compelled me to pray with them and ask forgiveness for slamming the refrigerator door or something silly." He handed me one of the glasses. I hesitated.

"You need this more than I do. Admit it, " he smiled.

I took the glass from him, and he toasted me. I raised the glass to my lips and downed it in one gulp.

He furrowed his brow. "Good, isn't it. Vintage, of course," he said, sitting back down. He carelessly pointed the gun, and I wasn't in any position to dive for it. He picked up his conversation as if he were now the patient, and I the doctor.

"I endured their cruel slaps across the back of my neck if I didn't speak the passages flawlessly. I was never allowed to have any friends because this world was too self-righteous, and they would tarnish my soul. And girls were out of the question." He cut his gun-bearing hand through the air. "Whores…all of them. My mother would say. Dirty, sinful succubus wenches looking to rob you of your purity." He nodded as if he agreed.

I shifted my eyes around the room. A slight movement at a window grabbed my attention, but I quickly snapped my focus back to the madman next to me, not wanting to reveal anything. He continued going on about his life as if we were having the best conversation ever.

"My parents allowed me to attend school, but mainly to help all the lost souls that walked the halls and spread God's word. I remember sitting outside in the hallway while my parents blasted my science teacher for teaching me that the world began with the Big Bang theory. The principal showed up and escorted them out of the building.

My parents chastised everything I learned in science class, but they had no choice but to accept the state requirements. If anything, it encouraged my parents to prove God's will in everything I learned at school. If I tried to counter their arguments with scientific proof, I would meet with my father's belt across my back."

When he lowered his eyes to take a sip of the whiskey, something moved in the corner of my eye. I glanced over at the window and caught a glimpse of a head peeking in. My soul lit up when I recognized the full head of hair and matching beard staring in my direction. Jeff.

"As it turns out, science became my favorite subject, regardless of my parents taking any opportunity to invoke the Holy Father in my science projects. My teacher grew accustomed to the religious references in my work, but the rest of the students never let me forget it. They teased and bullied me to no end, infusing my anger and hatred. Whenever I went home after another attack at school, my parents saw the anger in my eyes and only added to my fury by punishing me, insisting I had allowed the devil in." He snorted a laugh. "Maybe they weren't wrong." He spoke into the whiskey glass and took a solid gulp.

Jeff motioned with his hand, urging me to sit still. I shuffled in my seat, covering up the head shake I threw his way. I didn't want him to charge in while Lance was holding the gun. I lowered my hand below my knee and made a gun gesture with my fingers. He nodded but then vanished. I peered back at Lance, appearing oblivious to his new guest.

"As time passed, I learned how to appease my parents at home, keep quiet, and mind the kids at school. I also discovered ways to hide my love for science from them," he sat back in his chair, looking relaxed, as if keeping someone against their will was natural for him.

"After the whole ant thing, I went on to larger insects and even experimented with a snake. Not a rabbit, but you were close." He had a boyish grin. "Any science experiments were conducted in my room late at night or behind the shed."

I flinched when he sat up. The gun remained in his hand but rested on his lap.

“It wasn't until a quiet summer day spent sitting in the backyard reading that my passion for science blossomed into a love far beyond dissecting bugs.”

I sat leaning against the armrest, pretending to be entranced. "Then what happened?"

He perked up, appearing thrilled that I was invested in his story. "My neighbor's dog, a Rottweiler named Zeus, was sleeping under a tree in the yard next door when he started growling. Zeus was a beautiful animal- strong, obedient, and playful. I enjoyed playing with the dog through the fence, but when it came to wild animals such as rabbits, squirrels, and stray cats, the dog was no longer the gentle beast I grew used to, but noisy, curious, and a bully himself." He smiled up, acknowledging his compliment.

"When I looked over to see what Zeus was growling at, I saw a stray black cat wandering through the wire fence into Zeus's territory. It was a matter of seconds before Zeus trapped the cat in the corner. The foolish feline hissed and puffed its tail at the dog. Zeus attacked with full force, paying no mind to the claws slapping against his face. The dog snatched the cat up in its jaws and whipped it around with power, snapping its neck. The dog released the cat and loomed over the dead feline at his feet, relishing his victory. Then Zeus picked up the dead cat and played with it like a new chew toy."

"Amazing," I muttered through clenched teeth. I pretended to scratch my head and sneaked a look back at the window, but I didn't spot Jeff.

"I thought so, too!"

He drank the last of his whiskey and returned to the cabinet, pouring himself another. He quickly turned and asked if I wanted another.

"No. I'm good. Lightweight." He smirked and waved me off, filling his glass more than the last round.

"I was so amazed by the dog's passion for killing that I was jealous. Ridiculous as it sounds, I was jealous of both animals. I was intrigued to learn how the dog reacted when he had the cat right where he wanted it. Did he know when the cat's neck snapped and ended the furry feline's life? What emotions flooded his mind? If dogs could talk?" He studied me in the mirror.

"And what of the cat? Was it capable of knowing it was about to die? What flooded his mind at his last moment among the land of the living? It was as hypnotic watching the animals as it was watching you." He held the glass and turned back to me, annoying me with an admiring glare.

"So, what happened to your parents?" I asked.

He snapped out of his amorous gaze. "You know those candles I mentioned? I just lit the place up, causing a fire so big that my house burned down." He waved his hand as if it were no big deal. "My parents died in that fire. I got out, waiting until the fire was big enough before running to a neighbor's house. I was seventeen at the time."

He glared at me, and for a moment, I thought I was gazing into the eyes of a younger Lance. His eyes glazed over, his demeanor lightened, and I watched as he returned to reality.

"I'm sorry for what happened between you and your parents," I lied, "but how does that lead up to now?"

"Don't you see?" he said, "I want to understand what my parents were so obsessed with. I hate God; I have always hated God since I was a boy. My parents insisted I worship something I couldn't see, touch, or physically explain. I craved proof. I yearned for facts, for the experience. It's who I am, but they never understood that!"

"I can't help you find God. I don't know anything beyond the blackness when people die. It's like they all fall asleep." I wanted to grab him and shake him as hard as I could, knock some sense into him. He had a degree in reality, after all.

"Damn you! Why can't you understand me? I don't give a shit about God. Science is God. I want to learn about the science of death. I want to know every gripping detail. What does it feel like when life leaves their bodies? Do they fight it? Do they see anything around them? I want to know what you see at that moment in space and time when the body dies. You know it, and you can tell me!"

I was more at a loss for words than ever. He was demanding an explanation that I had no way of providing. The final moment? It's virtually indescribable. How does anyone describe it?

"I'm sorry, I don't know how." The room went utterly still, and his eyes glowed with fiery rage. I had to reconsider my approach to keep him at bay. I peered over at the window again. Still, there was no Jeff. I had to speed things up…

I dropped my gaze and clutched my head, pretending to lose my mind. He said he could read me. We'll see about that.

"I don't know how to get all these souls out of my head. I can't take it anymore. All this death is eating away at me, ripping me apart from the inside. Please, can you help me?" I knew that would appease him. He is so delusional that it probably wouldn't take much for him to lower his guard.

Lance moved in as if he wanted to console me. "I can help you. I can take it all away. I need you to put me in the right place in your beautiful mind."

"I'm just so afraid," I said in my best acting voice. "The dead follow me everywhere. All the people I profiled won't leave me alone."

The look on Lance's face suggested he had hit the lottery jackpot. "You can see them?"

"Yes. I never told anyone, but the victims are here, with me even now. They are all here, just as they died, and I think all those people are angry. That's why they won't leave me be."

"All right, this is good. We can work with this," he said, looking around. He turned his back to me, walked over to an end table, and pulled open a drawer. I stood firm, grabbed the back of the chair, and hurled it at him. The chair slammed against his head, causing him to fall and release Julian's gun. I dove for it, picked it up, and aimed it at him.

"You ignorant son-of-a-bitch, what makes you think I will ever tell you anything!" I stepped back and put him in my direct line of sight.

"You need me, Natalie," he said, rubbing his head and trying to stand up. "I don't doubt that you are trapped inside your head, and all those other people are syphoning your spirit. I can help you vacate them; I can help you regain your sanity."

"I'm not insane! Stop calling me insane!" I yelled at him, moving closer to put myself in better range.

"Natalie, listen to me. I know what it's like to be consumed by a force, not your own. I had to live my whole life that way, but I found a way to harness it. You can find a way, too. Just let me help you. For the last time, I'm begging you!"

"You are right. This is the last time," I said, turning the gun on him.

The front door burst open, and Jeff hurried in. We made eye contact for a moment before Lance turned and drew a second gun, shooting Jeff.

"Jeff!" I screamed as he clenched his chest and fell to the floor. I pulled the trigger, intending to shoot Lance, but nothing happened. Click. Click. Click. I checked the gun.

Lance turned on me, still rubbing his head. "Tisk. Tisk, you stupid idiot!" he breathed out. "Did you think I didn't notice him? You dumb bitch, how dare you think little of me." He pointed the gun directly at my chest. Julian's gun. I examined the one I was holding. "Now that you know it's not loaded, put it on the table." He waved to the coffee table a couple of feet from me.

I dropped the gun onto the hardwood and took a step toward Jeff.

"Ah, ah, ah, step back," he urged me with his gun. "There's nothing you can do for him. I don't think he will survive that one," he shrugged. "But let's hope he found Julian and called an ambulance before deciding to play cat and mouse; otherwise, Julian probably won't either."

"You are fucking piece of shit!" I half cried, half choked.

I looked down at Jeff, who was struggling to breathe. He gazed back at me, his chest heaving with every painful heartbeat as the life behind his eyes faded away.

"I've been called worse," he said, pointing his gun at me. He kneeled over Jeff, checked for a pulse, and then shook his head at me.

I let out a stifled cry as an unforgivable urge to rip Lance's heart out consumed me.

Lance surveyed Jeff's body. "At first, I was getting annoyed from yet another interruption, but now I realize this was all meant to be. We needed a new body."

"What are you talking about?" I forced down the vomit that was hovering in my throat. He killed my best friend. The little voice in my head groaned in anguish.

"I want to watch you do it. I want to watch you rip into Jeff's dead, lifeless body and dig inside his mind."

His excitement made me want to scream, but what was the point? "I knew there was a good reason why I couldn't stand you. You disgust me."

"Oh, come now, it's not like I'm making this all up. That's what you do, isn't it?" he asked, regarding Jeff's body as the cogs in his brain spun. "Rip into them?"

"Get away from him!" I yelled, stepping toward him.

Lance raised the gun. "Ms. Rhine, it would burden my heart if you made me pull this trigger again, but don't think I won't; and I wouldn't count on anyone coming to the rescue. After all, we are in the middle of nowhere."

My tear-blurred eyes locked onto Jeff. "He found us."

He froze and scrunched his face. "That is a good point." He kneeled and patted Jeff's clothes. "Ah, good. I can't seem to find a phone, so that settles that," he grinned.

I seethed at the sick bastard as he pulled Jeff's body out to a more open area on the floor.

"I'm not going to profile him," I said, more out of desperation than defiance.

"You will." A sickening smile crossed his face and turned my stomach.

Chapter Thirty-Nine

Sobs escaped one after another. Lance did this to him. He killed Jeff. Kyle's voice clouted me like a brick. "You have to stop him... what he did to other people and what he will do."

My eyes scanned Lance's body, imagining him kicking Kyle. Then my eyes went to his shoes—average size, tied down the front—precisely what was in Kyle's memory.

I inhaled and exhaled through a cough. The memory of how he was kicked repeatedly by those shoes lingered in my mind. "It was you," I muttered.

He kept his eyes down, but I knew he had heard me. "You killed Kyle," I shouted at him. I wasn't sure what I would do when the time came when I declared those words with confidence. I made the promise that I would get my revenge on the person who murdered my nephew, but I wasn't sure how. The urge to tear him apart was far greater than I imagined. After what he did to Julian and Jeff, I wanted to take every scalpel Mike had and slowly dissect Lance's brain the way he wanted to study mine.

Lance made eye contact with me. "I spent years trying to peer inside the minds of people. It's hard to explain this obsession. David mentioned that you were his drug. He took the words right out of my mouth. You are my drug, Natalie. I needed to know what you know, but you were willing to end the profiling. Julian was taking you from me; I couldn't let that happen. I have worked to get closer and closer to you. I even managed to get inside David's head and convince him how extraordinary you were. I made my obsession become his, and he did a marvelous job taking his pictures and reporting back to me."

He stood up. "He placed an interest in you far better than I expected until that bitch wife of his got in the way. Suddenly, David came to me complaining about his marriage issues. He said his wife threatened divorce if he didn't spend more time fixing his marriage."

I thought back to David. My mind pieced everything together, and I imagined David's wife's name on Lance's hit list. Then her last moments flowed through my mind. She did see her killer in the rearview mirror, and I recognized him from behind.

"You killed her, too."

He shrugged. "She was a vital piece to my delicious plan. And besides," he waved, "he, too, became obsessed with you. I was doing him a favor by removing her from the equation."

"You're even more disgusting than I first thought. You might as well shoot me. I will never profile my friend for your sick amusement."

"I could visit your sister," he said, singing his words.

I cringed at his mention of Nicole. "You even think of going near her…."

"Too late, already thought of it, so stop wasting time and do it," he nodded toward Jeff's body.

I kept my eyes locked on Lance as I stood. He was only four feet from me, and Jeff lay in the middle between us. I walked over to Jeff and pretended to find the best position for profiling. If he had David watch me, he would know how I began the profiling.

"You have him positioned all wrong."

Lance exhaled, eager to begin. "Then what is the correct way?"

"The victims were never moved. I have to profile them in the manner in which they died. If you want the best experience, that is."

He salivated, then gave me a questioning look. "He was shot. That's how he died. What more is there?"

"He has to be in the position he passed in," I said.

"You mean to tell me I must drag him back to where he fell?"

"Yes," I stated. He gave me his overused speculative glare. "Hey, you want this. This is how it must be," I said matter-of-factly.

"Fine. But don't try anything," he said.

I folded my arms across my chest, praying my plan would work. I watched him attempt to move Jeff without putting his gun down. Deadweight wasn't easy to move, as I expected. Lance struggled to lift Jeff by his shoulders but failed when the weight was too much. "Would you mind giving me a hand?"

"Not as long as you're dangling that gun. You might shoot me before I can start the profiling."

"You don't think I'm stupid enough to put it down, do you?"

I gave him a few sharp blinks. "You would be surprised at the kind of cooperation I may give after threatening to kill my sister."

He smiled, "Glad you're starting to use your common sense." He tucked the gun in his pants and motioned for me to pick a side.

I walked over and stood beside Jeff's body. Keeping my eyes locked on Lance's.

"We'll lift him together and put him back against the wall," he said.

I nodded as I contemplated my next move. Lance reached underneath Jeff's body. "Ready? One…two…three."

We started to lift Jeff together. Lance's face strained in concentration, and I used that moment to my advantage. I released Jeff and sucker-punched Lance in the chest with one fierce blow. He let out a choked gasp as he dropped Jeff's body. I dove on Lance, and as my fingers grazed the weapon, another shot went off. My body fell back as a sharp pain seared in my lower body. I slid down to the floor, grabbing the coffee table as Lance's footsteps closed in on me.

"I warned you, didn't I? Now, look what you made me do?" I saw him look around, holding his left arm close to his chest from the possibility of a busted rib.

I slumped on the floor, bleeding and unable to move. I tried to gasp for breath, but drawing air into my lungs felt too complicated. I had experienced this before when I profiled victims, but I would simply wake up. This time, it was me with a bullet lodged inside my body.

I saw Lance's shadow in the corner of my eye. I tried to follow his movements, but my consciousness was fading. The coldness crept in as my blood spilled from me. I'm not ready to die, I thought. My eyes closed as he reached down toward me.

"Do you have any idea how expensive this carpet was? Now you have blood everywhere!"

Chapter Forty

"Aunt Natalie, do you remember when we played in the woods, and there were all those rock piles that looked like forts?"

"Yes. Of course, I remember. I remember everything with you." Kyle and I walked together in the gray, holding hands and waving our arms playfully back and forth. It was only the two of us. No more ominous faces hovering, no more suffering. We walked a path through a wooded area, but there was no color to be seen. I couldn't hear the shushing of the trees. I felt no breeze and smelled no scents. I stilled for a moment, but Kyle kept guiding me along.

"Can we go back and see them again?"

"I would like that." I stroked his hair and laid my hand across his shoulder, pulling him in closer, craving his closeness.

"We can do many things here, you know." Kyle walked side by side, and I pulled him here and there, pretending I was incapable of walking. His laugh woke the trees around us, as if they were clearing a path.

I tried to cover a smirk, but I couldn't help it. This place was dull. Not scary, or dark, just…dull. It was like being stuck in a gray and white painting. "Like what?"

He mimicked my shuffling, then settled down and grabbed my hand in his. "Anything you want, just think about it, and we can do it."

"That sounds wonderful. Anything you want to do, my darling boy, I will spend forever doing it with you. Even if we are stuck in this place," I said, looking around. I pictured Heaven would be different, better. Full of color, life. I looked down at Kyle. At least I was with him, and that was all the life I needed. "So, what do you want to do?"

Kyle's face wiggled in complex thought. "Hmm. What do we have time for?"

I laughed at his absurd comment. Death was infinite. "Well, anything, you silly boy. I'm not going anywhere. I'm staying here with you forever," I reached out and pulled him into me. I kissed the top of his head and hugged him as tightly as my soul could muster. When I pulled away, I couldn't help but notice a sadness in his expression.

"What's wrong, Kyle? Aren't you happy?"

"Not yet."

My heart sank. I was here with him now, to keep him company and let him feel safe. I knelt at his eye level. "Kyle, do you know how much I love you?" I asked him.

"Yes, Aunt Natalie, you love me this much," he replied, stretching his arms wide.

I smiled, "Oh no, that is hardly my love for you. It's more like this." I also stretched my arms out and spun around in circles.

He laughed. "Wow, that's a whole lot."

"So, are you happy now?" I asked again, expecting a better answer. His face dropped once more. "Not yet," he said again.

"You're probably scared of this place, but you don't have to be. I'm here with you now, and I'm never leaving you. I will keep you safe forever!" I said, giving him a playful shake.

He jerked away and shouted at me, "Not yet!" His face was etched with anger.

"Why, Kyle? Why are you saying, 'Not yet?"

"Because I'm not done with you yet, you little bitch!"

My eyes rolled open. Paintings of melted clocks, skeletons, and what appeared to be a tormented shadow floating over a still figure hung all around me.

"Lance," I spoke out, feeling the intense burning as I breathed his name.

"I'm here and relieved that you are too."

I twisted my head toward the voice, but a couch blocked my view.

He sat at a desk, rustling around. "Oh, sorry. I hope you are comfortable on the floor. I wasn't about to have you bleeding on my nice leather furniture."

I winced from the painful burning. It felt like poison seeped into my blood, permeating my veins and organs, only to revisit the upper left side of my chest. "You shot me," the memory dawning on me.

"Yes, but if you recall, I warned you not to test me."

A chair creaked, and he drew closer to me. I tried to force my body to move, but every twitch was unbearable.

Lance dragged the couch aside and pulled a chair next to where I sat, bleeding. His attire was unconventional; he replaced his sweater vest and plaid dress shirt with a black long-sleeve V-neck shirt and black cargo pants.

My eyes met Lance's. "Why, Kyle? He was only a boy," my voice barely able to choke out the words. A volcano inside me erupted through my eyes, ears, and mouth. Every molecule was on fire. Even the floor beneath felt as if it were burning.

"I confess that I was the one who killed him, but he was an important piece to the puzzle inside that brain of yours." He sat there without expressing any genuine concern.

"Why?" I cried out. My body heaved from the heavy, forced sobs. I wanted to hurt him, to make him feel crushing pain, but I was unable to move, defenseless and defeated, all because of this man.

"Why? Why…why? That is the question, isn't it?" he sat back in the chair and crossed his legs. "I mean, c'mon Natalie, by now you have to have figured it out." He shook his head, perhaps surprised by the question, or further maddened into his psychotic episode. I couldn't read him anymore. He was no longer the good doctor, or even the annoying shrink. He was a demon, and he knew it.

"Let me say, for the record," he lifted his arms toward me defensively. "I didn't want to hurt the little guy. I was getting into my research, exploring the world of one, Ms. Natalie Rhine, and with our frequent visits, my desire to learn more was overpowering, to say the least."

Each word he said felt like a lesion on my soul.

"Do you remember during our first few sessions, you told me about your brother's drowning, how you would never profile another child that young again. Something about his recognition of his dying was different than an adult's last moments?"

He mistook a twitch for a nod.

“Well, that intrigued me.”

“No. You fucking bastard, you didn’t—”

He raised a hand. “Let me finish.” He stood from his chair and moved to stand next to the mantel. The only light in the room came from a gas fireplace, where a soft fire danced freely behind the glass wall. The light reflected off his features, darkening his eyes and clothes. He appeared to be more than a demon. I was convinced he was Lucifer himself.

“It's Julian’s fault, you know. I would never have taken it that far had he not forced my hand. David’s wife would have been enough to do my study.”

“You killed her to get to me,” I asked.

He stared down at the flames, possessed by a force that drove out all humanity he had left.

"Julian would never allow me near you during your profiling, so I needed someone who could get close. David was perfect. I convinced him you were special. To my surprise, it didn’t take much convincing, but he was getting sloppy- wasting my time, and as you well know, I don’t like my time wasted. What better way to make him do my dirty work than to give him the only reason to need you in his life?"

I fought to mend my mind and body. I needed this man to pay. The burning never subsided, but I welcomed it. I opened myself to the physical pain to block the anger, but it wasn't enough. Evil sat inches away from me. "Have I told you that you're a sick bastard?"

"I’m aware of what I am?" he said with divine arrogance. "More importantly, I am aware of what you were. You asked me over that awful excuse for coffee what my professional opinion was of you." He knelt, hovering just a few feet away. "Let me tell you my true opinion. You are the most incredible person I have ever met, but I don't believe you have a gift from God." He stood again, taking a few paces toward his desk, then turning on his heel. "No. Quite in fact, I think the big guy below gifted you that wonderful talent."

I shrank back, disgusted. "You don't believe in God, but you believe in the devil?"

"Well, something like that. There is a strange force of nature that makes humans do unspeakable things. I live for science, but even I have to believe in something."

"And I pray someday, that something will smile over you as you burn in hell!"

He pondered, obliged a smile that quickly faded, and sat at his desk.

"I've already had my fair share of hell. But you… well now… I told myself that if I got to experience your hell, well, damn, my whole universe would light up with possibility."

"He was just a boy. A fucking child."

"On the contrary, he was your last glimmer of sanity. You should be honored that I have taken such drastic measures to understand you better." He stood there, self-assured, oblivious to the chaos and destruction he had caused.

For the first time, I detected genuine sincerity in his voice, tinged with true insanity. I shut my eyes and tried to block out the world, his world, and the madness of it all. When I opened them again, I was no longer alone. They all stood there, waiting for me—all those people and their agony, eager to be released—David and his wife. Sherry Sweeney. Congressman Floyd. Darrel Brown.

All standing united together. Then my eyes fell on two young boys- Kyle and Nathan.

"Now you know my story. I want to hear yours, and this time, no holding back, or your sister will be next." He snipped, glaring with an award-winning smile. "So, tell me, my dear, how do you connect? How can you enter the minds of the recently departed?" he asked.

How do I get inside, indeed? He wants to know about death. He wants to know how it feels. So why don't I show him? I always wondered if I could, and here, with all of them patiently waiting, I knew what they were trying to tell me.

My eyes focused back on Lance's. He didn't show off his typical poised and straight stance, and his eyes reflected a sinister look. His hair was in disarray, but the utter calmness he possessed sent a chill down his spine. Only a psychotic can brag about killing and remain at ease. Only a soulless man can do what he did. Perhaps I should give him a soul or maybe a hundred.

I forgot about all the burning shooting through my chest. I made the sensation disappear and replaced it with a cooling one, covering every fiber of my being. I slowed my breathing and concentrated, keeping my eyes steady on Lance's. At first, his face held a smirk, eager for my knowledge. His calmness and lack of movement assisted with my task.

I centered myself around his entire frame. I drove my core to the perfect existential level of being. He wanted to know about my work, which involved extracting memories.

I would give him every one of mine and those who became a part of me. He would experience it all, all their pain and terror, all at once. My recurring dream, where the victims made me revisit the fear and torture of all their fates, made me realize they were showing me what I could do.

I crept down into my soul, into their souls. I imagined wrapping my fingers around the darkness, dragging it out of my body and into his.

Lance's eyes twitched at the corners as his smugness faded. He scratched at his neck as if something was crawling along it, and then rubbed his hand along his face. "Well, I'm waiting," as a bead of sweat rolled from his brow.

I remained steady as the souls floated out of me. I stared into his eyes, finding my doorway. The air grew heavy as every soul permeated his being one at a time. I saw them enter his body through every crevice they gained access to.

Lance moved around more frequently. He rubbed at his skin, and lines of sweat now rolled down the sides of his face. His fingers and legs twitched, but he appeared frozen in place, unable to move his arms or legs. "What are you doing?" he demanded. "Stop looking at me like that! What are you doing?" he cried out. Awareness flooded his entire face, and his eyes displayed a fear that frightened even the most sinister.

Blood started trickling from his nose as he finally broke from his paralyzed state and wiped his hand across his face. He tore at his chest, ripping his shirt, gripping his throat as nail marks tore away at his skin.

All the tension was released from my body, creating a strong sense of euphoria. Their pain was no longer mine. It all now belonged to him. "You want to know what I know. Now you will. You will know what it feels like to suffocate to death. You will see how the Congressman felt to be sliced open. How Sherry Sweeney felt getting stabbed over and over." They were all inside of him now. Showing him precisely what he wanted.

"Natalie! Enough! Stop what you're doing!" He lifted his arms in front of him, unnerved by the self-inflicted marks he caused, as well as the unaccounted-for blood that spilled from his very core. He guarded his head and body as if he were trying to stop a force from striking, or to shield himself from a bullet breaking through, as David and Michelle crept inside.

"That's for David and Michelle!"

He choked, spitting out small puddles of mucus as he lurched from a presence hitting him from behind. "That's for Kyle!"

His shrieks of pure torture were a pleasant sound to my ears. Grabbing at his head, chest, and face, everywhere he had skin, and clawing and beating away the attacks to no end. Mixed voices charged into him. I heard them all. The way the victims begged for their lives was as if they were all a part of death's chorus line. So, this is what happens when I profile the living. Interesting.

Lance darted around in circles, trying to find a way to stop it all. He fell against his desk, knocking over his precious antiques. The old telescope fell to the floor at his feet, and he lost all control over his body, falling hard with it.

My concentration didn't ease up. I spilled every memory into him, giving him visions of all the people who were now making their homes inside his head all at once. "This is for you, Kyle," I said aloud, “as promised.”

Lance lay helpless on the floor as his body jerked in every direction. His skin and eyes had lost almost all their color. My victory was sweet, and my revenge was effective.

The bullet wound in my abdomen burned, reminding me I, too, would succumb to my infliction. My loss of blood was just as significant. Then a strange loneliness enveloped me. They were gone. All those people who lived inside my head. Gone. My body was subdued to the darkness as life stilled.

Chapter Forty-One

The smell of mud and fresh-cut grass scented the air. A light, comfortable breeze swept through as the sun peeked through the pillowy white clouds—a perfect day for a funeral.

Nicole gazed at an oversized statue of an angel holding a child as the sun cast a warm glow on the wings, enhancing the sculpture's allure. The stone had the name Rose carved at the base, and the timeline only allowed the poor child a three-year lifespan. She wondered if perhaps her child was embracing an angel.

"It's so calm here and peaceful," she said quietly.

"Yes. I agree." Julian sat beside Nicole, making a muffled sound as he favored his lower right side from a recovering wound. He wore his dark charcoal suit with a baby blue dress shirt. She remembered Natalie saying how much she loved that suit—and the shirt brought out the color of his eyes. "It's a lovely place to rest in peace," he added, nodding to her that he was alright when Nicole reached toward him in concern.

Nicole turned away and locked her eyes on the angel as a tear ran down her cheek. Peace was all she ever wanted. Her gaze shifted toward the pearl-white casket displayed in front of her. Dozens of flowers in various shapes adorned the top, creating a beautiful array of colors. Nicole's mind captured a vivid mental image of the casket, which was now ingrained in her memory. She wished she didn't find it so beautiful.

"Thank you all for being here to send off an extraordinary person on this extraordinary day." The pastor began. "I remember when Kyle was a baby; I performed his baptism. As I poured the water on his head, I will never forget how he looked up and smiled the most incredible smile." The pastor held such kindness and grace in his features. "As he grew older, I would start mass, welcome all the Sunday school children to come up and talk with me. Kyle would sit down with the group. One day, when we assembled, I noticed him staring at Jesus displayed on the cross, and he asked how he got there." The pastor smiled at the crowd, fond of his memory. "He was always curious, but he took me by surprise when he walked right past me, up to Jesus, and said, 'Hey buddy, how did you get up there?" The group laughed at the pastor's story. Even Nicole let out a moderate chuckle.

Julian reached for her hand and squeezed. His face remained as solid as the stone tombs surrounding him. He no longer wanted to cry. He did all that at Lance's home when he found Natalie on the floor. Lance sat a few feet from her, begging in pained breaths for whatever it was to stop. He lashed around as if he warded off blows to his head and body, unaware Julian had entered the room.

An ambulance took Lance to the emergency room and treated him before admitting him to the psych ward for further observation. Forensics transported Jeff's body to the morgue, and his peers created a memorial outside the station in a brick garden. Mike and his team immediately began closing cases. Lance's notebook detailed all the events leading up to Kyle's murder. He easily discerned what happened to Jeff, and thanks to the gun used to kill David's wife, found in Lance's possession, he had enough to close that case as well.

Julian sat only a few feet from the casket that cradled the little boy's body. He wanted to drive back to the psych ward and beat Lance to a pulp for the hell he caused. He wished he could go back in time and realize Lance was insane. He could have stopped himself from putting Natalie in Lance's direct line of sight. His gut had told him something was off, but he refused to listen.

"And as for Natalie," the pastor said, "we say a prayer for her as well. She used her gifts to bring truth, justice, and peace to those who needed it the most, and I could not have been prouder of her. Her family couldn't be more proud of her, and I know all of you, standing here now, are proud of her for all she has done."

Nicole nodded in agreement. Life dealt their family a series of brutal blows, some more destructive than others. She wanted her sister now more than ever. She squeezed Julian's hand. He loved Natalie. She could see that in his eyes, and it made her smile. He did have beautiful eyes. She understood why Natalie was so enamored with him. He did what he could to protect and make her feel empowered, unique, and essential. She had a new sense of trust and respect for him.

Nicole thanked the pastor when the funeral procession came to an end, and the crowd dispersed. The caretakers arrived and finalized the casket before lowering it to the ground. Nicole watched as the pearly white box sheltering her son's body disappeared into the earth.

She laid Kyle's body to rest among their family. The tears welled, and she cried from the hardest recognition of not knowing how she would manage life without him. She fell to her knees, right between Kyle and Nathan's graves, and placed her hand against the grass. "Please take care of my son."

Julian knelt and pulled Nicole into a comforting embrace. "You need to take it one day at a time, and if you ever need anything, please don't hesitate to call me." He lingered for a moment, took one final look at Nicole, and then, with a low, muttered goodbye, he turned and walked away, leaving her to grieve.

Nicole stopped sobbing. She stared at the grave, wanting to have her sister beside her. She witnessed the persecution Natalie faced for being who she was. Often cut off from those around her and compelled to hide in fear. No one understood her. Natalie lived a way of life below that of an average person, so Nicole made a promise a long time ago never to follow that path.

Her eyes roamed over the names of her family members. Years of her life rested right here before her. Many were taken before their time. A bloodline so strong there was no denying who she was. Not anymore. She looked over at her grandmother's grave. "I'm sorry, Nana, but I can't hide anymore."

Nicole stood and cast her eyes over the vast forest of gravestones that spanned the cemetery. Sunlight shimmered across the grass, and patches of color from laid flowers were seen here and there. It was a beautiful place—quiet and peaceful.

She drew that peace within her body to overpower the chaos that raged around her. She raised her head toward the sun, soaking in its incredible warmth as it permeated her skin. She listened to the birds in the distance and smelled the freshly dug earth. She opened all her senses to the world around her and absorbed everything that was there. Her fingers started to twitch, and her body shook in a rhythmic tremor.

Everything shifted around her as heat rose from the ground beneath her, creating a sensation of a warm blanket enveloping her body. The stones marked with her family's names shook in unison. "This is who I am. This is what we all are." Nicole collapsed to the ground as everything around her stopped.

The caretakers saw Nicole fall over and ran to her side. "Ma'am, are you okay?" one of them asked. Nicole lay on the ground, stroking the grass against her skin, waiting for the air to reenter her body. She opened her eyelids to the sunlight but reflected only darkness through her blackened eyes. The man closest to her fell back and uttered a "whoa."

"Ma'am, do you need me to call for an ambulance?" he asked.

Nicole didn't hear him. The warmth permeated her whole body—in every muscle, vein, and cell. Her pupils slowly adjusted back to normal, and she felt the light flow through her entire body. She raised herself, not even looking at the two men standing over her.

"That won't be necessary." She only turned once and smiled at her son's grave.

When she climbed into her car, she turned back and read the words written on the gravestone with the hovering angel.

Come to me, child, for I will hold you. Eternal peace is your playground.

Chapter Forty-Two

Six months later

Joshua Lance sat in his room reading a book. The orderly knocked on the door, informing him he was due for his appointment.

"Ready when you are," he said. The door opened, and a tall, African-American man walked into the room, followed by a second behind him; neither appeared to be the sort he wanted to trifle with. Lance set his book down on the table next to his chair and stood up, fixing his clothes. He checked his reflection, fixed his hair, and smiled back at himself, pleased with his appearance. His outfit included a tailored white collared shirt, pants, and tennis shoes. The uniform was pristine, without a single mark or wrinkle.

"Ah, Maxwell and Daniel, how good to see you. Regardless of popular opinion, I do rather enjoy the services you fine men give. When my time is through here, I will insist you work for me," Lance said, pointing his finger in a self-assured manner.

The two men gave him a smug look as each escorted him through the halls of the ward to his psychiatric evaluation.

"I assume you're telling us you will behave yourself this time. Although I do rather enjoy putting restraints on you," the first orderly said to Lance for only his ears to hear.

Lance's smile faded, and his eyes remained fixed straight ahead. "That hasn't been necessary for quite some time now, nor will it be necessary in the future. I'm doing much better."

Lance walked with a buoyant stride through the halls. Due to his connection with doctors in his hometown, he was sent to a medical facility in a different state so that he wouldn't receive any preferential treatment. Although unfamiliar with this hospital, he still treated it like his comfort zone, acting as if he were there to counsel instead of needing counseling.

"That's up to the doctor to decide," the second orderly said, swiping his ID card to access a security door.

The three men walked down multiple hallways before stopping at a desk. "Lance is here for his appointment."

"Good morning, Walter," Lance said to the older man behind the desk.

Walter looked up from his computer. "Joshua," he answered, then dropped his head.

"How did your grandson do at his school science fair?"

"Very well, thank you." Walter didn't give him any eye contact. There was no entertaining a madman on his schedule.

Lance lightly banged his hand against the countertop. "Well, that's good to hear. Did he add the parts I recommended?"

"He's only eight. Adding in your ideas is hardly appropriate for a boy his age."

Lance appeared a little taken aback. "What do you mean by 'hardly appropriate,' Walter? It is never too young to start a boy out knowing about things like that. Listen to me, I...."

"Learned at an early age, yeah, we know," all three men said.

Lance shut his mouth, stunned.

Walter shook his head. "He can wait over there. There's a new physician assigned to him."

Lance cocked his head at Walter in disbelief as Max and Daniel pulled him toward a chair. "A new one, why? I thought things were going well with Dr. Macavoy."

"I don't ask, I schedule," Walter responded.

The orderlies forced Lance to sit in a chair. "Thank you," he said, giving both men a stern look as he pulled his arms out of their grasp. He adjusted himself and fixed his shirt. "I hope you all realize this may be the last time you see me. Dr. Mac and I were on the same page. He knew I was not sick or insane. A man of science knows a man of science."

"Give it a rest," Max said, looking toward the door to the doctor's office.

"Fine, fine. I'm sure this one will consider all the work Mac and I have done and sign off on my release." Lance's confidence returned, along with his smile.

Walter turned his head toward the orderlies and rolled his eyes. Both men smirked back at him.

Lance sat quietly in the hall, waiting, when a buzzer sounded off at Walter's desk. "The doctor is ready to see you now," he said without looking at him.

"Walter, it was nice working with you." Lance gave a half-bow, disappearing into the office.

The office was modern yet straightforward. Ecru walls, accented with soft yellows and greens, decorated the room with minimal effort. Miniature, colorful fake plants sat on shelves and bookcases, while a large, thick-paned window let the daylight filter through the glass, minus the bars covering the outside. The room was four floors up, providing a decent view of the grounds below.

Lance took his usual seat, and the orderlies stood behind, observing him. A door leading into a second room opened, and a woman with lovely brunette hair tied into a French braid entered. She wore a beige two-piece suit and smiled toward the orderlies.

"Thank you, gentlemen. I can handle it from here." Both men gave her a cautious look.

"Ma'am, this one has been known to make attempts."

She turned her head and regarded him, giving him a cautious look. "He won't be making any attempts of the sort. Not unless he wants to spend countless hours of his life sedated." She turned toward him. "Do you?"

Lance smiled and shook his head, accompanied by a hand gesture. "No ma'am. You can expect nothing but the utmost professionalism from me. I can assure you of that."

She turned back toward the orderlies and gave them a reassuring nod.

Yes, ma'am, we will be outside," and they both turned and left the room.

Lance waved over his head without turning in their direction. "Remember, when I leave here, you can both come and work for me," he yelled.

Max snickered as he shut the door. Lance focused his attention on the female standing a few feet away.

"Well, let me start by saying I'm surprised to be working with a new psychiatrist." He judged the woman as she sorted through the paperwork. "And I want to say I do not see why we would not work well together. After all, we are both doctors."

She looked at him impassively. "I am a practitioner. You are not. You relinquished your license when you went on a killing spree."

"A piece of paper doesn't make a person who they are. It simply gives them a title for the public to recite," he said. "But I am an expert, nonetheless, and I hope you will respect that."

The woman tossed her head up unamused, grabbed a file, pen, and pad, and sat in a chair angled a safe distance away. She heard Lance's faint growls of anger.

"I would like to know why Dr. Macavoy is no longer my appointed psychiatrist."

"You needn't concern yourself with Dr. Macavoy. The state reassigned him."

"And you are?" he asked, looking for a name badge.

The woman blinked at Lance and smiled, "I am now your court-appointed psychiatrist."

Lance's face dropped. "I see."

She turned her attention toward the window behind her. It was a dreary spring day in April. Trees were starting to bud as the warmth stayed around during the days. On the grounds below, patients at lower risk wandered the area for fresh air and exercise.

"Excuse me. I believe I asked your name and am still awaiting an answer."

The doctor turned back toward him. He had that simple Mr. Rogers air.

"I am the victor of one's thoughts; suffered over those poisoned from their judgment," she said.

He peeked up. "That was lovely. Where did you hear that from?" he asked, offering her a smile.

"My sister."

"Well, it sounds like she had a way with words."

"She had a way with people."

Lance relaxed a bit in his chair. "I, too, have a way with people. I bet she and I would get along swimmingly." He crossed his legs, rested his elbows on the armrests, and clasped his hands together.

The doctor pondered his words. "She wasn't very fond of psychiatrists or doctors."

"That's a shame to hear. We doctors do more good than anyone gives us credit for." He eased his mindset into therapy mode. "Do you have any shared interests with her... Doctor, sorry, I still didn't get your name?"

"We share quite a bit in common. And it's Rhine. Dr. Nicole Rhine."

Lance's smile disappeared. His eyes twitched at the corners. The air in the room was still, and the world outside was quiet. Lance's hand reached up and wiped at his nose. When he saw the blood on his fingertips, his eyes fixated on the woman across from him. "Shall we begin?" she smiled. Her pupils were so wide that her eyes appeared completely black.

Epilogue

Julian carried a bouquet through the hospital doors, making his way down the branching hallways, passing room after room until he reached his destination. He pushed open the door and was greeted by the steady beeping of the heart monitor. He walked across the room and replaced older, wilted flowers with the new ones he had brought. A nurse walked into the room moments later. She had a tenured air about her and was often assigned as the day nurse to the room.

"Good morning, Captain. How are you doing today?" she asked, walking over to the whiteboard and making changes. She erased the night nurse's name and replaced it with her own. Then she turned and greeted Julian with a weak smile.

Julian finished arranging the flowers. "Work is keeping me busy, and I feel like I've aged ten years. Other than that, I'm doing fine. Thank you for asking."

"Well, you don't look like you've aged one bit."

Julian smiled and turned to look at the numbers on the monitor. "Any changes?"

"No, not yet, but I suppose no news is good news in this case." She tapped several buttons on the monitor, changed the saline bag, and adjusted the drip flow. When she finished, she stood beside the captain and patted him on the shoulder.

"Her wounds healed well. Now, it's just a matter of figuring out what keeps her from waking up. Too bad we can't figure out what is going on inside that head of hers."

Julian walked over to the side of the bed and looked down at the sleeping beauty. He smiled, "I couldn't figure out what was going on inside her head long before she ended up here."

"Well, I believe that everything happens for a reason. Whatever is keeping her asleep, perhaps it's for the best. Give her the time she needs to heal what's inside."

Julian kept his eyes locked on Natalie.

The nurse smiled back at him and nodded, "I'll be around in a few hours to check on her," she said, leaving Julian alone.

Julian saw the nurse leave the room out of the corner of his eye and waited for the door to close behind her. He lowered his head and whispered in a soft, delicate voice, "It's being handled. You take all the time you need."

He kissed her forehead, then pulled a chair up. "I'll be waiting for you."

www.ingramcontent.com/pod-product-compliance
Lightning Source LLC
Chambersburg PA
CBHW020532020726
47494CB00006B/1730

* 9 7 9 8 9 9 9 1 5 9 6 1 8 *